Slowly the shadowy figures █████████████ f the path to the door and escape. Darryl and Gary backed away from the approaching ghosts until Darryl's back hit the wall of windows. His eyes darted around in terror. There was no place to go.

Joe Bob Renfro moved up beside Troy. "Jump," he commanded in a hollow tone.

For a moment Darryl thought he had mistaken the word. He looked fearfully at Gary who was climbing onto the narrow windowsill. "Hey, man! We can't jump from here! It's three stories down!"

Troy moved silently to Darryl and reached out his hand. In the moonlight Darryl could see the frayed edges of his cuffs and the sunken skin beneath Troy's eyes. He looked as if he had been dead for months. As he had been.

Darryl scrambled onto the sill next to Gary. "Don't make us jump," he pleaded. "Don't do this!"

"Kill," Joe Bob muttered.

"Die," Misty whispered. Brooke's gray lips moved with her. "Die. Like we did."

"Like we did," the others repeated.

Darryl heard a crashing sound as Gary's weight against the window broke the glass. Before he could react, Gary grabbed his arm, pulling Darryl out the window with him. Together they fell, their screams tearing the air. High above him in the English room, Darryl saw faces fill the windows.

As his eyes glazed over in death, they began to disappear.

THE UPRISING
ABIGAIL McDANIELS

ZEBRA BOOKS
KENSINGTON PUBLISHING CORP.

ZEBRA BOOKS are published by

Kensington Publishing Corp.
475 Park Avenue South
New York, NY 10016

First Printing: March, 1994

Printed in the United States of America

Prologue

The low fire glittered in Kevin Donatello's black eyes. He snapped his head around in response to a sound in the darkness beyond and had to brush back the forelock of his ebony hair so he could see. A girl stepped hesitantly forward, and the firelight made her long red hair glow. "Finally," Kevin said. "Where are the others?"

"They're coming." Brooke Wright stepped closer to the fire.

"Aren't you forgetting something?" Kevin said in a controlled voice. He never let the others see his nervousness.

"Heil," she said as she raised her right arm in a stiff salute.

"That's better." Kevin watched as she sat opposite him. He had had doubts that Brooke would follow through. For a moment he felt a twinge of gratitude, but it was swiftly followed by derisive thoughts. Brooke was his follower and she believed in him. It was only fitting that she should be part of the Grand Sacrifice.

That's how he thought of what would happen that night. Grand Sacrifice. It would be grand indeed if it worked. The full moon crested almost directly overhead as the others began to arrive. Each dutifully greeted him with, "Heil," then took his or her appointed place in the circle around the fire. Kevin didn't acknowledge them by so much as a flicker of an eyelash. He was convinced of their blind obedience, and now that Brooke was in the circle he was sure of hers as well.

Troy Spaulding was the last to arrive. Kevin watched as he sat beside Brooke. Their eyes met for a moment, then Troy looked away. Kevin knew that Troy and Brooke had dated the year before but had since broken up. Troy had told Kevin that sometimes he wondered if Brooke still had feelings for him, but was afraid to ask. Troy didn't have to say anything else; Kevin knew Troy's ego was too fragile to risk rejection by asking Brooke if she still cared for him.

"The circle is complete," Kevin declared as he had at the beginning of every meeting. He looked at their intense faces. Twelve followers. Thirteen, counting himself. But he couldn't really count himself as a follower, since he was the leader and the inspiration behind the group. In the far distance he heard an eighteen-wheeler pass on the highway. Crickets sang in the summer grasses all around them. He glanced at his watch. In two hours his world would never be this ordinary again.

"I almost couldn't get out," Misty Traveno said. She was painfully shy and even now found it hard to talk in the circle. "My parents were still up. I went out the back door."

"Mom and I went shopping for school clothes today," Brooke said as she glanced nervously around the circle. "I couldn't tell her I wouldn't be needing them."

"Your sister can wear them," Bubba Holt said in his gruff voice. "Tracy is about your size."

Brooke looked at him. Bubba automatically tried to hide the crankcase grease that perpetually rimmed his fingernails. Under ordinary circumstances Brooke and Bubba would never have had cause to exchange a word. "We would have graduated next year."

Kevin saw doubt ripple over the other faces. "We have something better in store for us," he reminded them quickly. "We're the chosen ones."

Troy pivoted his well-muscled body so he could look directly at Kevin. "How do you know?" he asked. "How can you be so sure this will work?"

"I know it will. Do you doubt my authority?"

"No," Troy answered hastily. "Not that. It's just that some of us, well, we don't all have as much faith as you do."

Kevin lifted his face toward the moon and his black hair fell behind his shoulders. His raised his thin arms toward the sky in a gesture of reverence. "Give this doubter a sign," he commanded. He waited. After a moment a hot breeze sent the fire guttering and dancing. He hadn't doubted that something of the sort would happen. It always did if he waited long enough, and his followers always believed it to be a sign, no matter if it was a breeze or an owl call or whatever. He fixed Troy with a cool gaze. "Do you still doubt?"

Troy shook his head and looked around uneasily. He might be the football team captain and the most popular boy in school, but Kevin had discovered his weakness. Troy was afraid he was gay and was terrified that others might find out. Kevin knew he had nothing to fear from him.

Brooke shifted, and her long hair caught the light of the campfire. She was so beautiful Kevin almost hated to think he would never see her again. "We've all believed Kevin so far and he's never been wrong," she said. "If we doubt, we'll mess it all up." She turned her dark blue eyes in Kevin's direction for assurance.

Kevin nodded silently as if he were a father giving approval to a precocious child. He was reasonably certain that no one else in the circle knew Brooke's secret. Like Troy's, he had discovered it by accident. Brooke was an alcoholic and had been suicidal on more than one occasion. He had found her one night behind the field house after a football game, still in her cheerleading outfit, clutching a bottle of pills. She had just broken up with her current boyfriend and saw no reason to continue living. Before Kevin came along, she had intended to take the pills and put an end to all her doubts and cravings. He owed Brooke a great deal because she was the one who had put the idea of the group into his head.

For years Kevin had been interested in black magic and demonology. He had bought every book he could find on the subject and had experimented with various spells and incantations. Finally, at the beginning of the last school year, he had discovered an old volume of Satanism and had at last found his goal in life.

The book was mouldy and all but falling apart, but its words had touched a need in Kevin. A need to be special, to be different from everyone else. And the book had told him how to accomplish this.

It described a Grand Sacrifice, a sacrifice that went beyond the usual decimation of a cat or dog and involved more than a jumble of words that might or might not work. Even though he didn't follow the beliefs of Wicca, he thought of himself as a warlock, and this sacrifice was to be the ultimate in any warlock's life. This sacrifice would grant him powers that few dared to seek.

That was when he had started gathering followers. Brooke had been the first, though she didn't know that. He had kept his choices secret until the first time he brought them all together. On the surface, they were an unlikely group. Brooke was popular and as rich as Tiffany Matthews, who was sitting on Kevin's right. Bubba Holt was the son of a poor mechanic, and Toni Fay Randall's parents didn't seem to have a source of income at all. Eddie Ray came from a middle class family, but he was as wild as an outlaw, and Joe Bob Renfro was downright mean.

Jimmy Frye was on the football team with Troy and showed promise of becoming a professional athlete, but he was riddled with depression. Jeanne Wrayford was so shy she had never had a date and likely never would. Ellis Johnson was so thoroughly average most of his own classmates didn't know his name or recognize him on the street. Kathy Alsop was a scholar and would possibly have been the school valedictorian, but she, like Jimmy, was too depressed to care. Finding Kathy had completed Kevin's circle.

He smiled at each of them individually. "Tonight is the night we've all waited for. Tonight we join the

9

ONES WHO HAVE GONE BEFORE." He liked to talk like that, as if his words were capitalized. He knew the others were impressed by it as well. "Have each of you decided where it's to be done?"

Toni Fay spoke up, her voice soft but determined. "I'm going to the pond beside my house. I've always gone there when something important has happened to me."

"I've always loved theater," Misty whispered. "I'm going to the auditorium."

Troy looked at her. "I'll help you get inside the building."

"So everyone knows where?" Kevin looked around the group at the nodding heads. "Do you all know how it's to happen?"

"I'm going to that damned garage," Bubba said in a gravelly voice. "I figure it's only fitting that it happen there. It's the only place my old man ever speaks to me."

"Same here," Joe Bob said. "My garage, at home. And won't my folks be surprised?" He grinned mirthlessly and glanced around the circle as if daring anyone to challenge him.

"Valium," Ellis said in a low voice, then louder, "Lots of Valium. That's for me."

"I've chosen my car," Brooke said with a toss of her red hair. "I love that car. I'd like to take it with me."

Kevin smiled and nodded. "Okay. It's all set. Does anyone have any questions?"

They all looked at each other and collectively shook their heads. Jeanne's eyes were large and fearful. Kevin looked at her questioningly, and she reached in her jeans pocket and showed him a bottle of Seconal. Kevin nodded.

"Where will you be?" Brooke asked. "What will you use?"

"I'll be here," he replied. "I'll use my mind."

A murmur ran around the group. Kevin knew he had them in the palm of his hand. He stood and stretched his arms upward as if he would embrace the moon. "The time has come." He pointed in the general direction of Pleiades. "When the moon has passed the Seven Sisters, it will be too late."

The others stood and made the stiff arm salute. Kevin saluted them back. "Until we meet again," he said with promise glittering in his eyes.

Slowly they faded into the blackness. Soon Kevin could hear their car engines start and the sounds of their departure. He sat down by the fire and crossed his arms to wait.

Troy Spaulding drove Misty Traveno to the darkened high school and parked in the slot reserved for the principal. For a moment they sat in silence staring at the school building. At last Misty said, "I've never been here after hours. Have you?"

"Just for ball games and the like. Never when nobody else was here."

Misty looked at him through the darkness. "Are you afraid?"

Troy frowned, because he was scared half to death and figured she must have known. Misty could be too perceptive. "Let's go."

They left the car and circled the school to the gym door. Misty tried to open it. "It's locked."

"Of course it's locked." Troy shifted his grip on the sack he carried and reached in his pocket and pulled out a key. "I told Coach Hodges I wanted to come over this afternoon and work out. He thinks I'm getting in shape early for football season."

Misty made no comment and ducked her head. She never went to football games. Until she joined Kevin's group, she had rarely talked to anyone in the school. She wasn't one for idle conversation.

Troy put the key in the lock and turned it. When he pushed the door open, the odor of gym lockers and sweat socks came to him. He usually enjoyed that smell because it aroused the spirit of competition within him. "Can you find your way to the auditorium?"

Misty nodded. "I could find it with my eyes closed." She hesitated. "Where will you be? Here?"

"I haven't decided yet," he lied.

"Well, I'll see you when the group is together again." She gave him one of her private little smiles and walked away.

Troy listened to her footsteps echoing across the basketball court, then heard the clang of the door on the opposite wall. He gave her plenty of time to move away, then headed for his English classroom. He had chosen this place because it was in this room that he had first had his doubts about his masculinity and because he had a secret love of poetry that no one, not even his closest friends—maybe them especially—had guessed existed.

The door was locked as he had thought it probably

would be. He didn't mind. In a way it was fitting that it should be this way—locked out from where and how he wished to be. He sat on the floor and opened the sack.

On the dark highway west of town, Brooke Wright lifted her hair in the wind and reveled in the pleasure she got from driving her convertible. She loved this car and kept it as clean as she kept herself. As familiar road signs and landmarks streamed past, she pressed harder on the accelerator; Brooke had always loved to drive fast, and she had received numerous speeding tickets to prove it. As she neared the stretch of road she'd chosen, her smile disappeared. The road lay straight and flat before her, the landscape marked only by one lone tree. She pushed the accelerator to the floor and gripped the wheel with fierce determination, her eyes fixed on the tree.

Minutes later on the other side of town, Toni Fay Randall slipped off her tennis shoes and socks and gazed at the moonlit cow pond. Across the barbed wire fence, she could see the house where she had lived all her life. It was dark and squat in the night, surrounded by a dirt yard that was shunned even by weeds. She looked up at the moon and saw it was nearing the spot where she knew the Pleiades to be. Slowly, she walked into the cool water and felt the soft mud squish between her toes. She waded deeper.

* * *

Kevin Donatello stayed beside the fire and watched it diminish to a guttering remnant of its former brilliance. Mentally he reached out to all the twelve. A flame of excitement was growing in him. Had it started? He consulted his watch. Nearly midnight. It might almost be finished by now. He didn't have any doubt that it would be over by midnight.

Carefully he started chanting the mantra he had learned from the black book. His mind reached out to grasp the souls of the others and to pull them to him. They were the most important people in the world, more dear to him in their way than his parents or anyone else he had ever known. They were the Great Sacrifice. As he honored them and drew them back to him, he thought for a minute he could feel his power increasing, building as they gave up their own bodies and surrendered their power to him.

Not for a moment did Kevin consider dying. No, his part in this sacrifice was to live, and to live more powerfully than he had ever lived before. They couldn't, wouldn't, understand. That's why it had been so important to let them believe he was entering the pact with them. If he died, there would be no point in the deaths. Kevin had to chuckle at their naiveté. They were to die so that his power would increase until he was the One described in the Satanic book. He laughed to think how amazed everyone in town would be when they saw the change in him.

He stood with his arms stretched toward the moon until his hands were bloodless and his shoulders ached. At length, he let his hands drop to his sides and gazed at the moon one last time. When he checked his watch again, it was well past midnight. The time had passed.

Cautiously he moved and flexed his muscles. He didn't feel any different than he had before.

Kevin circled the dying fire. Reaching out with his mind, he tried to raise the flame; the coals winked back but refused to do his bidding. Had something gone wrong? He tried to recall the exact wording of the passage in the book. Had he omitted some step? Forgotten some incantation? No, he was positive he had done it all perfectly.

That meant the others had failed him somehow. Had one not been able to follow through? Had some method taken longer than was expected? He had more or less left the methods up to his followers. Had that been a mistake?

He glared up at the night sky. He was no different than he had been before!

The first body found was that of Toni Fay Randall. She was discovered by her brother when he went out at dawn to feed their cow. She was floating face down in the pond behind their house. At first he didn't know what to think. He had never seen a dead body before and since he knew by the clothing it was Toni Fay, he thought she must be playing some sort of prank. But she wasn't.

Brooke Wright's car was found twisted around the lone tree on the road frequented by teenagers who wanted to test the prowess of their cars. She was pronounced dead at the scene and her name was withheld until her parents and sister could be notified by the authorities.

As the sun rose, more bodies were found, all apparent victims of suicide, and none of whom seemed to have any connection with the others. The town of Maple Glen, Missouri was gripped first in shock and denial, then horror. The last two of the twelve who took their lives were found in the high school building. Misty Traveno had hanged herself from a rope on the stage of the school auditorium, and Troy Spaulding had washed down about fifty Seconal capsules with a fifth of bourbon in the hall outside the English classroom.

The only person who knew the answer to why this had happened was Kevin Donatello, and he wasn't talking. He was too busy trying to figure out what had gone wrong and how to prevent it from going wrong the next time.

Chapter One

Tracy Wright parked her car as near to the grave as the winding road permitted. For a long time she sat staring out the window at the pale marble headstone. Then the summer's heat got the best of her, and she left the car.

She hadn't been here often, and she had never before come alone. For a moment she was almost afraid to approach the grave. The cemetery seemed too still, too silent.

She told herself she was being foolish and walked briskly to the side of the grave. Now that the cemetery caretakers had covered it with grass, only a careful eye could tell it was a newer grave than the ones on either side. Its headstone looked new and clean—and forbidding.

"Brooke Lucinda Wright," it read. "1976–1994."

An irrepressible smile tilted Tracy's lips. Brooke had hated her middle name. She was the first girl born into their family, and following a longstanding tradition in their family, her middle name was the same as their mother's first name. Tracy used to tease Brooke about how glad she was that she was the second born and had a middle name that didn't make her cringe. Brooke disliked the name so much that she almost died whenever she heard it. At that thought, Tracy's smile was replaced with a grimace of guilt. That was a terrible thing for her to remember when Brooke really was dead.

Tracy turned her attention to the beautiful flowers in the ornamental vase that sat beside the headstone. They were real, from their own garden, not plastic. Tracy detested plastic flowers. Her mother came here often and always brought fresh flowers, but autumn was approaching, and Tracy wondered what she would do for flowers then.

Life hadn't been the same since Brooke's death. A full month had passed, but Tracy still felt as if she were living in a dream—or a nightmare. She and Brooke had been close, for all their differences, and she missed her desperately.

"It's worse at night," she whispered to the headstone. "Remember how we used to lie awake and talk after Mom and Dad thought we were asleep? I don't have anybody to talk to anymore. Well," she amended, "I still have Amy, but she's not the same as having you."

In the silence she could hear a bird calling from far away in the trees that bounded the cemetery.

Where had Brooke gone when she died? That question had plagued Tracy's nightmares since the deaths. It was particularly troubling because no one could answer it for certain. Tracy knew that her preacher and her parents had an opinion about it, but she wasn't so sure she believed in a Heaven where Brooke would be an angel and sit on some cloud and play a harp. The thought was ridiculous enough to make her smile again. She could just picture Brooke tossing her long red hair at the idea and leading the other angels in a protest.

Tracy touched her own hair. It was blond and long, though not as long as Brooke's had been. It hung perfectly straight to past her shoulders and refused any attempts she had ever made to coax curls into it. Brooke had inherited the blue eyes, not Tracy. Hers were an ambiguous hazel—brown one day and green the next. She was accustomed to the fact that Brooke had been by far the more beautiful, more accomplished and definitely smarter of the two of them.

Tears began to well up again in Tracy's eyes. This time they were tears of pity for herself rather than tears of sorrow. She wasn't sure which hurt more.

Since Brooke had died, her father had also changed, and Tracy couldn't understand that. It was as if he never had time for her anymore. She tried to put the thought out of her mind. There was no point in blaming that on Brooke, though Tracy did. In life Brooke had had everything. It seemed in death she still had it all.

Tracy was worried about these thoughts. Was it all right to be angry at her dead sister? It certainly didn't seem like something she should be feeling, and Tracy was thankful that her parents couldn't know this. But lately when she thought about Brooke, her thoughts drifted to angry issues instead of grief. That was why she had come alone to the cemetery. She hoped the sight of Brooke's grave would make her thoughts more acceptable. It hadn't.

19

Tracy turned and went back to the car, the grass and tombstones a blur through her tears. Before she got in, she looked back again. "I miss you," she repeated. "I just wish everything could be the way it was before." Again she wondered why Brooke had done it. She had had problems, sure, but who didn't? Tracy would have traded problems with Brooke any day and been glad for the exchange. At times she felt as if she were being swamped by her own troubles. So why had Brooke killed herself?

There was no answer. Tracy got into her car and started the engine. A glance at her watch told her she'd have to hurry to get home before her mother returned and asked her where she had been. At least that was what her mother would have done before. Since the deaths, Tracy's mother had been different. Far too different. That was one of Tracy's greatest problems. She drove away from the grave and out of the cemetery without giving it a backward glance.

Tess Bowen looked around her new home and tried to find enjoyment in her freedom. She had been divorced for nearly nine months, but she still felt as if part of her were missing.

She had put most of her things away, but boxes of various sizes and shapes still cluttered the rooms. Moving was difficult even if a person had someone to help them. Alone it was a monumental task.

Coming to Maple Glen had, however, put distance between Brad and herself, and that made it worth the effort. She had continued teaching through the end of the school term, but working in the same school with

20

him and seeing him in the halls between classes had been difficult, especially since she knew by the grapevine that he was sleeping with the new history teacher, a girl fresh out of college. She told herself she didn't mind and that she was lucky to be rid of him. The last part was true. Brad had never made marriage easy. Nevertheless, a tear welled in her brown eyes, which she quickly brushed away.

She wondered what her new school would be like. She had seen it, of course, but that hadn't given her a feel for the students and other teachers. Every school had a personality of its own, she had noticed. The building was impressive. It had been built early in the century and looked as if it would still be standing square and solid centuries in the future. It was a nice change from her previous school with its pastel panels and row upon row of uninteresting windows that had been thoroughly modern in the 1950s.

Maple Glen was also a refreshing change from the busy streets of St. Louis. Nestled in Missouri's rolling hills as if it were comfortably settled in the palm of a giant hand, Maple Glen looked like the perfect hometown, the sort you'd find pictured on ribbon candy tins at Christmas or used as the setting for a nostalgic movie. Tess hoped it would prove to be as peaceful as it looked. Her life could use some peace and quiet after the year of conflict that led up to her divorce.

Glancing at her watch, Tess decided she had time to run by the school and put away the supplies she had bought the evening before. The principal, Mr. Crouthers, had been surprisingly lenient in telling her to get whatever art supplies she needed and that the school would reimburse her. Tess appreciated the lack of red tape. In her old school she would have had to fill out forms, formally request the supplies and then, as likely as not, still have to buy them herself.

Although she hadn't seen her homeroom yet, the principal had given her the list of supplies already there. It seemed the last teacher had been fond of making written inventories at the end of the year. Tess hoped she wouldn't be expected to do the same. Her previous school had spoiled her on that count.

Not wanting to press her luck with the new system, Tess had bought only a few boxes of colored markers and assorted pencils and tape—the sort of things she could be sure of needing, no matter how organized the last teacher had been. Pencils always disappeared and tape dispensers had a habit of walking away with the students. She considered waiting to carry the supplies to her art room the following Monday when school would start, but she wanted to see the room and get acquainted with the materials that were there.

She retrieved the sack of supplies she'd left in her hall closet, ran a brush through her short brown hair and went out to her car. She had been lucky in finding a house only five blocks from the school. On nice days she could walk to work, yet it was far enough from the school to be isolated from the traffic of students and parents. The neighborhood was quiet, and her street was lined on both sides with large trees whose leafy branches arched across the pavement to form a virtual canopy. Her house was a typical one story brick with a lawn that looked as if it had been established and carefully tended by a gardener. After years of apartment living, this was like paradise.

When she reached the school, she was relieved to

find she wouldn't be there alone; another car was already out front. She parked her car beside the other one and headed up the sidewalk carrying her sack of supplies. Now was as good a time as any to meet one of her fellow teachers.

The steel entry doors were locked as Tess had expected them to be. She fished in her purse for several moments, then found the key the principal had given her and let herself in.

Once inside, she turned off the alarm system as she'd been instructed to do, then paused and listened. She could hear sounds coming through the door next to the principal's office. "Hello?" she called out, not wanting to walk in and startle someone.

"I'm in here, in the teacher's lounge," a voice called out.

Tess opened the door. A rather formidable-looking woman with dark gray hair arranged in a style that had been popular several decades before was wiping clean a glass coffee pot. "Hello," Tess said. "I saw a car out front and thought someone was here.

"It seems as if I live here. You must be the new art teacher," the older woman said as Tess came into the room. "I'm Hannah Mitchell. I teach English."

"I'm Tess Bowen." She put down the sack she carried, smiled and looked around the room. She hoped she didn't look as nervous about this new job as she felt. Tess had never been comfortable in new situations. "It's going to take me a while to find my way around, I guess."

"It won't take long. This building is old, but its floor plan is pretty simple. You'll be surprised how soon you'll know where everything is. Trust me."

"I came by to put away some art supplies. I hope I'm not disturbing you." Although the woman seemed friendly, there was something odd about her that left Tess feeling like a trespassing student. She wondered if the school had some sort of restriction about teachers wearing jeans in the building during hours when classes were not being held.

"Not at all. I like company," Hannah replied as she knelt and fished out one of the two cans of coffee stored under the counter. "I only live a couple of blocks away, and I'm the one who usually sees to it that there's coffee and creamer and so forth here in the lounge. Since we didn't have the second semester of summer school, I wasn't sure what I'd find."

Tess looked at her in surprise. "There was no second semester? Why not?"

Hannah straightened and surveyed Tess from head to toe with blatant curiosity. "You haven't heard about it?"

"Heard about what? I only moved here three days ago." It was the troubled look in the woman's eyes that had left Tess feeling uncomfortable.

For a minute Tess thought the woman would refuse to answer. Finally she said, "We had some deaths here last month. Everyone was so upset, the principal canceled classes for the rest of the summer."

"I never heard of such a thing," Tess said. "He actually canceled school? What about the state requirements? Surely it would have been better for the students to have their lives proceed as usual."

"The people who died were all students."

Stunned, Tess sat on the arm of a stuffed chair.

24

"How terrible! Mr. Crouthers didn't mention it to me. You'd have thought he would have told me."

"He probably assumed you knew. It was on the national news. They even did a segment about it on *60 Minutes.*"

"I didn't watch much television this summer. I've been involved in a messy divorce, and it's taken all my energy. That's why I moved here to Maple Glen. I'm trying to make a new start."

Hannah looked as if she couldn't comprehend how a person might not have heard about Maple Glen's tragedy. "That's why the position of art teacher came open at the last minute like this. Mrs. Larson was kin to one of the students, a boy named Troy Spaulding. She was due to retire anyway, so she told Mr. Crouthers that she wouldn't be back."

"Please don't think I'm callous, but I'm having trouble understanding how a death, as tragic as it is when it's a child, could have such far-reaching results."

"There wasn't just one death." Hannah turned away as if the words were painful to her. "There were twelve."

"Twelve? What on earth happened? Was it a school bus wreck?"

"I really can't talk about it." Hannah shut the cabinet door and turned to leave. "I'm sorry, but it still hurts me too much. I knew all the students and was rather close to one or two of them. They were all enrolled for my classes this coming year." Hannah paused. "They would all have graduated in the spring." She lowered her head and walked quickly toward the door.

25

"I'm sorry. I didn't mean to upset you."

Hannah stopped and looked back. "I know. You haven't done anything wrong." Taking a deep breath, she said, "I haven't talked to anyone about this since it happened, but I have to learn to face it. School starts next week, and I'll almost certainly have to talk to the students about it. I guess I may as well start now." She sat on the nearest chair. "The deaths were all suicides."

"Suicide!"

"At first there was talk that it might have been a mass murderer, but they all died at approximately the same time, all in different locations, and some by means a murderer wouldn't think of using."

Tess didn't know what to say. "How could that happen? Twelve?"

Hannah nodded. "The police assume it was some sort of suicide pact, but I think that's impossible. They didn't have anything in common, those students. While they knew each other, of course, none of them were close friends. The boy I mentioned earlier, Troy Spaulding, had dated one of the girls, a pretty girl named Brooke Wright. She was one of the cheerleaders last year, and he was captain of the football team. But they had broken up before school was out and apparently weren't dating any longer."

"That's incredible! I had no idea anything like this had happened here. Maple Glen seems so peaceful!"

"We're trying to get on with our lives. It's not easy."

"I don't know what to say." Tess felt stunned. "I can't believe Mr. Crouthers didn't tell me about this when I applied for the job."

"We all were afraid Maple Glen would get a bad

reputation. He probably decided you knew and weren't affected by it, or maybe he thought he was lucky to find a teacher to take Mrs. Larson's place at such a late date and didn't want to take any chances on losing you. Other than myself, she had been teaching here longer than any of the others. I know he was concerned about finding a replacement."

"It sounds like this won't be an easy year."

"No, it won't be easy for any of us. To tell you the truth, I'm almost dreading the beginning of classes. Maybe we should have kept the school open this summer, I don't know. At the time, it seemed like the right thing to close it. No one wanted to be here or to have to think about the tragedy more than was necessary."

"You said you were close to some of the students?"

Hannah nodded. "When you've been teaching at a school for as long as I've been at this one, you know all the students. I even taught some of their parents. I was particularly close to Troy Spaulding. I taught a junior class last year in addition to my senior ones and he was in it. He was a good boy and a better than average student. I always had the feeling he was really listening to me. They all don't, you know."

"I know."

"Brooke Wright, the girl he used to date, went to my church. I've known her all her life. She was such a lovely girl. Popular, too. Cheerleaders always are. I suspect her mother was guilty of pushing Brooke too much, but the girl showed so much promise. Brooke was the only girl in school with long red hair, and it was about the prettiest hair I've ever seen." Hannah pulled her thoughts back and smiled self-consciously. "You get attached to some of the students. You try not to show favorites, but you can't help having some that you like better than others."

"I know. After I decided to come here, I realized I would miss teaching some of the students in the school I was in before this one."

"It's hard, getting a divorce and moving to a new town at the same time."

"Yes, but my ex-husband is also a teacher at that same school, and I couldn't handle seeing him in the halls every time I turned around. Like I said, it was a messy divorce and there were hard feelings all around. I saw our friends choosing one side over the other, and I knew I had to find a new start."

"I've been a widow for years. I considered moving away when Willard died, but it would have been a mistake for me. I've lived in Maple Glen all my life." She hesitated. "After this summer, I've wondered if it might not have been better if I hadn't. Then I wouldn't have known the students so well."

Tess felt uncomfortable with the older woman's confessions. She wasn't used to people who opened up so quickly. "I guess I ought to be taking these supplies to my room and let you get back to what you were doing." Tess picked up the sack she had been carrying.

Hannah nervously laughed, as if she felt foolish for letting a stranger see her vulnerability. "You must think I'm a silly old woman for carrying on like this."

Tess smiled. "No, I don't think that. You must be a good teacher. Otherwise you wouldn't care so deeply."

"Do you mind being in the school alone? I was just about to leave."

"No, I don't mind. It will take me a while to inventory what's in my room and to organize it the way I want it. I didn't know anyone would be here at all."

"I'll be running along then. It was nice meeting you."

"Thank you. I'm glad to know someone's name and face before we're bombarded with students. The beginning of school is always frantic."

Hannah smiled. "If you need anything, my homeroom is 317."

"Thanks." Tess followed the other teacher out the door and they went in separate directions. After the outside door clanged shut behind Hannah, the school was eerily silent.

Tess went purposefully to the stairs, telling herself she didn't mind being alone in the building. It was likely, she thought, that other teachers would be coming to their homerooms in preparation for the arrival of students on Monday. This had been standard procedure in her former school.

The stairs were divided by a low wall, making one lane for going up and another for going down. Tess went up the right side, her footsteps echoing around her. At the top of the stairs, a long hall stretched before her. Behind her were the stairs to the third floor. She still heard no sounds but her own.

Reading the numbers over the doors, Tess went down the locker-lined hall. The janitor apparently had been busy, for the aging tile floor gleamed with a coat of new wax, and although the walls above the lockers needed a fresh coat of paint in a more modern color, they were free of graffiti, which was more than could be said of the school she had moved from.

For a minute she longed for the more up-to-date

building of her old school with its newer design and modern facilities. But Brad was there with no intention of leaving the school or its new history teacher, and she was reminded how glad she was for anything that put distance between them.

The art room, number 203, was the second to the last room on the left. She unlocked it with her key, and the door swung open easily. She was pleased to find the room sunny. There were two rows of tables with four chairs at each table. Her desk sat at the front of the room and both it and the teacher's chair bore evidence of years of wear and tear. At the back of the room were shelves that served as a room divider between the classroom and the area for mixing paint.

Tess carried her supplies to the back and started putting them away on the shelves. Her predecessor, Mrs. Larson, had left everything tidy. The bottles of glue were grouped on a shelf with construction paper and a box of scissors. Rows of large cans of powdered tempura paint were arranged according to color. Tape, crayons, pencils and markers were on another shelf, along with boxes of woodworking tools.

As she stretched on tiptoes to put the markers she'd bought on the top shelf, the hairs on the back of her neck stood up. Instinctively, she jerked her head around to look behind her. The room was still empty, but she could have sworn someone had come in. Feeling foolish for being so nervous, she turned back to her work and started to inventory the woodworking tools.

Wood carving made a mess, but she had found students enjoyed making block prints out of sections of four by fours. In her old school, students had been forbidden to carry knives and she assumed it would be the same in this one. Carving with the tools she provided gave the students the experience of carving safely.

Again she thought she felt someone near her, and she turned abruptly, but found no one else there. Nevertheless, she felt uneasy. The building was large and old and she told herself this had put her nerves on edge. But she was determined to finish her tasks before leaving. She would frequently be here after hours to set up crafts and art projects, and she couldn't allow herself to be afraid of the building.

She added her new pencils to the ones already in the can and realized she was moving silently as if she were afraid of being overheard. She made an effort to move more naturally. There was no reason to be afraid here. None at all. The downstairs doors locked automatically and only someone with a key could get inside.

At that instant, she heard a locker slam shut out in the hall. She jumped and her heart began to race. Telling herself it had to be another teacher, she went to the door and looked out.

The hall was empty and all the lockers were shut firmly. "Is anybody here?" she called out, trying to make her voice sound authoritative, despite her nervousness. There was no answer.

She forced herself to go back to the shelves in the rear of her room. For a long minute she stood there, her eyes turned toward the door. Had her mind been playing tricks on her? She knew of nothing else that would make the sound of a locker being slammed. The other classrooms in this hall must certainly be for teaching history and math and the like—they weren't likely to have anything in them that could sound like a locker being closed. Besides, she had called out, and

31

surely if another teacher was in one of the adjacent rooms she would have gotten an answer.

Tess finished putting the contents of her sack in place and was glad to leave the room. The hall seemed longer than before, but she knew that was because the window that lit it was behind her and the stairs at the far end only looked dark by comparison. She had not bothered turning on the hall light when she came in, but wished now that she had, since the light switches were all at the top of the stairs. She told herself not to be silly and hurried ahead.

As she was going down the stairs she heard sounds coming from the floor above. She couldn't quite identify them. They were almost like words, but muffled and too low to quite make out their meaning. She paused, her hand gripping the rail of the partition that divided the stairs. "Is there anyone up there?"

When only silence returned, she told herself there was no reason to go up and check, and she felt somewhat relieved. The building was old. Maybe it made strange noises. Tess hurried down the remaining stairs, reactivated the alarm system, and went out the front doors. Only then did she realize she was holding her breath and trembling.

A panic attack, she told herself. She had had them occasionally. It would go away soon. But she looked back at the metal doors and was glad she didn't have to go back inside until others would be there with her. Telling herself she would soon be accustomed to the building's creaks and groans, she managed to walk sedately to her car.

* * *

32

Lucy Wright called out to let her husband and daughter know she was back from shopping. Going to the kitchen table, she eased her purchases out of her aching arms then touched her graying brown hair to be sure it was still neatly combed. She hadn't expected to buy so much, but school would start for her daughter the following Monday and she wanted her to be ready. "Tracy, come look what I found for you," she called toward the den.

Her teenage daughter ambled into the kitchen. These days Tracy always looked sad.

Lucy opened the first sack. "Blouses were on sale at Bendalls. This will match your plaid skirt. See?"

Tracy picked up the blouse halfheartedly. "It's pretty. But my skirt is shades of red and this blouse is blue. I almost never wear blue."

For a moment Lucy was confused. Of course. Brooke had been the one to wear blue. Her eyes stung with tears.

Tracy managed a smile and said, "Thanks, Mom. It'll go great with my new jeans. Everything goes with jeans."

Lucy stared at the blouse. "I feel so stupid. When I was in the store I forgot . . . Maybe you should exchange it. Get yourself something else." Lucy turned away so Tracy couldn't see her face. How had she forgotten even for a moment that Brooke was dead?

Tracy stood there awkwardly, still holding the blouse. "Mom? Are you feeling all right?"

"Of course I am," Lucy said more sharply than she had intended. "I just bought the wrong color, that's all."

Tracy reached in the sack and took out two hairbrushes, one pink, the other blue. She held them silently in her hand, then laid them on the table to reach into the other sack. "You bought two of everything."

Lucy sat in the nearest chair. What had happened to her? She barely remembered being in the store at all. "I wanted you to have all you'd need," she said unconvincingly.

"Two hairbrushes?"

"One is for me," Lucy lied.

Tracy sat beside her. "Mom, I think you should see a doctor."

"I'm not sick," Lucy snapped. She had to think. What else had she done while she was out? Had she spoken to anyone and mentioned Brooke as if she were still alive? She had caught herself doing that before. "I've been under a lot of stress since . . . this past month. We all have."

Tracy reached out to pat her shoulder. "I know. It's been terrible. But we have to put it behind us. We have to go on."

Lucy glared at her. "How can I? Your sister is dead!" She still had trouble saying that. "I can't just put it out of my mind and act as if she never existed. If only we hadn't bought her that car." She leaned her elbow on the table and rested her forehead on her palm. A headache was starting to throb behind her eyes.

"It wouldn't have mattered," Tracy said softly. "That's what the counselor said. If she was determined to do it, we couldn't have stopped her."

"Don't talk like that!" Lucy pulled away. "It was an accident, I tell you. I know it was a coincidence, but that's all it was. An accident. Brooke had no reason to kill herself."

Tracy looked uncomfortable, as if she disagreed but didn't want to argue about it. She had always been less inclined to argue than had Brooke. Lucy didn't like to recall all the heated words she and Brooke had exchanged. Lucy had always said they were as different at oil and water. Brook had been beautiful and talented from the cradle, whereas Tracy was more usually described as a "late bloomer." But despite their differences, they had been close.

"I miss her, too," Tracy said as if she knew what her mother had been thinking. "At times my room seems awfully lonesome without her in it." She sighed. "I went through her clothes and took out the things I'd like to keep."

"We'll keep all of them," Lucy said quickly. She couldn't bear to part with the clothes Brooke had worn and touched and loved. "We have plenty of room."

Tracy looked disturbed. "Mom, we talked about this. Dad and I both agree that it's going to be better to get most of her things out of sight. We miss her too much. When I open her closet and all her clothes are still hanging in there, it makes me feel terrible. And it's not good for you, either."

Lucy heard her husband coming into the kitchen and glanced at the door. Ross stopped in the doorway, and she knew he must have heard all they had said. She tried to pretend nothing was wrong. "Go put your things away," she said to Tracy. "I'm going to start supper now."

"Lucy, you've got to get some help," Ross said as he

picked up the blue hairbrush and blouse. "Let me call Dr. Hudson. He said he'll manage to work in all the parents who need him. He helped me get through it."

"How can you stand there and say you've gotten over Brooke? Are you trying to tell me that you no longer miss her? That you don't still listen for her to come in?"

Ross gently drew Tracy from the chair and nudged her toward the door. Tracy took the hint and left the room. Ross sat where she had been and took Lucy's hand. "Honey, I still miss her. I always will. But I've come to grips with the fact that she's gone. You haven't. We're worried about you."

"There's no need to be," Lucy said stiffly. "There's nothing wrong with me."

Ross didn't answer.

Lucy frowned at him. "I'm not crazy, you know."

"No one said that you are."

"No, but you've hinted at it pretty strongly lately. All this talk about seeing Dr. Hudson! Don't you think I know what you mean by that? You think I'm having a nervous breakdown or something."

Ross was silent so long Lucy gave him a sharp look. "Honey, we all miss Brooke. We'll probably never know what happened to make her or the others do such a thing. But do you think she would want you to refuse to get help or to go on with your life?"

"I have no idea what you're talking about. I just came back from the store. I'm getting Tracy ready for school. That's getting on with my life, if you ask me."

Ross picked up the blue blouse. "Let me make an appointment for you with Dr. Hudson. If he tells us you're okay, I'll never mention it again."

36

Lucy stood and stalked to the sink. "I have work to do."

For a while Ross sat there watching her, then he sighed and left the room. Lucy put her palms on the countertop to steady herself and leaned forward. Was he right? How could she sometimes forget that Brooke wasn't still living in the house?

This wasn't the first time she had accidentally bought something for Brooke since the accident—she refused to think of the car wreck in any other term. The week before she had found herself buying a type of sandwich meat that no one else in the house ate but Brooke, and the diet colas she preferred. Once, she had come home to discover she had bought two sweaters and a skirt in the colors that would have been perfect with Brooke's red hair but all wrong with Tracy's blond hair. Before anyone else could notice what she'd done, she took the clothing back to the store and exchanged it for clothing Tracy would wear. The clerk had given her a peculiar look but hadn't asked any questions.

Lucy straightened, found herself steady again and began moving about the kitchen, automatically cooking supper and remembering how good it had been before the accident when Brooke had friends over and how she had practiced cheerleader yells in the den on rainy days. How Brooke and Tracy had laughed over certain boys and hoped others would ask them out.

She thought about Troy Spaulding. Brooke had liked him a lot the year before. Now he was dead, too. Could he have had any bearing on Brooke's death? He was found in the school, like the Traveno girl. Was there a connection there as well?

She set the table, still moving on automatic pilot. Could Brooke have left a suicide note in some unlikely place, like the attic or a closet? She hadn't thought to look in places like the coat closet since it had happened in July. It seemed unlikely that Brooke would do that, but none of it made any sense.

Lucy left the meat cooking and went to the coat closet. She could hear the TV in the den and at times she was sure she could hear Tracy and Ross talking in low voices. They seemed to do that often of late. Had they always done that and she just never noticed?

She opened the door of the coat closet and started going through all the coat pockets, not just the ones belonging to Brooke, but every coat, sweater and jacket. When she found nothing in the pockets, she started searching the shelf.

"Mom? What are you doing?"

Lucy turned to see Tracy staring at her, her eyes wide and frightened. "Nothing. I was just looking for something." She shut the closet door and went back to the kitchen.

The meat was burning in the pan but Lucy pretended not to notice as she moved the skillet aside. It wouldn't hurt any of them to eat overdone meat. She had too much else to think about. To Tracy she said, "Call you father. It's ready."

Tracy was looking at the table. For a minute Lucy didn't see what was wrong, then she silently went to the place where Brooke used to sit and removed the place setting there. She didn't meet Tracy's eyes. It was only a mistake. Nothing else. She couldn't worry about that now. Methodically she began to dish up the vegetables and carry the bowls to the table.

Tracy sat on the twin bed she always slept in at Amy Dennis's house and hugged her knees to her chest under her nightgown. "I'm dreading the start of school."

"Yeah, me too." Amy was sitting at her old-fashioned dresser trying to find a new style for her hair. "What do you think?" She piled it on top of her head and a brown tendril drifted down to her shoulders.

Tracy managed to smile. "It looks like you combed it with a mixer."

Amy sighed and let her hair fall. "You're so lucky to have straight hair. Mine won't do anything but go its own way."

"Yeah, right. Like mine won't."

"But yours always looks so smooth and shiny. Everybody wants blond hair."

"I don't mind the color. Brooke's was prettier. Everybody says so."

"You don't see many people with red hair that long. It was beautiful." Amy looked at her friend in the mirror. "You still miss her a lot, don't you?"

"Of course I do. That's a dumb question," Tracy snapped.

"You don't have to take my head off." Amy turned back to her own reflection.

"I'm sorry. I had a problem with my Mom tonight. She set Brooke's place at the table again." Tracy forced Amy to meet her eyes in the mirror. "Don't you tell a single soul I ever said this!"

39

"You know I won't. If you can't talk to your best friend, who can you talk to?"

"Mom also bought Brooke some more clothes and a hair brush."

"No!" Amy's eyes were wide.

"What am I going to do? Why does she keep doing things like this?" Tracy fell back on the bed, her arms spread, her hands dangling over the edges of the mattress. "People are going to think she's crazy. And she's not," she added.

"I know she's not." Amy was loyal to a fault. "Have you tried to talk to her?"

"Sure I have. It doesn't do any good. Nothing does."

"Has she talked to Dr. Hudson? My Mom says he's real good."

"I guess she has. I don't know." Tracy rolled over onto her stomach. "I went to the cemetery today."

"You did? All by yourself? I'd have gone with you."

"I know. I just needed to be by myself." She paused a moment and decided she couldn't trust even Amy with the admission of her angry thoughts about Brooke.

"I just don't think that's a good idea. I know you loved Brooke and you miss her, but you have to get on with your life."

Tracy glanced at Amy's back. She could remember a time when a month seemed like a long time to her, too. "She would have graduated next spring."

"And we'll graduate the following spring. Where are you going to college? I just can't decide."

"I haven't even thought about it. I'd love to get away from Maple Glen. I can tell you that."

"God, me too! I won't ever come back here. Except for visits, that is." Amy put her head to one side. "Maybe I ought to cut my hair. What do you think?"

"I like it long. That way you can wear it up or down or whatever. You cut it short in the fifth grade and you hated it."

"I remember. It looked awful. My hair always looks awful!"

Tracy smiled. "No, it doesn't. Here. Let me try." She got off the bed and came to stand behind Amy. "I saw Jason Cook today." She knew Amy had had a crush on Jason for weeks.

"Was Britanny Sinclair draped all over him?"

"Not this time. He's so cute!"

"I know! I wish he'd ask me out. I don't even like Britanny. Do you?"

"No way!" Tracy was also loyal. "I think she wears contacts to make her eyes that color."

"I wouldn't put it past her."

Tracy brushed Amy's hair back from her face. "I'm going to try to French braid it."

"Great!"

Tracy picked up a strand of Amy's hair and twisted it with a strand from the other side. "I wish school would never start."

"Me, too." Amy's face fell. "I really dread it. It won't seem right with so many of the senior class missing."

"I know."

"Why do you suppose they did it? I mean, it wasn't like they ran around together or anything. Brooke wasn't still dating Troy. None of the others ever dated at all, as far as I know."

41

"Mom says Brooke's death was an accident, that it was just a coincidence that her car hit that tree the same night as all the others died."

"Was it, do you think?"

Tracy was quiet for a time. "No. She didn't have any reason to be out there on that road all by herself. Nobody ever goes out there alone. It's always to race or sit on their car hoods under that tree. She wouldn't have had any reason to be there in the middle of the night all alone. That makes less sense than if she meant to do it."

"Ouch! That's too tight."

"Sorry." Tracy loosened her grip on Amy's hair. "Graduation this year will be awful! Somebody told me Kathy Alsop was even in the running for valedictorian."

"Was she? I knew she was smart." Amy frowned. "I hate to say this, but will they still use the auditorium? I mean, after Misty Traveno hung herself there and all."

"I guess they'll have to."

Amy shivered. "She was always so weird! I won't be able to go in there without thinking about her."

"Well, Troy was found outside the English room, and you'll have to go to class there every day."

"I know, but I always think of him being in the gym. He was so good at sports. Why do you suppose he was outside the English room of all places?"

"I have no idea." Tracy looked at Amy in the mirror. "I'm sort of scared to go back to school. Do you know what I mean?"

Amy nodded. "Yeah. I am, too."

"Sometimes I'm not sure I know who I am anymore."

Amy looked puzzled. "What do you mean?"

Tracy didn't know how to explain it, so she changed the direction of the conversation to the safer subject of which boys they hoped to date the coming year. But she still felt lost and confused inside.

Chapter Two

As the students came through the door to the art room, Tess felt her nervousness easing. These boys and girls looked no different than those she had taught for years. Although the setting was different and the students unfamiliar to her, all else was the same.

She waited behind the scarred desk for the second bell to ring. The boys and girls were staring at her and speculating about her in whispers. She ignored them. All new teachers went through this gauntlet of inspections. Would she be stricter than Mrs. Larson had been? Would she expect more or less from them?

When the bell rang she stood and faced the class, her attendance book in her hand. "My name is Mrs. Bowen. This is my first year in Maple Glen High as I'm sure you all know." She gave them a small smile— enough to appear friendly but slight enough to keep the necessary barrier that separated her from them. If she later wanted to let some of the students know her better, she could let down more defenses then. Tess knew from experience that it was easier to maintain discipline if she preserved distance from the students.

"I'm going to call the roll and put names with faces. It may take me a few days to learn you all, but by the end of the week I should know you." She consulted her book. "Kelly Nelson?"

A mousy girl at the front table held up her hand, then lowered it quickly. "Here." She glanced around to see if anyone was laughing at her.

"Lester Conroe?" The giggles told her Lester went by a nickname. A large black boy held up his hand and glared at the gigglers. "Do you prefer to be called something else?" she asked.

"Everybody calls me Mojo."

Tess picked up a pencil and made a note. "Very well, Mojo."

One by one she clicked off the students. As she did she found herself watching a rather peculiar girl in the back of the room. The girl was sitting quietly at the end of the last table, apparently daydreaming as she stared at a spot just past Tess's shoulder. Tess glanced around to see if there was something behind her that she wasn't aware of but found nothing that might have been the focus of the girl's attention. So far, the girl hadn't answered to any of the names. She only sat there, her long red hair draped over one shoulder and her skin paler than any of the other girls'.

When Tess reached the end of the list, she looked back down at her attendance book with a frown. The pale girl hadn't responded. Was she in the wrong classroom? "I'm sorry, but I don't seem to have you on my . . ." Tess stopped in midsentence.

The girl was gone. She couldn't have possibly left the room without Tess seeing her. Had she slipped into the work area? Tess felt the others' eyes following her as she went to the back of the room. She looked behind the wall of shelves that screened the sink and supplies from the rest of the room. No one was there.

Prickles of apprehension began crawling up the back of her neck. She told herself someone was playing a joke on her. New teachers often had to weather this. Going to the table where the girl had sat, she fixed the two boys there with a cool gaze and said, "Where did the girl go?"

They looked at each other in honest confusion. "What girl?" Mojo asked.

Tess straightened. Had her eyes been playing tricks on her? Impossible. But she believed Mojo and had no other explanation. "Never mind. Today we're going to sketch. You'll find paper and pencils on the shelves. I try to avoid traffic jams at the supplies, however, so I'm going to ask," she glanced at the roll book, "Mary to hand out the paper and pencils."

A girl at the second table stood and went to the supply area. Tess glanced at her to be sure she was finding everything as she added, "I don't accept sketches or drawings of any kind in ballpoint pen. When we start our pen and ink work, you'll be asked to use India ink and pens which the school will furnish."

The boy sitting by Mojo said, "Mrs. Larson let us draw with whatever we wanted to use."

Tess gave him another small smile to soften her words. "I'm not Mrs. Larson. I insist on pencil drawings." She ignored the muffled groan. Some rebellion was to be expected. As Mary passed around the paper and pencils, Tess returned to the front of the class. "If any of you have any problems, you're free to come to

46

me. If you need another sheet of paper or break the lead in your pencil, you may take care of that need without permission as long as you do so quietly." She had given this speech so often to so many classes she knew it by memory.

Her eyes went back to the place where the red-haired girl had been sitting. Where had she gone? And why hadn't Mojo and the other boy seen her? She gave the assignment for the day's sketching and pretended to be busy with papers at her desk. Who was she, and how had she been able to leave the room without Tess seeing her?

The morning flew by. The other two classes were much like the first. Tess had known they would be. The students' names and faces were already connecting for her. Tess had always been good at remembering students, and she knew this would give her an edge at this new school. At lunch she sat with the other teachers at the table along the back wall of the cafeteria and looked at the students. The red-haired girl wasn't there, but it was possible she had a different lunch break.

She turned to the middle-aged man sitting closest to her. "We haven't met. I'm Tess Bowen, the new art teacher."

The man smiled. "Ed Hudson. I'm not exactly a teacher. I'm the school counselor. Or at least I am on Wednesday and Friday."

"This is Monday."

"I know. In view of the deaths last summer, I thought it might be prudent for me to be here on the first day of school. In case any of the students need to talk, you know."

47

Tess nodded. "Mrs. Mitchell told me about the tragedy. I missed seeing any mention of it on TV and had no idea such a thing had happened."

Ed looked at her as he chewed his broccoli casserole. "I'm surprised Fred Crouthers didn't fill you in on it when you were hired."

"I suppose he thought I knew or that it wouldn't affect my job."

Ed shook his head. "I'm afraid this will affect all of us for a long time."

The woman sitting beside him nodded. "It certainly will. I still can't believe it. All those young people! What could have caused them to do such a thing?" Her eyes were troubled and her face looked as if it might pucker into tears at any moment.

Tess averted her eyes and wondered again why she hadn't been told about the deaths before she took the job. Was it only that the principal was insensitive to a tragedy of this magnitude or was it that he had been afraid no one would take the position if they connected the deaths with Maple Glen High? Tess would have taken the job under any conditions, but he couldn't have known that. This job opening had saved her from having to teach at the same school with her ex-husband. Not many positions came open so late in the summer.

A tall man with an athletic build joined them and sat on Tess's right. He grinned at her and said, "You must be the new art teacher. I'm Lane Hodges."

"I'm Tess Bowen." She realized she was staring and looked away. He was more handsome than the average man, and she wondered if her reaction was an unusual one.

48

"Lane is our coach and history teacher," Ed told her. "He stays busy this time of year."

Lane grinned again. "I'm busy all year," he corrected goodnaturedly. "We have more sports than football, you know."

Ed smiled back. "But none more important." To Tess Ed explained, "Maple Glen went to the finals last year and there's hope we will again."

"I hope you're right," Lane said as he buttered his bread. "Losing Troy and Jimmy could cost us."

"Troy and Jimmy?" Tess asked.

Lane and Ed exchanged a look. "They were two of the students who died last summer," Lane explained.

"Troy Spaulding and Jimmy Frye," Ed said as if that explained it. "Troy was team captain and one of the best athletes Maple Glen ever produced."

Lane shook his head. "He and Jimmy weren't particularly close friends. I still find myself wondering why it happened."

The woman beside Ed said, "I do, too. I just doesn't make any sense, if you ask me. None of those students had anything in common. Not a single thing!"

"There must have been something," Ed replied. "We might not ever find out what it was, but twelve suicides on the same night can't be a coincidence." He added to the woman, "If you want to come in and talk to me during your off period, I'll be in my office."

The woman laughed nervously and glanced at the others. "I'd feel so silly doing that. I wouldn't have any idea what to say."

Ed smiled. "I'm hoping more of you teachers will take me up on this. After all, your lives have been affected by this too, and the counseling won't be for free much longer."

"It's like a sale," Lane told her with humor sparkling in his eyes. "I know how you like sales."

The woman blushed and laughed but said in a low voice, "Maybe I will stop by after all. My off period is coming up."

"Great. I don't have anyone scheduled then."

Tess listened and wondered. She had never talked to a counselor unless she counted the marriage counselor that hadn't helped put her marriage back together, but she would have gone to one if it had been her students that died. She was reminded again that Maple Glen's attitudes were rather smaller than its population warranted.

"Where did you move here from?" Lane asked her.

Tess glanced at him to be sure he was talking to her. "I'm from St. Louis."

"The big city," he said with a smile. "Maple Glen must be quite an adjustment for you."

"A bit, but I'm enjoying it. I don't miss the traffic at all. I had a half hour drive in heavy traffic to and from school. Here I live close enough to walk."

"You must have bought the Franklin house."

Tess stared at him. "I believe it *was* owned by a family named Franklin. How on earth did you know that?"

"For one thing, there haven't been that many houses for sale within walking distance of the school, and I noticed the sign was gone from the yard. I live just past it and over a block. We're practically neighbors."

"I guess I'm not used to small town living yet." She

50

pushed her plate away and put her spoon in her jello. "I like the students," she added quickly. "Several of them show real talent."

The woman leaned forward again and said, "We have so many talented students here. By the way, I'm Janis Denkle. I teach speech and drama." She was a youngish woman with dark hair and a receding chin. Her brown eyes looked warm and friendly.

Tess acknowledged her with a smile and nod. "It may take me a while to get to know all of you. I hope you'll bear with me." A thought struck her. "By the way, can you tell me anything about a girl with unusually pale skin and long red hair? She showed up in my first period class and somehow left the room without me seeing her. I guess she was in the wrong class, because she didn't answer to roll call."

Janis glanced at the other teachers. "When you first started talking, Brooke Wright came to mind. She was the only girl in school with long red hair."

"Brooke Wright? That name seems familiar."

"She was one of the twelve students," Ed said. "It couldn't have been her."

"No, of course not," Janis said hurriedly. "Maybe we have a new student I haven't met yet."

"That could be it," Tess agreed. "I just can't see how she left the room without me seeing her."

"She sounds like she's got some fast moves," Lane put in. "We could use her on the track team." He grinned at Tess and winked to include her into the joke.

Tess found herself smiling spontaneously for what seemed to be the first time in days. She thought she might enjoy this new school once she learned her way

51

around. Certainly everyone was friendlier here than in her old school.

After they had all finished eating, Lane showed Tess where the conveyor belt was that carried the dirty dishes back into the kitchen, then headed back to the gym after separating from Tess. His schedule was always arranged so that his senior history classes met the first two periods in the morning and he'd have the rest of the day in the gym.

The gym, built many years before, was out back of the school. As in many small towns, high school athletics was a vital part of the community, and the sports equipment was kept in near-perfect condition. At times he wished his history books were updated so diligently.

He let himself into the gym and didn't bother to lock the door behind him. The next class would be starting soon and it would save him some steps to leave the door open. He skirted the gym floor, his footsteps echoing around him. He liked the feel of being alone there. The gym and locker room were separated from the classrooms by a hall and lockers, and he enjoyed the privacy from time to time.

The locker room was in the back of the building and served both the boys and the girls as their P.E. classes were separately scheduled. There were several showers which Lane suspected were used more often by the girls than the boys, despite his orders for everyone to shower before returning to classes. Past that were the lockers with benches and the equipment closets.

Lane went to one of the equipment closets, unlocked the door with one of the many keys on his key ring and stepped inside. The room smelled of leather and plastic and sweat—odors he was so familiar with that he seldom noticed them. He flipped on a light switch and went to the shelf where the volleyballs were kept and started examining them.

Behind him he heard a faint sound, and he paused to listen, but heard nothing. Thinking it had been only his imagination, he picked up a pump and started airing up one of the volleyballs. The whooshing noise of the air rushing into the ball filled the room. When the ball was firm again, Lane started to put it back on the shelf and get another one to air up, but stopped again to listen. This time, instead of silence, he heard a noise that sounded as if it was coming from out in the locker room.

Remembering he had left the gym door unlocked, he put the pump down and went out into the locker area to see who had come in. "Who's in here?" he called out. It wasn't time for class yet, and all the students knew they weren't allowed in the gym early. No one answered.

Lane had almost concluded it was his imagination when he heard the sound again. It was a strange noise, almost as if someone were whispering but in so low a voice that only parts of the words reached him. Was there someone moving about just past the first row of lockers?

Although Lane wasn't nervous by nature, he felt an icy shiver run down his back. If someone was there, why weren't they answering? Again he heard a sound, this time as if someone was moving about in sock feet—a sound that was almost too soft to hear and that was impossible to locate.

Lane put the volleyball under his arm and walked

silently toward the rows of lockers. If someone was in here, he would remind them of the rules and send them on their way. Loitering could not be allowed; there was too much a student could get into here in the locker room.

Cautiously, he peered around the end of the row of lockers and found he was alone. For a minute he felt confused. How could this be? He put the ball on the floor and went around the next row of lockers. In no time he had retraced his tracks to the gym door and was positive no one else was in the locker room. Again the sound came from the first bay of lockers. Frowning, Lane hurried back, intent only on finding the student or students and sending them packing.

There was no one. He looked around in frustration, then realized the area wasn't as he had left it. On the end of the long bench was a football jersey. As he picked it up, the number thirty-four seemed to leap up at him.

Trying not to show the fear that coursed through him, Lane hurried to the office he shared with the female P. E. instructor and unlocked the door. He crossed the small room and jerked open the cabinet. He had removed two football jerseys from the storage room before school started—the jerseys that had belonged to Troy Spaulding and Jimmy Frye. He hadn't wanted anyone wearing them at least for a year or so and had considered retiring both numbers permanently. Only one jersey, still neatly folded, remained where he had left them both. The other was in his hand.

Number thirty-four. Troy Spaulding's number. As Lane stared at it, he heard another noise behind him.

He wheeled about, prepared to strike out at the sick-minded prankster, but saw nothing for a second. Then the volleyball he'd left in the locker room bounced through the doorway of his office, almost scaring him to death. As quickly as he could get his feet to move, he hurried to the door and looked out. A cold chill raced through him as he realized he was completely alone.

"How's it going?" Amy asked as she sat beside Tracy at the cafeteria table.

"Okay, I guess. Did you get Mr. Davis for math?"

Amy wrinkled her nose. "Yes. Did you?"

Tracy nodded. "I had English this morning. It was weird. I kept thinking about Troy, and I felt like everybody was staring at me. Because of Brooke, you know."

"That must be rough."

Tracy shrugged and tried to pretend she didn't mind. "We're going to fail math. You know that, don't you?"

"I knew it as soon as I saw I had Mr. Davis. He's the meanest teacher in this school. He's even worse than Mrs. Mitchell."

"I don't think she's so bad. She gave us homework though."

"Homework! On our first day of school?" Amy sighed and poked her fork into her red jello. "I hate school. If my parents wouldn't kill me, I wouldn't even consider going to college."

"I thought you wanted to get away from Maple Glen," Tracy teased.

"I do. But I'm not anxious to get away by going to college. If high school is this tough, think what college will be like!"

"Yeah, I've thought about that." Tracy glanced around the cafeteria and her eyes met those of a boy in a black tee-shirt with a picture of a rock group printed on the front. He was boldly staring at her. Tracy hastily looked away. To Amy she said, "Who's that boy over there? The one wearing the Poison Needle shirt?"

Amy glanced with studied casualness across the room. "That's Kevin Donatello. You don't think he's cute, do you?"

"No!" she lied. From the disgusted tone of Amy's voice Tracy didn't want to seem too interested in the boy. That was one of the unwritten rules in being best friends.

"Neither do I. He was in my English class last year, and he's really weird! I mean major time."

"Why is he staring at me so intently?" Tracy was afraid to look back at Kevin, but she could feel her skin crawl as if someone was staring at her.

"Beats me. Just ignore him."

Tracy tried, but it wasn't easy. She picked at her food for a few minutes, then glanced back. He was gone. She relaxed and hurried to finish her meal before her lunch hour was over.

Tess finished the first day of school, glad it had gone so smoothly, and as she left her classroom, her steps echoed down the vacant hall. Apparently, the teachers at this school left almost as quickly as their students, and already the building felt empty. Feeling uneasy, she picked up her pace. As she passed an open door, she was glad to see that Janis Denkle, the drama teacher, was still in her room. Janis waved and smiled. Tess waved back. Although she felt foolish in admitting it even to herself, she was relieved not to be the last to leave. She wasn't sure why, but the old building played havoc with her nerves.

She left the building and was walking down the sidewalk when she saw Lane coming in her direction. They met at the corner. "We're going in the same direction," Lane said. "Mind if I walk with you?"

"Of course not. I'm glad for the company."

"I was curious about what you'd said at lunch regarding the red-haired girl, so I checked with the admissions office. There are no new girls at all this semester. I have to admit I'm wondering who the red-haired one could be."

Tess glanced up at him. "I'm surprised you went to all that trouble. After all, there must be a dozen girls in the school who fit that description."

He was silent for a few steps. "You said her hair was long. How long was it?"

"That's the first thing I noticed about her. It must have reached past her waist. You don't see hair that long very often, much less hair that shade of red. It was coppery, like a new penny. She was quite pretty but awfully pale." Tess laughed. "I thought all teenage girls tried to tan during the summer."

Almost mechanically, Lane said, "Brooke wore her hair in that style. She had the longest hair in school. Her sister's hair is past her shoulders, but not nearly as long as Brooke's. And her sister is blond."

Tess shrugged. "It couldn't possibly be Brooke, so I don't see why everyone keeps telling me about her. I hate to sound callous, but I'm surprised her name keeps cropping up in connection with the girl I saw."

"I know it's impossible. She just keeps coming to mind though." He was quiet for a while. "The deaths hit everyone hard. I guess I'm still not over the shock. Maybe I ought to make another appointment with Ed and talk to him."

"I didn't mean to sound rude. Were you close to Brooke?"

"Not really. Everyone knew her, of course. She was head cheerleader and she dated Troy last year. I knew Troy well." He paused as if he were thinking.

"Can you tell me about the deaths? Since everyone's still talking about them, I feel I need to know more about them."

He drew in a deep breath as if it still bothered him to think about it. "They died mostly in different ways. A few people tried to say they were murdered, but that never held water. No one takes a student to the school and kills him by making him wash his mother's sleeping pills down with bourbon."

"One of them did that? At school?"

"Two were found in the school. Troy mixed pills and booze. A girl named Misty Traveno hung herself on the stage in the auditorium. I'd have said they hardly knew each other, but the doctor said they died at about the same time so they must have gone there together."

"How terrible! I had no idea any of them died in the school."

"The others were at home or around town. Brooke

58

drove her car into a tree. Some say it might have been an accident, but I don't agree. The road out there is perfectly straight and that's the only object she could have found to run into."

"What about the others?"

"Some took massive overdoses of prescription drugs like Valium. One cut her wrists, one shot himself. They used all sorts of methods. Some were good students—Kathy Alsop might have been the valedictorian if she'd lived. Bubba Holt stayed on the edge of flunking every course he took. Some were popular, others probably never had a date in their lives." He shook his head. "There's no rhyme or reason to it, as far as I can tell."

"There has to be. Twelve kids don't decide out of the clear blue to kill themselves and all coincidentally pick the same night to do it. That makes no sense."

"None of it does. That's partly why it's so hard for us to deal with. It could have been any of the kids. Or it could happen again."

"Surely not!"

"I'd have said it couldn't happen once. But I'll bet all the parents are thinking that and wondering if this is just the beginning."

"I can see Ed will have his hands full," she said. "Surely no one really believes it could happen again. It was a tragedy, but most tragedies of this proportion only happen once."

"That's what we're all hoping."

"Do you have a child in the school?"

He shook his head. "This is the first time I've been glad of that. I'm divorced and my son lives in Atlanta

59

with his mother." He made eye contact with her. "How about you? Do you have a family?"

"No. I'm fresh from a divorce and have no children. I came here looking for a new start."

"Looks like you found one." Lane smiled down at her. "The night life in Maple Glen is just about zero, but there are ball games and movies. Maybe we could go to one together."

"I thought you're the coach. Won't you have to sit with the team?"

"Sure, but I don't have to ride to and from the game with them. Maple Glen is friendly, but it can get lonely in the evening. I know because I moved here after my divorce."

"You did? I guess we have something in common." She smiled up at him. "I haven't had time to get lonely yet, but I can see how that will happen once I finish moving in."

"If you need any help, I'm in the phone book. I'm not great at putting things away, but I excel at hauling things to the attic."

"Can I ask you a question? Did any of the students live in the house I just bought?"

"No. That house was on the market before all this happened."

Tess felt a rush of relief. "Good. I'm not superstitious or anything like that, but I was wondering if something terrible had happened there."

"The housing market is slow here. Not many people move to or from Maple Glen. That's why I say it can be lonely. The people mean to be friendly, but most have known each other all their lives and forget that a newcomer may feel left out."

"How long have you been here?"

"Ten years. I'm still considered new around here though. That's the way it is in Maple Glen. Residence is measured in generations."

"It's just the sort of town I was looking for. I loved it the minute I first saw it. All the sleepy streets and huge trees and people who still sit out on their front porches. It looks like the sort of town Norman Rockwell would have painted."

"Up until this summer, it was."

Tess left the sidewalk and walked onto her front lawn. "This is as far as I go."

"I'll see you tomorrow. I go to school early. I'm the one who usually has to supervise the students in SOS—that's how we punish students who are determined to disrupt class. I doubt I'll have any kids for a week or so, but you'd be surprised how quickly the troublemakers get started."

"No, I wouldn't. I've taught for years." She smiled and added, "Would you like to come in for coffee?"

"Thanks, but I have a lesson plan I need to finish before tomorrow. Can I have a rain check?"

"Sure. The offer is open any time. We newcomers have to stick together."

"Right." He grinned as he turned and walked away.

Tess went to the side door and paused for a moment to think before unlocking the door. It had been a long time since she had wanted to talk to a man on a personal basis. At times it seemed as if she and Brad had been married forever. Finding her way around the single scene wasn't going to be easy—she glanced over

61

her shoulder for a last glimpse of Lane Hodges—but it could prove to be interesting.

Kevin Donatello waited on the school grounds to see which way Tracy would go. To his satisfaction, she seemed to be walking home. He jogged to catch up to her and fell in step with her.

"Do you want something?" she asked without a shred of friendliness.

"Whoa! I just wanted to walk with you." He had never paid much attention to her before, but he was intrigued by the fact that Brooke had been her sister. "Okay?"

"I guess so."

They walked in silence for a few steps. "I saw you in the cafeteria today," he said.

"I know. You were staring at me." Tracy didn't give him so much encouragement as a glance.

"You're pretty."

She looked directly at him. "No, I'm not."

"I said you are, didn't I? I ought to know. I'm looking right at you."

Tracy kept walking, but at a faster pace.

"Hey, are we in a race or something? You're walking so fast we can't even talk." He caught her arm, and she allowed him to slow her down. "There. That's much better."

"My mom worries if I come home late."

"So does mine. Big deal. They get over it."

Tracy frowned at him. "That's pretty selfish."

He shrugged. "I'd rather be with a pretty girl than

my mother. Are you going with anybody in particular?"

"No. I'm not interested in sports, and that's all the boys around here seem to think about."

"Not me. I don't even go to the games."

She gave him a long look. "No?"

"I'd like to see you sometime. Okay?"

"Maybe."

He walked for a minute, considering his next move. "One of the things I'm interested in is power."

She laughed. "Power? Excuse me?"

"Don't laugh. I'm serious. Don't you ever wonder about things like that? What makes one person more powerful than another? About the universe and how to use it?"

"How to use the universe?" Tracy stopped walking and stared at him with her head tilted in curiosity. "Are you on something?"

He laughed and shoved his hands into the back pockets of his jeans. "No way! I don't do drugs."

She didn't look convinced, but she resumed walking.

"I'm talking about natural highs. Meditation. Things like that."

"I don't know how to meditate."

"I could teach you."

Tracy looked interested at last. "You could?"

"Sure. It's not that hard. A bunch of us get together and meditate, talk about the universe's power, things like that. Would you like to come?"

"I don't know. Who else would be there?"

"Sorry. Our names are secret."

"What on earth for? We all know each other, more or less. Maple Glen isn't that big."

"I know. There wouldn't be anybody there you don't go to school with. But some of the kids are afraid somebody might make fun of them for being interested in this stuff so we agreed not to tell anyone unless I think they would be a good addition to the group."

"You're the one to decide this?"

"I'm the leader." He watched her profile. "How about it?"

"I have to think about it. When are you getting together?"

"I can't even tell you that."

Tracy paused at the corner. "I don't know. It sounds sort of weird, all this secrecy. You know?"

"Yeah, but if you join us, wouldn't you want your name to be kept secret? That way the jocks can't tease you or come barging in and ruin our gathering."

"Maybe I'd like that. Can Amy Dennis come, too?"

Kevin shook his head. "We only let in one new member at a time. That way we can get used to each other and learn to trust ourselves."

"I'll have to think about it."

Kevin reached out and pushed a strand of her pale hair over her shoulder. "You do that." He gave her a wink and turned and walked away.

He knew she was intrigued. All girls were fascinated by secrets. He had told her enough to know if she was really interested, but not enough for her to know too much too soon. All that would come in time. He had done this before. Kevin had just started gathering his next group.

Chapter Three

"Hitler began his empire by taking over the territories occupied by German-speaking people—Austria and western Czechoslovakia. By March he had control of the rest of Czechoslovakia and in the beginning of September he attacked Poland. That's when Britain and France declared war." Lane Hodges turned from the European map he'd been using for illustration to his history class.

In the second row Kevin Donatello was watching him with rapt attention. The other students lounged in their chairs in varying degrees of disinterest. History wasn't a popular subject, only a required one.

Kevin's hand shot up. "Mr. Hodges? Isn't it true that Hitler was ruler over a nation larger than any since Rome?"

"Since ancient Rome, yes."

The boy's eyes were shining with zeal as if he were hearing a litany he well knew. "Then Hitler was one of the world's greatest men."

Lane studied the boy as he answered. "That depends on your definition on greatness. I don't consider a madman and murderer to be great, no matter how much territory he commanded."

"How can you say he was a madman? He had to be brilliant to conquer all he did. As for him being a murderer, he didn't do anything Roosevelt and Churchill didn't do. People have died in all wars."

Lane carefully put down the chalk. Up until now he hadn't paid much attention to Kevin. He had seen the boy from time to time in the halls, but Kevin was the sort that was easily overlooked. "Hitler's regime was responsible for the deaths of approximately six million people who weren't soldiers."

"Jews," Kevin said, his mouth drawing up at one corner.

"Men, women and children. That was about a third of all the Jews living at that time. These weren't soldiers. That's what makes me say Hitler was a murderer."

"There are always casualties in war," Kevin said with a shrug.

Lane moved to his desk. The exchange was making him uneasy. Several of the other students had revived enough to stare at Kevin. A few of them rolled their eyes upward as if they had heard him express this or a similar opinion before. "In 1931 Japan seized Manchuria, which is a north-eastern province of China. By 1937 they had taken several major cities along the coast and controlled the coast line."

Lane continued. "Italy's aggression began with Mussolini invading Ethiopia in Africa. Much of Hitler's rise to power was modeled on that of Mussolini, called El Duce."

Kevin was leaning forward in his desk as if he

couldn't hear enough. The glittering in his dark eyes was taking a fanatical turn. "Wasn't it Mussolini that said, 'War is to the man what motherhood is to the woman'?"

"Yes, he did. He also said that peace is depressing and the negation of all the fundamental virtues of man." Lane tried to lighten the tone. "We all know better than that. Man isn't a killer by nature."

"Some are," Kevin said calmly. "Who's to say they aren't the most highly evolved?"

"Anyone with a working brain," Lane answered sharply. He couldn't let a student take over a class room, especially not to voice such contemptible ideas.

"But it's obvious that some countries and some people are superior to others." Kevin glanced around as if he expected to see some of the students agree with him. "Are you saying America isn't superior to, say, Libya?"

"You're confusing military strength with evolution. Our constitution says 'All men are created equal.' Not that all American ones are."

"What about women?" Kevin challenged.

The classroom was perfectly quiet. All the students were alert now. Lane came from behind his desk and leaned against the front of it. "That reference is to mankind, not to the two sexes. This isn't a philosophy class, Kevin. Let's get back to World War II."

Kevin said nothing, merely nodding for Lane to continue.

"Mussolini also was interested in recreating ancient Rome. He built neo-Roman buildings and even renamed the Mediterranean Sea. He called it *Mare Nostrum,* or 'Our Sea'."

Although Lane picked up his lecture at the point where he had left it off, he kept his attention on Kevin. He had never had a student quite so interested in any subject, and he knew it had nothing to do with his ability to teach. There was something in Kevin that was different and unsettling. Lane preferred the usual lack of interest to this fevered excitement that Kevin was exhibiting.

Lucy Wright had spent the morning cleaning her house. She seldom did that these days and didn't realize she was doing little more than moving things about. Since Brooke's death she had felt no desire to do much of anything.

She opened the door to the room Brooke had shared with Tracy. The twin beds were neatly made. Tracy liked order and usually kept the room clean, even when Brooke had been alive. One side of the room had a lived-in look, while the other was starting to seem empty. All Brooke's rock posters had been taken down, but Lucy hadn't been able to abide having Tracy's country-and-western ones put in their place. Atop Tracy's bed were several old stuffed animals that she'd treasured since her childhood. Brooke's bed was bare.

Lucy drifted into the room and sat on the edge of Brooke's bed. How many times over the years had she come in and sat at this same place to talk with Brooke about some problem she was having or to take Brooke's temperature if she was sick or to tell her good night? Lucy had lived in this house all her married life.

Brooke had slept in this bed since outgrowing the baby bed.

Lucy lovingly stroked Brooke's pillow and her nubby bedspread. Tracy had picked out the matching spreads; Brooke hadn't been interested for some reason. Lucy thought it probably had been because she was preoccupied with boys or school or cheer leading. Brooke had been extremely popular. Everyone had liked her.

At times Lucy had noticed that Brooke seemed absentminded—Tracy had said she was "spaced-out," whatever that meant. Occasionally Lucy had wondered if Brooke was secretly drinking. Now she felt guilty for ever having had such a thought. Brooke had been a wonderful daughter, a good student. She had been voted most popular for the last three years and probably would have been selected again her senior year as well. Of course she hadn't been drinking alcohol.

Lucy rose and listlessly went to the walk-in closet that both girls had used. Tracy's side was neat and orderly, all the blouses hanging together, all the jeans and skirts in their places. Brooke's was no better than it ever had been. Lucy knew Tracy had gone through her sister's things and had taken the ones she wanted, but she regretted having allowed her to do that. It made Brooke's death seem so final.

Automatically she reached out and straightened a blue dress on its hanger. Brooke had loved blue and had worn it more than any other color. Tracy's side of the closet was a riot of different colors, with red and black being slightly predominate. Lucy had often heard the girls teasing each other about blue being

Brooke's signature color and how Tracy was pleased to let her have it. She supposed it was because Brooke's eyes had been such a beautiful shade of blue. Tracy's eyes were hazel like her father's, just as she had his blond hair.

Methodically Lucy started straightening Brooke's side of the closet. There were so many clothes! Brooke loved clothing and seldom threw anything out, and she easily had twice as many clothes as her sister. Tracy wasn't particularly interested in being stylish. She had rather make a style of her own. At times she looked more like a gypsy than a student of Maple Glen High.

As Lucy hung Brooke's clothing straight and smoothed the fabrics on the hangers, she let herself pretend last summer hadn't happened. This was a fantasy she indulged in more and more often. She pretended it was a year ago and Brooke was starting her junior year in high school, Tracy her sophomore one. Brooke was still dating Troy Spaulding and Lucy could still hope they would eventually marry.

Troy had been perfect for Brooke. Both were popular and incredibly attractive. As a couple they were striking. His letter jacket with all the patches proclaiming him team captain, all-state quarterback and so forth had swallowed Brooke, even though she was tall. Lucy had thought Brooke was the prettiest girl she had ever seen. At times she had found it hard to believe she could have given birth to such a beauty. Brooke—and Tracy as well—looked more like Ross' side of the family.

Lucy touched her own face and wondered if she had ever been as pretty as Brooke. She knew she hadn't, but at times she pretended she had, that years had removed her beauty, that at one time she had broken as many hearts as had her eldest daughter.

When she was finished straightening Brooke's clothing, she started on her shoes. Brooke had loved shoes almost as much as she did clothing, but had taken little care to keep them arranged. Tracy's shoes were all in boxes labeled with their color and style, but Brooke's were a jumble of empty boxes and assorted shoes. Dutifully, Lucy boxed Brooke's shoes and stacked the boxes with the labels facing out. Bending for one last look, she noticed several books on the closet floor in the back corner.

She ducked under Brooke's long dresses and brought them out. They were obviously schoolbooks since they had covers on them in the school's colors, but she had no idea what they were doing in the back of the closet. Lucy smiled and shook her head at Brooke's lack of organization. She imagined Brooke coming in from school and tossing the books on the floor of the closet, inadvertently pushing them beneath the clothes to get them out of sight, then forgetting where they were.

Lucy took the books back downstairs with her. She couldn't remember what classes Brooke had this morning, but it seemed likely that she would need her school books. Locked firmly in her fantasy, Lucy put the books in the car and drove to school.

Tracy had English next period and that meant she had to go to her locker on the first floor, then race to the third before the bell rang. She and her friends with lockers in the same location had often wondered if this was a method devised by the school to make it more difficult on students, or if it was simply a curse from having a last name that started with a letter near the end of the alphabet. She hurried with the stream of students who were going down the right side of the stairs. On the left side of the dividing partition were students pressing toward the upper floors. Although they had five minutes, Tracy was always sure she would be late, and she hated to be the last into the room.

She rushed to her locker and spun the combination lock, hoping this morning it wouldn't be as cantankerous as it sometimes was. All her friends agreed that the school purposely chose locks whose combinations were difficult to remember, and Amy swore she knew for a fact that Mr. Crouthers ordered the locks to that specification from some factory in Maine. Tracy finally found the right sequence of numbers and the lock snapped open.

Her locker was as neat as her closet. She had always liked order and felt uneasy if her things were out of place. Amy teased her about it all the time. She had even chosen a plaid bedspread so she could line up the edges perfectly. Tracy supposed she might take it to extremes at times, but she hated anything to be in disarray.

With her fingers fairly flying, she adjusted the paisley scarf she wore about her shoulders so the fringe was even on her moss green sweater. The day wasn't really cool enough for a scarf, but she had hit upon the combination that morning and was afraid she might forget it by the time fall temperatures arrived. She touched the clip that held her long blond hair back from her face to be sure it was still straight. The mirror she had hung in the back of her locker told her that her makeup needed no touch-up.

She took out her English book and notebook and slammed the locker door shut. Her watch said she had two minutes to climb three flights of stairs and run down the hall to the English class. Already the halls were emptying of students. Tracy knew she wasn't supposed to run in the hall, but she jogged back in the direction of the stairs.

"Tracy?"

She turned and was amazed to find her mother coming toward her. "Mom? What are you doing here?"

"I had to bring Brooke's books to school. Do you know what class she has now?" Lucy gestured with the books she held. "I guess I could go by the office, but I hate to bother them if I can find her on my own."

Tracy felt a creepy sensation rising up the back of her neck. "Brooke's books?"

Lucy nodded as if she didn't understand why Tracy was being so uncooperative. "She doesn't have P.E. this period, does she? I've never liked going into the gym." Lucy laughed. "I didn't even like it when I was in school here. Do you remember I went to school here, too?"

"Sure, Mom." Tracy shifted her books so she could take the three that had belonged to Brooke.

Lucy stroked the cover of the top one as if she were reluctant to let it go. "Maybe I ought to find her and give them to her myself. You'll be late if you do it. I know how you hate being late. Remember how you never were tardy all the time you were in grade school?"

"I remember." Tracy was growing more concerned every moment. Didn't her mother remember Brooke was dead? Why was she here talking about all these things in the past?

"You'll be sure and find Brooke? You promise?"

Tracy didn't know what to say. "I promise." She had read somewhere that it was good to humor a person who didn't seem to be connected with reality. The tardy bell rang but Tracy scarcely heard it. "Maybe I ought to go to the office and call Daddy."

"He's at work." Lucy looked confused. "Isn't he at work?"

"Mom, you're scaring me. Come on, let's go to the office."

"No, you're late as it is. Here, give me the books back and I'll take care of it."

"Mom, you can't find Brooke. You know she's—"

"Hush!" Lucy demanded, frowning at her. "You just hush. Go on to class now and hurry. Maybe the teacher won't notice you're late." She took the books from Tracy and started back the way she had come.

"I can't just walk off and leave you! Where are you going?"

"I'm going home, of course. Now you go to class. This isn't at all like you—to be late." Lucy tucked Brooke's books under her arm and walked purposefully toward the door that led to the street.

Tracy stood staring after her. Slowly her eyes started to fill with tears and she brushed at them impatiently. She couldn't worry about this now. Amy had said Mrs. Mitchell was giving a pop quiz in English today, and Tracy knew she was already in trouble for

74

being so late, but she couldn't move. Was there something terribly wrong with her mother?

Her dad had asked her opinion as to whether her mom seemed all right, and she hadn't been sure how to answer him. Her mother still cooked meals, but she no longer cleaned the house. At times she called Tracy by Brooke's name or set too many plates on the table, but hadn't she occasionally made mistakes like this before Brooke died? Surely everyone slipped up once in a while. She wondered if she should go to the office and call her father.

The outside door closed behind Lucy and Tracy blinked. The halls were oddly quiet and she had the sinking feeling of being in a place where she wasn't supposed to be. She couldn't go to the office and give them a plausible explanation without telling them the reason she wanted to call her father. It would never do to let Miss Billings know her mother had brought Brooke's last year's books to school thinking Brooke would need them. Miss Billings was the biggest gossip in town and would tell everyone she knew that something was very odd about Lucy Wright.

Pushing the tears back down, Tracy ran up the stairs. By the time she reached the third floor she was breathing hard and could use that as an explanation for her teary eyes and flushed cheeks. She dashed down the hall and into the English room.

Mrs. Mitchell paused in the act of handing out the pages of the quiz. "You're late." She peered at Tracy over her reading glasses and waited for an explanation.

"I . . . my locker was stuck. I couldn't get the lock to work." She hurried to her desk and slid into it, her cheeks blazing with embarrassment. She had never had Brooke's flair for being the center of attention.

"All right," Mrs. Mitchell began, seeming to have accepted Tracy's explanation, "We're taking a test over the chapter you were to read for today." She put the correct number of papers on the front desk of every row, and the students each took one and passed the others back.

Tracy took a page and sent the others behind her. The mimeographed words were a blur, and she couldn't remember anything she had read. She took out a pen and started to read the first question.

The day crawled by. By last period Tracy was more upset than she had been earlier. After thinking about her mother's actions all day, she could see just how odd it had been. This was more than simply calling Tracy by the wrong name. Even as her mother was leaving, she hadn't realized Brooke wasn't at the school. No slip of memory lasted that long.

Tracy stared down at the pen and ink drawing she was supposed to hand in at the end of art class. She had already smudged it, and she had been as careful as she could be. There was no way she could hide the mistake or finish it by the end of the period. That, on top of the English test she had bombed, was enough to make her cry. She wondered if she had made a big mistake that morning by not calling her father as soon as her mother left. What if Lucy had gone home and done something awful or was run over on the way home or had forgotten where she lived and was wandering through the streets, still carrying Brooke's books? Tracy felt thoroughly guilty.

She was aware of someone standing beside her and

she looked up to see the new teacher, Mrs. Bowen, looking at her work. Quickly Tracy dipped her quill into the ink bottle and went back to the drawing.

"I like what you're doing here," Tess said. "You've filled the space well, and it shows liveliness." She wondered why the girl only ducked her head as if she were embarrassed. Tracy Wright had never struck her as one of the shy students. If anything, Tracy always talked too much in class. Something was clearly bothering her. Tess glanced at her wristwatch. "Tracy, can you stay for a few minutes after class?"

Tracy nodded without speaking and bent lower over the drawing.

Tess went back to her desk after slowly passing by the other students. She remembered that Tracy's sister had been one of the students to die during the summer. It wasn't unlikely that Tracy was suffering and unable to talk to anyone about it. Tess was sure she, too, would have found it hard to go to the school counselor when she was Tracy's age and under such circumstances. And teenagers could be so hard on one another. Tracy might be afraid of being teased if she went in to talk to Ed Hudson. Perhaps she needed someone to listen to her problems.

At five minutes before time for the dismissal bell, Tess had the students start to clean up their projects. She watched to be sure the quills were all washed and replaced in the boxes. The students moved about with the usual clatter and giggles, all but Tracy. Tess was glad she had asked her to stay behind. Something was obviously wrong.

The bell rang and the students swarmed for the door. Tess sometimes wondered how such lethargic teenagers could be galvanized into action at the sound of a bell. She could hear them in the hall, laughing and calling to friends.

Tracy remained seated at her table. Tess went to her. The pen and ink drawing lay on the table and Tess pulled it toward her.

"I didn't have time to finish," Tracy said. Her eyes didn't meet Tess'. "And I smudged it here." She pointed at a barely perceptible thickening of a line.

"That's hardly noticeable. It may be unfinished, but it still deserves a good grade. Is that what's worrying you?" She knew it wasn't. Tracy had been preoccupied the entire class.

"Yes." Tracy sighed. "Can I go now?"

"Are you sure you don't need to talk? I know I'm new here and you don't know me as well as you know the other teachers, but sometimes that makes it easier to talk."

"How did you know I needed to talk?"

"I may be new here, but I've been teaching several years. I can tell something is bothering you." She hesitated. "Is it about your sister?"

Tracy's eyes darted to Tess' and then looked away. "I guess."

"I never knew her, but I guess you must miss her a lot."

Tracy nodded and her fingers absently turned the drawing in circles on the table. "We always shared a room and it seems weird not to have her around."

"Have you talked to Dr. Hudson about it? I hear a lot of the students and teachers have."

"I've talked to him."

"How are your parents taking it?"

78

"Dad is okay, I guess. I mean, he misses her and all, but he's all right."

"And your mother?"

Tracy pushed back in her chair and frowned at the table. Tess knew she had hit the source of the problem. After a long moment Tracy said, "She came by the school today."

"You're mother did?"

Tracy nodded and started playing with the fringe that edged the colorful scarf she wore. "She was bringing Brooke's books to her."

Tess felt the fine hairs stand up on the back of her neck. "I beg your pardon?"

"She couldn't seem to remember that Brooke is gone. I didn't want to call Dad and have Miss Billings know about Mom." She glanced up at Tess. "You aren't friends with Miss Billings, are you?"

"No, I barely know her."

"She's the worst gossip in town. Anyway, I didn't want her talking bad about Mom, so I couldn't call Dad. Now I'm scared that I didn't do the right thing."

"Does your mom often do things like this?"

"Lately she has been. Not this bad, but she forgets. She even bought Brooke a blouse the other day. She said she bought it for me, but it was blue." When she saw Tess didn't understand, she added, "Brooke always wore blue. I don't like that color very much."

"I see."

"And she set a place for Brooke at the table three times this week. I mean, I could understand if she did it once, but *three* times? How could she do that?"

"I don't know. Has she been to see Dr. Hudson? It sounds as if your mother might need someone to talk

79

with." Tess was no expert, but she thought Lucy Wright sounded like a woman who needed professional help.

"I'm wondering if she's having a nervous breakdown or something." Tracy slid lower in the chair. "I know she misses Brooke. So do Dad and me, but she still has me! Why does she have to think about Brooke all the time?" She sighed. "That sounds awful. I didn't mean it that way."

"I understand. I think you should tell your father when he comes home. It sounds like the sort of thing he should know."

"Okay." Tracy sat straighter. "Can I go now? I don't like to be late. Mom might worry."

"Sure. But if you need to talk, come to me. Okay?"

Tracy finally smiled, though ever so faintly. "Okay. You won't tell anybody what I said?"

"No, I won't." She watched Tracy leave the room. It was hard on the ones who were left behind. Even though she was personally untouched by the tragedy, Tess could see its results everywhere. The students seemed to swing between being difficult to control to being too quiet. She couldn't imagine what it must have been like the morning after the deaths were discovered.

Feeling the need to be with someone, she closed her room and hurried downstairs. The other teachers were leaving for the day, and she exchanged good-byes with several as she went toward the gym. She didn't know if Lane Hodges would be there or if he would be on the field with the football players at this hour, but she wanted to be with him if she could. Lane always had his feet so firmly planted on earth. She couldn't imagine him being spooked by echoes and odd shadows in the old school.

The gym was silent and she knew he must have gone to the football field, but she decided to look in his office since she had come this far. The smell of new wax on the basketball court reminded her of her own school days. Although she had grown up far from Maple Glen, some things were universal to schools.

She went into the locker area and thought she heard a sound further back. "Hello? Is anyone here?" She didn't want to walk in on some student who might be dressing. No one answered. "Mr. Hodges? Is that you?"

A muffled sound that could have been an affirmation came to her. She let the gym door close behind her and went toward the back. "I didn't know if you'd be here or not." She rounded the shower area and started down the rows of lockers. "When are you going to the field?"

Again the sound came to her. "What? I can't understand you." She walked more purposely, positive Lane was in his office.

The rows of lockers were empty and silent. Tess had never been fond of walking into areas she couldn't see clearly before entering. She supposed that came from spending her life in cities, and she told herself that was foolish. Nothing could hurt her here. "Lane?"

His office was empty. She could see that through the glass embedded with wire mesh. The desk chair was pushed up to the desk and lights were out. "Are you in the storage closet?" She could see no reason Lane would go in there and close the door behind him. "Lane? Answer me."

81

The sound came again but this time she couldn't tell if it came from the closet or from behind her. Tess glanced behind her, then started backing up, her senses alert. That wasn't Lane's voice. Trying not to panic, she turned and headed back in the direction from which she had come. She made her steps measured. If anyone was in here, it had to be a student playing tricks on her. Nothing else made any sense. She couldn't let a student send her running from the lockers.

The muffled voice came again, only this time accompanied by the click of a locker being easily closed. She had just passed the last row of lockers, and she knew no one was there. She walked faster.

By the time she reached the gymnasium she was walking as fast as she could. The door to the locker area had closed behind her but she could swear she heard it open again. She looked back. The door was closed. Taking a steadying breath, she walked toward the outside door. In the echo of her footsteps she thought she heard someone else walking. This time she didn't look to see. She was too intent on getting out into the sunlight.

When she finally reached the door, she dared a glance behind her. No one was there. With her heart racing painfully, she made herself look more closely. She was positive she had heard a voice and there was no way to come or go from that end of the building except for the way she had taken. Besides, she had heard the click of a locker and nothing else sounded quite like that. She recalled she had heard a similar sound the first time she had been in the old building. The footsteps could have been an illusion, she told herself. The gym had a large echo. She closed the door, tested to be sure it locked behind her, and hurried in the direction of her house.

Hannah Mitchell was working late in her room. She often did that. It was easier to grade papers here than to carry them all home. Since there was no one waiting for her at home, she had formed the habit of working as late as it took.

When it started getting dark, Hannah turned on the lights. She still had several tests to finish. Some of the students had written far more than was necessary, probably in hopes of stumbling on the correct answers by sheer number of words. She picked up her red pen and started to read the next page.

From the corner of her eye, she saw a movement and she glanced up, startled. The room was empty, of course. No one was left in the building. The janitor had even gone. She knew this because he always made a pass through the halls to be sure no lights were left on. She had told him good night as she had on many other occasions. It was no secret to her that some of the students believed she actually lived in the school and slept in her supply closet.

A soft sound came from down the hall and Hannah frowned. Had some students slipped back into the school? She had surprised vandals several years back and had no fear of confronting them. She stood quietly and tiptoed to the door to listen.

The sound came again but she couldn't quite tell what it was. It was so soft she was a bit surprised that she had heard it at all. She opened the door and looked

83

out. The hall was nearly black. The janitor had left the stairway lights on for her, but their illumination barely reached past the stairwell. She squinted and tried to see through the darkness. "Who's there?"

After a moment she made out a shape. It was motionless and only visible because it was darker than the other shadows. Hannah frowned and said, "I can see you. What do you want?" There was no answer. "You have no business here after hours." She made her voice as stern as possible. The shadow neither moved nor spoke.

Uncertainly Hannah straightened. Was that someone or was it only her imagination? The hall light switch was at the end of the hall near the stairs, and she had no way of seeing into the shadows. When several seconds passed, she decided it had to be a trick of the light. No student would stand there so silently or so still.

She went back to her desk, but she couldn't get her mind back on the tests. Several times she jumped, sure she had heard more noises in the hall. Vague shapes seemed to move just at the edge of her vision. Feeling thoroughly uneasy, she stood and picked up the ungraded tests. She would finish them at home. She had nothing else planned for that night. Telling herself this had nothing to do with the tricks her mind was playing on her, she took a deep breath and went out into the hall.

As before she saw the shadow. It was vague, but she could almost swear she could make out a shoulder, the neck and part of a head. Gathering all her courage, Hannah snapped off her classroom light and proceeded down the dark hall just as she had for years.

84

She didn't allow herself to quicken her pace, even when she heard a barely perceptible sound behind her.

At the top of the stairs she flipped on the hall lights and looked back. The hall was empty and silent. Hannah stood for a minute, convincing herself no one was there. Then she turned off the lights. At once she saw the clear silhouette of a teenage boy standing near the door to her room.

Hannah drew in her breath sharply. No one was there! She was positive of that. But she still saw the shape, and she recalled that she had often seen Troy Spaulding standing in that exact posture. It had been distinctive of him to stand with his arms folded over his middle and his hips thrust slightly forward. Troy Spaulding had died in the hall just outside her classroom door, just where the shape seemed to be.

Hannah turned and hurried down the stairs, not caring that she was showing her fright or that some student must be playing a trick on her. This went beyond a harmless prank, in her opinion, and she didn't really believe there could possibly be anyone in the building except her.

She was out of breath by the time she reached the outside door, but felt the need to stop and regain some composure before going out where others might see her. What she had seen was impossible. It was only her mind playing tricks. Hesitantly she turned and looked back into the black building. With the stair well lights out it was impenetrably dark; she couldn't have seen someone if he'd been standing only two feet away. The thought sent her hurrying through the door and out into the streetlight's glow.

Although she had never been afraid of the dark in

her entire life and she was usually as undaunted in the empty school as she was in her own living room, Hannah rushed through the streets, looking neither to the left nor to the right.

"Alone." The whisper ran down the dark hallways and up the stairway. "Alone."

"Gone," a whisper answered, rising from the auditorium.

Slowly they arrived and formed in vapors too fine for a mortal eye to see. Troy looked from one pale, still face to another. Brooke's red hair had a barely perceptible tint, her eyes looked too pale to be as blue as they had been in life. As in life, Misty Traveno hung back from the others, her mop of curly hair almost visible. "Alone," she whispered.

Troy glared down the hall. It wasn't supposed to have been like this. They weren't supposed to be dead, and Kevin was supposed to be with them.

"Kevin," Brooke sighed, her wispy voice trailing into the shadows. "Kevin."

He knew what she meant. Since that night their thoughts had been fused together. A single word was as good as a conversation. "Kill," he whispered, his eyes sparking in the darkness, then disappearing. "Kill!"

For the first weeks they had been apart, but in the last few days, they had found their way to the school. First Brooke had arrived, her eyes vacant and her face pallid. Next Toni Fay Randall, her hair still appearing wet from the water in her father's cow pond. Jeanne Wrayford had been the last to arrive, her movements

86

sluggish as if she still bore the effects of the massive dose of Valium she had taken.

Now they were together, and they were gathering strength from one another. Troy couldn't have said how it worked, and he didn't care. It was enough that they were already so strong they could be seen when they willed it. The only problem was that sometimes they could be seen when they didn't want to. Troy could have sworn the English teacher saw him as she was leaving.

"Cheated," Misty whispered. The word ran around the gathering. They edged closer.

"Cheated," Joe Bob Renfro hissed, his gaunt face becoming a mask of rage. "Kill!"

"Kill," Troy agreed. He turned his head and looked down the black hall. He could see as easily in the darkness now as he had been able to see in the light when he was alive. They were strong and growing stronger. "Soon."

The word swept like a breeze among the shadows and down the echoing hall. "Soon."

Chapter Four

"What sort of turn-out do you have here for Parents' Night?" Tess asked Lane Hodges as she walked from the parking lot with him.

"Usually it's pretty good. Not everyone will come, of course. That never happens anywhere. But the people here mostly know each other at least on sight and that makes for a good turnout. Was it like that in your other school?"

Tess laughed. "If we got half a dozen parents we considered it a success. My old school district wasn't well-knit either socially or economically. We had problems with attendance, drugs, concealed weapons—you name it, that school had it."

"Cities are different from small towns, I guess."

"I think it was more the school district. The boundaries were placed wrong, I think, and the kids didn't feel like a unit. The other schools in St. Louis didn't seem to have this much of a problem, as far as I could tell. That's one reason I wanted to come to a small town. Maple Glen seemed perfect."

"It was until last summer."

Tess didn't answer. She had noticed that no matter what the conversation was, the subject always seemed to drift back to the suicides.

"I'm hoping I have one student's parents in particular," Lane continued. "It's a boy named Kevin Donatello. Do you have him in art?"

"Donatello. No, the name's not familiar in connection with a student. I'd certainly remember that name in an art class." She saw Lane's confused expression. "Donatello was a famous Italian painter."

He laughed. "I was thinking of the Ninja turtle."

Tess smiled and shook her head. "Sad, but true. Why do you want to meet his parents?"

"I'm concerned about Kevin. For some reason he's obsessed by World War II. So much so that I'm concerned that he needs professional counseling. He gets an odd look in his eyes, almost like a religious fervor and launches in on Hitler's good points."

"I didn't know there were any." They were nearing the gym and their steps slowed. Behind them the parking lot was illumined by tall streetlights that cast a peculiar orange glow over the cars.

"That's why I'm concerned."

Tess looked at the door to the gym. "I came down to find you the other day after school. The gym was unlocked and I could have sworn I heard someone in the locker area, but when I looked, no one was there."

"The gym was unlocked and I wasn't there? Neither were any of the other coaches? That's strange. We never leave it open. There's too much expensive equipment that could take a walk."

"I called out and thought I heard someone answer."

89

"You know how gyms echo. I wonder why it was unlocked."

"It was empty so I guess one of the other coaches had left for a moment for some reason. I gather nothing is missing."

"Nothing." He seemed preoccupied.

"Are you to meet the parents out here or in the history room?"

"In the history room. I'm not sure any of the parents would come all the way to the gym." He glanced at his watch. "It's almost time."

"My room is all ready. I stayed after school to put up the pictures and set out the sculptures and so forth."

"There wasn't much to do in my room." They walked briskly down the hall and up the stairs.

It seemed odd to be in the school after hours. The windows were dark squares and there was a sense of expectancy in the old building. Tess could hear the sounds of activity coming from the classrooms and occasionally one teacher called to another as they completed last-minute tasks.

At the door to the art room, Lane paused. "I guess we should have driven over together. We live so close to each other, there was no reason to take two cars."

Tess smiled. She was used to driving half way across St. Louis to reach the school. In that sense, everyone in Maple Glen lived close to her. "I should have called and suggested that. Next time."

"Right." He seemed reluctant to go, but moved away in the direction of his history room. She knew he was becoming interested in her, and she liked the way that made her feel.

Tess went into her room and turned on the lights. A glance at the tables showed her that it was all just as she had left it. She had put out work from every student, and each was clearly labeled with the student's name and class period. The parents were encouraged to meet all their children's teachers, and in her former school the art room had been a favorite stopping place. She hoped it would be that way in this school as well.

A few minutes before seven, Tess heard conversations in the hall that indicated the parents were arriving. Her first visitors were Tracy Wright's parents.

"Tracy is doing well in class," Tess said as she picked up a clay figure their daughter had sculpted.

Ross Wright took the figure from her and showed it to his wife. "Look. It's a clown."

The woman touched the clay, only marginally interested, then looked around the room. "Nice."

Tess remembered the day Lucy Wright had come to school with her dead child's schoolbooks. Even if Tracy hadn't confided in her that day, Tess would have seen something was wrong with the woman. Lucy's eyes were haunted, and she seemed to be searching for something. Tess pointed to the clown and said, "See the proportions and the stance? She's put a liveliness in all her work."

"So Tracy is doing well?" Ross asked.

Tess nodded. "She's one of my best students."

"Is this all the work?" Lucy asked.

"No, I only put out a sample of each student's work. I picked the one I considered to be best or one that has special interest for the student. Is there something in particular you're looking for?"

Lucy shook her head, but she continued to search the pictures on the wall above the chalk board.

Tess found herself staring at Lucy and hastily turned to Ross and said, "Lately Tracy seems preoccupied. Her work hasn't suffered and I'm certainly not saying she's a problem in class—far from it—but she seems to be worried about something."

Ross shifted uneasily and glanced at his wife. "You must know her sister was one of the ones . . . well, we lost her this past summer."

"Yes, I know, and I'm so sorry. No, this must be something else. I'd have expected her to more depressed at the beginning of school. This is the third week and it seems to be getting more pronounced."

"Brooke was so good in art," Lucy said almost as if to herself. "She was really talented. She's said she wanted to major in art in college."

Ross looked uncomfortable and gave his wife a warning glance.

"Do you have any of her things here?" Lucy moved to the next table to read the names.

Tess said, "No, these are only from this year's students. Brooke would have taken all her work home at the end of the last school year." When Lucy made no comment or sign that she had heard, she said to Ross, "Is Tracy with you?"

"No, she had a date tonight. You know how teenagers are." Ross laughed but the sound wasn't mirthful. "She seems to think she sees enough of the school every day."

"I can't blame her."

Lucy picked up a pen and ink drawing and was

92

studying it closely. "Is this one of Brooke's? It seems familiar."

Ross went to her and gently took the drawing from her. "Let's go see Tracy's English teacher."

Lucy looked around as if she were surprised to find herself in the art room. She smiled at Tess and held out her hand. "It was so nice to meet you. I hope you like it here in Maple Glen."

Tess shook her hand. "I'm sure I will."

"I've lived here all my life," Lucy continued. "So has Ross. We went to school in this very building. I sat at the table over there by the window. Mrs. Larson was the teacher then. Do you know her?"

"No, I've not had the pleasure."

"She seemed old, even when I was in school. Ross, how old would you say Mrs. Larson is?" Lucy's forehead puckered as if the question were very important.

Ross tried to laugh. "I have no idea. She's had gray hair for as long as I can remember."

"Brooke says she's older than dirt," Lucy said. "That's the way she puts it."

Tess was concerned about the woman. Her husband was clearly worried as well. Lucy moved away to look at some of the chalk drawings near the supply area and Tess said to Ross, "Is she all right?"

"Lucy? Sure, she's fine. She's holding up pretty well, considering." He continued to watch her.

Tess knew she was overstepping the boundaries, but she said, "Tracy told me about her bringing Brooke's books to school. I know it's none of my business, but I feel I should say something since Tracy is one of my students. Perhaps it would be a good idea for Mrs. Wright to see Dr. Hudson. I know he's talked to several of the teachers and students and has helped them get over the shock."

Ross frowned at her. "Lucy is fine. I suggested that she see him, but she says there's no need. Tracy shouldn't have told you about that. Lucy has lapses of memory. That's all."

Tess stared up at him. "I'd say bringing Brooke's books to school was more than a lapse of memory."

"Lucy is high-strung. Always has been. Naturally she took Brooke's death hard, but she'll get over it. She's from hardy stock." He didn't look as if he were all that convinced, however.

"If there's anything I can do, will you let me know? I'm afraid this is what's behind Tracy's inability to concentrate. I'm not trying to pry, Mr. Wright. I'm only concerned for Tracy."

"Thank you. Lucy will be fine." He held out his hand and took Lucy's as she walked nearer. "We have to be going now."

"Thank you for coming," Tess said as she watched them leave. She couldn't help but wonder if the man was embarrassed and was pretending everything was fine or if he was in denial because he couldn't handle the idea that his wife was losing her grip on reality. Either way, she was more concerned about Tracy than she had been before meeting her parents.

Hannah Mitchell's English room on the third floor was not as easily accessible as the other classrooms, and she wasn't too surprised that few parents climbed the extra flight of stairs to come to her room. She had asked for a room on a lower floor for the last several years, but one hadn't been available. As she looked around the room she wondered why she was still teaching. She had reached retirement age, yet she returned every year.

She had been in this room so long, she sometimes thought the students would still continue to come here for English, even if she were given a room on a lower floor. English had been taught in this room for as long as anyone could remember. As a child, this was where she had studied English. For years she had equipped a veritable army of boys and girls with verbs, nouns and poetry. Without her input, many of her students might never have heard the name Charles Dickens, let alone have read any of his work. She considered English more important than any sport ever played.

Hannah looked around the room and shook her head. For all the importance of her subject, she seldom saw parents interested enough to climb the three flights of steps she and their children scaled every day. At times Hannah was resentful of that.

A muffled noise from out in the hall drew her attention, and she looked up expectantly. When no one came in the open door, she went to it and looked out. No one was there. The sound she'd heard must have come from the lower floor. She was directly over the chemistry lab and sometimes she could hear the clattering of glassware and occasionally caught a whiff of something they were brewing up—most often noxious and offensive odors. That was another reason she wished she had a different room.

As happened often these days, her eyes drifted to the area outside her room next to the locker, where she had thought she'd seen someone standing that night she was grading papers here alone. Now, with the hall light on, it seemed ridiculous that she had frightened herself so badly that evening. Hannah was embarrassed that it had happened and was glad no other teachers knew about it. She thought she must be getting old indeed if she was starting to imagine people lurking in shadows.

"Next I'll be looking for burglars under my bed," she scoffed to herself. Since she lived alone, she had developed the habit of talking to herself when no one else was around. It was sometimes pleasant to hear a voice, even if it was her own.

She looked at the large clock in the hall and compared the time on it to her watch. As always, they were in perfect sync. In thirty minutes she could close up and go home.

Now that she had admitted to herself that no parent was likely to make the effort to come to her room, she heard a couple coming up the stairs. Judging by their shortness of breath, she knew they would have an appreciation for the climb she made every day. On first sight, she recognized them as former students. The woman's maiden name had been Semple, and the man was Harvey Nelson. They had been among the popular crowd during their school years, but their daughter, Kelly, was too shy to assert herself.

Hannah smiled in greeting. "Margaret, Harvey. It's been a long time."

Margaret nodded. "These stairs seem to have gotten steeper. Remember how we used to race up them, Harvey?"

He grinned. "We were in better shape in those days. How are you, Mrs. Mitchell?"

96

"I'm quite well, thank you." She stepped aside and ushered them into her room. "I had hoped you'd come tonight."

"Oh? Kelly's not in trouble, is she?" Harvey said as he looked around the room, avoiding eye contact with his former teacher much the same as he'd done as her student.

"Kelly? Of course not. No, she's a perfect student, even if she's a bit quieter than I would prefer."

"We sure weren't, were we? Harvey and me were always into something." Margaret said with a wink at her husband.

"Yes, you certainly were." Hannah had hoped that as Margaret matured she would have taken more to heart Hannah's efforts to correct her common grammar mistakes, but she hadn't bet money on a positive outcome. Years of experience had shown her that students who couldn't or wouldn't learn to speak correctly in school rarely improved later. She had done all she could for the girl when she was in her English class.

"Now, Mrs. Mitchell, what did you want to tell us about Kelly?" Harvey asked.

"She's always been shy, goodness knows, but lately she seems more withdrawn."

"How can you tell? She seldom says two sentences in a row," Harvey said. "We've talked about it with her grandparents."

Margaret joined in. "I don't know how we managed to have a girl who was so shy, but she's always been that way." Margaret seemed perplexed.

"I've known Kelly almost all her life," Hannah said. "I wouldn't bring this up if I weren't concerned. Lately when I ask her a question, she seems afraid to answer. She wasn't that shy last year."

Margaret's brow puckered. "She was friends with Toni Fay Randall, you know. She took all those deaths hard."

"We all did," Harvey added with a glance at his wife. "Kelly often spent the weekend with Toni Fay, usually at our house."

"We live close to them," Margaret reminded Hannah. "You can see the Randalls' pond from our side pasture."

"It was a terrible tragedy," Hannah agreed.

"They had planned to spend the next weekend at our house. At times it's still hard to believe it all happened."

"I knew the girls were friends, but I had forgotten you were neighbors as well. I guess that could explain why Kelly is having trouble this year."

"Sometimes I see her out in the pasture, just looking toward that cow pond," Margaret said. "I try to keep her occupied, but I work and I can't be with her as much as I probably should."

"Most mothers work these days," Hannah told her. "You can't feel guilty about that." She had never had children of her own and couldn't understand why some mothers seemed to believe they should spend every waking moment with their offspring. "She'll become more independent if she has to rely on herself from time to time. I think that's healthier."

"I'm sure you're right." Margaret didn't look as if she were sure of that at all.

"But she's already so shy." Harvey frowned as if he were trying to figure out how to change that. "I've

98

encouraged her to get a part-time job so she'll learn how to mix with people, but she's so timid she won't go to an interview."

Hannah's smile faded. "I didn't realize that. I assumed she could do that. She must know practically everyone in town."

Harvey tried to explain. "Her shyness isn't limited to strangers. Why, even at family gatherings, she hangs back like a shadow. She used to at least try to play with her cousins, but now that she's a teenager, she just ignores them. We find her hiding in the barn, reading a book, while all the other kids are running around and having fun."

"Reading is fun to many people," Hannah said dryly.

"I suppose, but wouldn't you think it would be more fun to talk and giggle with your cousins you haven't seen in months? She can read any time."

Hannah was puzzled. "I hadn't realized it was so severe. If you like, I'll talk to her. Maybe she'll confide in me. She may find Dr. Hudson too intimidating."

Margaret laughed. "That's an understatement! Kelly would never be able to make an appointment and go talk to him. I know because I've suggested it to her. She almost cried at the thought."

"I'm glad we had a chance to talk," Hannah said as she heard footsteps in the hall and the hard breathing of another pair of intrepid parents. "I'll do what I can on this end. Call me if there's anything else I can do."

Margaret nodded and Harvey said, "Thanks. We'll do that."

As they left, Hannah turned to greet Mojo Conroe's parents, Tyrilee and Lester Sr. Like the Nelsons, Hannah had also taught them in school, as well as Mojo's older brother and sisters.

Meantime, in the history room, Lane Hodges was talking to Becky Donatello. "Kevin is an interesting student."

Becky seemed relieved. "I'm so glad to hear that. Since his father and I divorced, he's been, well, different. I was afraid he might be a problem in school."

"No, he's not disruptive. I didn't know you and Mr. Donatello had divorced."

"It happened during the summer. With all else that was going on, I guess the news hasn't spread. He's been transferred to Sykeston, so we don't see him very often. I think that's good, but Kevin must miss him."

"He hasn't said if he does or not?"

Becky looked down as if she were embarrassed. "We . . . don't talk much. I'm having to work two jobs now, and when I come home, Kevin is often out." She tried to smile. "You know how teenagers are. They spend as much time away from home as possible."

Lane smiled to put her at ease. "I know. I did the same."

"So did I."

"There is one thing I'm curious about, though. Is there some reason why Kevin is so engrossed in World War II Germany?"

Becky looked confused. "No. Is he?"

Lane nodded. "That's all he wants to talk about in class. We're studying World War II and he talks almost as much as I do. I was wondering if he's mentioned his interest in the subject at home."

"I'm embarrassed to admit it, but I don't really know what his interests are." Becky pushed her dark hair back from her face. "Now that you mention it, though, he does have a lot of books on Germany and Hitler. He even has a swastika flag on the wall of his bedroom."

"He does? Don't you think that's odd?" At times Lane couldn't understand where parents were coming from. It was as if Kevin's mother barely knew him.

"At first I did, now I hardly think about it. It's rather colorful, and I assumed that's why he wanted it."

"Where did he get it?"

"I have no idea. I suppose he sent off for it in the mail. He does that often. Packages are always arriving and letters are leaving. I don't pay much attention to it. Not really."

"I see."

"Since the divorce I've had my hands full," she said as if she felt the need to defend herself. "His worthless father certainly doesn't do anything to help, especially since he moved away. I'm having to raise Kevin all on my own!"

"I know that must be difficult for you. Does he see his father often?"

"No way! That worthless sack of—" Becky stopped herself and glanced at Lane. "He never writes and he's too cheap to call Kevin. He hasn't even sent my child support money this month, and it's nearly three weeks late! I've told Kevin that we're well rid of him."

Lane made no comment. He knew most kids felt torn in a divorce and that this could account for some of Kevin's unusual behavior. "Is your ex-husband interested in Nazi Germany?"

Becky gave a mirthless laugh. "Him? I doubt he

knows where Germany is. He's not interested in anything but himself. Himself and football on TV. I guess it's good that Kevin is taking an interest in history. Right?"

"I'm concerned about the amount of time he spends thinking and arguing for Hitler's cause, frankly. Has anything else happened to him lately that could cause him to obsess on this?"

Becky cocked her head to one side for a moment. "There was the divorce, like I said. Then there were those kids that killed themselves."

"Was he friends with any of them? Close friends, I mean?"

"I don't know. Like I said, I'm working two jobs and it's all I can do to get through the day. He could have half the town over, and I wouldn't know about it if I'm at work. As far as I know, he didn't hardly know them."

"What about last year? Was he interested in Hitler before his father left?"

"He's been gone from the house nearly a year, off and on. He would leave me and come back, leave and come back. Me and Kevin have been by ourselves almost a year, all told. I've been working two jobs ever since that worthless scum moved out the first time. I saw the handwriting on the wall, you might say."

"So you don't know if he was into this last year or not?" Lane tried to keep the disgust out of his voice. Some parents took such little interest in their children that they didn't deserve the titles of mom and dad.

"The swastika flag is new. He got it during the summer. He's always been a big reader. Don't ask me who he got that from."

"As I said, Kevin isn't a discipline problem and his grades are holding steady at a B average. I was only concerned about his interests."

Becky shrugged. "I guess if he's doing okay grade-wise I can't complain. Right?"

"Thanks for coming in."

She gave him an uncertain smile and said good-bye. Lane was glad to see her leave. With so little supervision, it was no wonder Kevin was developing some unusual interests. He must feel as if he has no restraints at all, and in a boy Kevin's age, that could spell trouble.

As Tess had expected, many parents had come by her art room. All parents seemed to be eager to see what their children had made. Mojo's parents had been especially pleased at the unlikely and amazingly delicate drawings made by their son. Although Tess had not admitted it to them, she had been no less surprised. On the surface Mojo looked as if he had never entertained a gentle thought in his life.

Rather than leaving as soon as the last of the parents were gone, Tess stayed behind to put away the artwork so she wouldn't have to return to the school early the next day. She was pleased when Lane poked his head in her door to tell her good-bye, and although she was aware of the building growing quieter, she didn't think about possibly being the last person left in the building.

Ten minutes later, she finished straightening her room and gave it one last glance before turning off the light and stepping out into the hall. At first she was perplexed to discover that no one else was there. All the doors to the other rooms were closed and the glass transoms above them were dark. Ahead of her, she noticed that the light in the stairwell to the third floor was already out, leading her to assume Hannah Mitchell, too, had already gone home.

Tess refused to think about being alone and closed her ears to the faint, rustling noises that she could hear in the shadows behind her and from the floor above her. Lowering her head as if that would hasten her exit, she hurried down the stairs.

The ground floor was also dark, except for the light beside the door that led to the street. She had come in the far door that was nearer the parking lot, but she was reluctant to walk down the dark hall to reach it. The sooner she was outside, the better she would feel. She turned out the light on the lower stairs and the one that lit the lobby. The blackness was almost complete.

She thought she heard the muffled clang of a locker closing high above her. For a moment, she considered going back to investigate, but her nerves couldn't take it. No one was up there. Surely no student would want to vandalize the building so badly that he would stay behind in the eerie darkness. As she walked along the sidewalk out in front of the building that led to the parking lot, she fished in her purse for her keys. In St. Louis, she'd learned that it wasn't prudent not to have her keys in hand before leaving a lighted building at night, but staying in this particular building, even with the lights on, long enough to find her keys, had seemed a greater threat.

As she found her keys, she rounded the corner of the building and easily spotted her car; it sat alone on the

104

parking lot. She wondered why no one had bothered to tell her she was the last person left in the school, but decided everyone else was accustomed to being there alone from time to time. She felt foolish for being so alarmed. Maple Glen couldn't possibly be more threatening than the school district she had moved from.

She put her key in the lock and opened the door. As she pulled the door open, she saw a shadow move in the area between the gym and the main building. She hesitated. Who was that? As she watched, another shadow joined the first. Her heart started to race. Hastily, she got into her car, slammed the door and pressed the switch that operated the electric door locks. As she fumbled trying to put the key into the ignition, she watched the shadows. Fortunately, neither of them moved.

Finally, she got the key into the ignition and twisted it to the start position. She heard something clicking, but the engine failed to start. With a deep frown, she tried again. For several days she had thought there was something wrong with the ignition switch, but she hadn't expected it to stop working tonight. Fearfully she looked back at the shadows. Were there more of them?

When it became obvious the car wouldn't start, Tess took a deep breath and got out of the car. "Jason Cook?" she called out as she squinted at the darkness. "Is that you?" The shadow had broad shoulders and narrow hips and bore a slight resemblance to Jason. If it was Jason, she knew she had nothing to fear. "Jason?" she called again, but no one answered. "Who's there? I can see you, so you may as well answer me." Again, she got no response, but the shadows shifted as if they were listening to her words.

She looked down the street for a passing motorist or help of some sort, but to no avail. Since she didn't live very far from the school, the most logical course to take was simply to walk home. If whoever was in the shadows wouldn't come out when she called, they might not venture any closer as she walked away. All her years of city experience, however, warned her of the potential danger. Her mouth was as dry as cotton, and she was so frightened that she was shaking. Her only other alternative was to stay in the car all night or until the shadowy figures left. That choice was even less palatable.

Tess opened the car door and stepped out. Pretending not to care that the shadows were watching her, she shut the car door and walked toward the street. Her ears were tuned for any sound other than that of her own fast steps, and in only seconds she was positive that she heard footsteps on the tar and gravel surface of the parking lot. She refused to turn and look. If the students following her—and she had to believe the shadowy figures were just students—were trying to frighten her, she couldn't let them see how well they were succeeding.

As quickly as she could move without running, she hurried down the sidewalk. Barely audible sounds were following her; she was certain. In the darkness between street lights, she dared a glance back. Several students were following her. She didn't recognize any of them, but was slightly relieved to see some were girls. With girls in the group, the boys probably weren't bent on rape. She continued to move as quickly as possible, however. The students were too quiet and their faces were too intent.

By the time she was on her block, she was almost running. Her ankles threatened to give way because of the strain of walking so fast in high heels, but she couldn't allow herself to slow down. A glance back told her they were closer, though they didn't seem to be walking any faster than they had been.

She was gripping her house key so tightly that her fingers had gone numb and she was afraid of dropping it in the dark. When she reached her drive, she ran, not caring what it might look like to the students following her. She jammed the key into the lock and turned it. Almost falling into the house, she slammed the door behind her and leaned against it as she turned the handle of the dead bolt, securing the door.

Her heart was pounding in her throat so hard that she could hardly breathe. Slowly Tess turned and looked out the single pane of glass set high in the door.

Standing there in silence on her front walk were the students who had followed her. The porch light was on their faces, and she was startled to see the girl she had noticed on the first day of school—the one with unusually long red hair, the girl who had somehow disappeared before Tess could ask her name. They weren't moving or speaking to each other, only staring at her house.

Tess turned away from the door and tried to reassure herself that they couldn't get inside. She had been careful to lock the back and side door, and she never opened her windows, even on nights warmer than this one. She told herself she was safe, but she didn't feel it.

After several minutes, she dared another look. The front walk was empty. She didn't know when the students had left or where they had gone, but she was relieved that they were no longer standing out there, staring with that unnatural silence at her house. Who had they been? She thought by now she knew most of the students at the high school at least by sight, but except for the red-haired girl, she had never seen any of them. She resolved never to be the last to leave the school again.

Kelly Nelson had been wanting to see this particular movie for several days, but seeing Kevin Donatello come in and sit a few rows from her took her mind off the screen. In the weeks since Toni Fay Randall had died, Kelly had thought about a number of things she had heard.

She and Toni Fay had been best friends in spite of Kelly's shyness, partly because they were neighbors and partly because Toni Fay could see past Kelly's crippling shyness to the girl beneath. Best friends always shared secrets, and one time when she was spending the night, Toni Fay had hinted that she was in a new club. Kelly had asked questions, but all Toni Fay could tell her was that they had something really special planned and that she would never be the same after that. She had also revealed that the group was led by Kevin Donatello.

Since that time Kelly had watched him. Because of her natural aptitude for disappearing in any crowd, Kelly had been able to observe him without him once detecting her interest. At first he hadn't done anything particularly strange. He had walked Tracy Wright home once and had frequently talked to a tall girl named Mona Dupree. He seemed to be friends with Darryl Watson and Gary Valdes, but he never sat with them in the cafeteria or talked to them in the halls.

But by giving all she had seen careful thought, Kelly had started to put it all together. None of the students who had died had seemed to have a connection with one another, just as Kevin had no easily discernable connection with Tracy, Gary, Darryl or Mona. Kelly doubted that anyone other than herself had noticed Kevin with any of them.

When she thought back on it, she had seen him talking to Brooke Wright behind the football stadium one day. At the time she had thought they were talking almost by accident, but Brooke was one of the suicides. It was possible that Kevin was the missing piece in the riddle of why the suicides had occurred.

Kelly still missed Toni Fay a great deal. Toni Fay was the only close friend Kelly had ever had, and she had been almost inconsolable in those first few days after her death. If she could find the answer to why it happened, she might be able to avenge Toni Fay. For Kelly didn't think for a minute the suicides had been a coincidence.

As she watched, Tracy Wright entered the theater and sat a row or two in front of Kevin. He waited a few minutes, then moved up beside her. Kelly was suddenly more interested in them than in the movie. As soon as enough time passed for her move to be unnoticed, she went forward and sat directly behind Kevin.

The movie was turned up too loud for her to hear what Kevin was saying to Tracy, but Kelly was watching his lips. By straining hard, she could make out most of what he was saying. Tracy was pretending to watch the movie, but Kelly was sure she was listening to Kevin.

Kevin was telling her that he had talked to the others in some group and that they wanted Tracy to be one of them. This was so similar to what Toni Fay had told Kelly that she gasped. She had been right!

After a while, Kevin left Tracy and moved to the other side of the theater where he sat alone. Kelly watched carefully, but he didn't speak to anyone else. When the movie was almost over, he got up and strode up the aisle. Kelly was out of her seat and following him before she gave her actions any thought.

She caught up with him outside. "I want to talk to you!" She was as surprised as Kevin at the vehemence of her words. "I know what you're up to!"

Kevin whirled on her and stared. "I know you. You're Kelly Nelson."

"That's right. I was Toni Fay Randall's best friend," Kelly said with more than a trace of pride. "Her *very* best friend."

"Oh?" He took a step closer.

Kelly refused to back away. "We talked. She told me everything."

His black eyes seemed to glitter. "Let's go get a malt and talk about it."

She shook her head. "I don't want to go anywhere with you. I just want you to leave Tracy and Mona and the others alone."

Kevin's hand shot out and caught her arm. "What did you say?"

She tried in vain to pull away from him, suddenly frightened. "Let me go!"

He looked around as if to see who might be watching them, then pulled her to him as if they were a couple. He wrapped his arm around her shoulders and held her in a viselike grip as he forced her to walk. Kelly was too frightened to scream or even to fight back. At his black car, Kevin opened the driver's door and pushed her inside.

Kelly scrambled across the seat, but he grabbed her before she could get out the opposite door. She cowered against the door. Why had she said anything to him? She realized now she should have gone to her parents and told them what she knew. "I haven't told anyone," she said as he slammed the driver's door. "I promise I haven't."

"Maybe you'd better tell me what you're talking about." His voice was cold and cruel. She didn't dare disobey.

"Toni Fay used to talk to me. She said she was a member of some group. That it was supposed to be a secret."

"What did she say the group was?"

Kelly wasn't sure how to answer that. "Just a bunch of kids, I guess."

"What does that have to do with me?"

Her mouth was so dry she almost couldn't speak. "Nothing, I guess. Let me go, Kevin. I won't tell anybody. I promise!"

As he started the car, she tried to get out again, but he grabbed her and sped away. Once the car was moving so fast, she was afraid to try to escape. Without speaking he drove toward the city limits.

111

"Let me go! Just let me out of the car! I'm real good at keeping secrets!" She watched the street lights stream past. How fast was he driving? "Kevin, are you listening to me?"

"Shut up. I'm thinking."

She tried to be quiet. Maybe that was why he was driving. She had often heard her father say he liked to drive around and think. Maybe Kevin didn't mean her harm at all.

Kevin didn't dare let her go, but he didn't know what else to do with her. Certainly he couldn't trust her. If she would confront him in front of the movie theater, she might do it again when there were people around. Besides, as scared as she was, she would be sure to tell her parents or somebody. Girls did things like that.

Automatically he drove down the road he always took to get to the meeting place. When he made the next turn, he unexpectedly found himself on the dirt road that led directly to the meeting place. In fury he struck the steering wheel. Why hadn't he been thinking about where he was going? Now she knew where the meeting place was. It couldn't be seen from the dirt road, but if she had figured out his connection with Tracy and Mona, she could figure this out as well.

He stopped the car and pulled her out the driver's door. She protested but he didn't listen. There was no longer a choice. He had to be certain that she wouldn't tell. That she couldn't tell.

After dragging her through the brambles for several minutes, they emerged in the clearing. In the center was the blackened area where he always made the fire. Kelly was crying now and hiccuping softly.

"Where are we?" she asked.

"You tell me."

"Is this where you and Toni Fay and others used to meet?"

Kevin glared at her. She was too stupid even to try and trick him. He felt his strength growing as it always seemed to in this place. "That's right, Kelly. This is the place."

She shrank away from him, but he held her wrist tightly.

"Don't you want to see it? I thought you were so interested." Sarcasm tinged his words. How could he do it? What could he use?

"Kevin, please let me go. I won't tell anyone you're the leader. I swear I won't!"

"You even know that? Toni Fay was a real blabber-mouth!"

Kelly seemed ready to faint. He yanked her to him. His fingers closed around her throat, and he pressed with his thumbs as hard as he could. He felt the cartilage give, and she fought frantically, her mouth opening and closing against no breath. He was strong, and she was unable to break free. A delicious exhilaration flooded through him. Kelly made a choking noise and her eyes rolled back in her head. He held her throat a while longer, then let her lifeless body fall to the ground.

For a long time he stood there staring at her. It had been so easy. Just like in the movies. His own breath was coming in ragged gasps, as if he had been running.

When he was certain, from her failure to move, that she was dead, he went back to his car and got the shovel he always had with him in case the fire got out of hand. Kicking the black embers out of the way, he started digging.

It took him longer than he had expected. Kelly wasn't a large girl, but he had to make the hole deep enough so that no animals would dig her up. When she was buried, he shoveled the embers back in place. After another fire, the ground would look as if it had never been disturbed.

Kevin lifted his head and looked up at the moon. "Give me her energy. Give me her cunning!" he pleaded. He waited until the unseen forces had had ample time to bestow them upon him, then he went back to his car. He didn't give Kelly's grave a backward glance. All the way home he sang at the top of his voice. Kevin had never felt such a rush of excitement as he had at knowing he had singlehandedly snuffed out Kelly's life. This, he thought, was what the dark gods must have felt during the suicides. He was almost jealous.

Kelly was missed at once, since she so rarely went anywhere. Her parents were distraught, but the police could do nothing. Her body hadn't been found, and as far as anyone knew, she had no enemies. The police finally declared her a runaway. Her parents didn't believe it, but they had no other explanation. They told their friends and other family members that Kelly had been inconsolable since Toni Fay Randall's death and that she must have felt she couldn't stay in Maple Glen any longer. Everyone agreed that this must have been the case. After all, Kelly had been so reclusive; who really knew what she thought or felt?

114

Kevin never let on by so much as the flicker of an eyelash that he had known her at all. But whenever he lit the bonfire for his new and growing group, he thought about Kelly's body lying under the ashes and smiled.

Chapter Five

"It really scared me," Tess said to Lane as they walked to school the morning after Parents' Night.

"And you have no idea who the students were?"

"I didn't recognize any of them. Apparently they only wanted to scare me. I was wearing heels, and I'm sure they could have caught up with me if they'd wanted to harm me." She shivered at the memory. "One thing that frightened me so much was their silence. They weren't talking or making sounds like a group of teens usually do."

Lane frowned. "You should report this to Mr. Crouthers. We haven't had a problem with gangs in Maple Glen, but one may be forming."

"I'll go by there before I go to my room."

"And you say you didn't recognize any of them?"

"That was the odd part. True, I've only been here a short while, but I've always been good at remembering names and faces. You'd think I'd have known several. I had seen one of them before, though. It was the girl I asked about my first day here. You remember—the one with the long red hair. She came to my room by mistake."

"I haven't seen a new student by that description, but she would have to have been new not to know that yours was the art room. Even if she had never been in the school before, I should think she could tell it wasn't set up for English or history. That's pretty obvious."

"Nevertheless, she was with the ones who followed me home last night."

"I don't think it's a good idea for you to go home alone that late. Whatever motive they had, you shouldn't take the chance."

"I won't do it again. That's for sure. I've already called a garage to repair my car." She grimaced. "I'm trying to get the hang of doing the things Brad used to do."

"If you need me, you can call me."

"Thanks." She looked at the school building as they approached it. In the daylight, it merely looked old. "Brad would have said last night was all my imagination. That the kids just happened to be going my way."

"It doesn't sound like that to me. Promise you'll talk to Mr. Crouthers?"

"I promise."

They went into the school and parted ways at the second floor hall. Tess went to her room and started taking out the projects for first period.

"Tess? Could I see you for a moment?"

She glanced back at the door to see Janis Denkle, the drama teacher. "Of course. Come in"

"I hate to disturb you, but I wanted to discuss the scenery for the play."

117

"What play?"

"Didn't you get the memo?" She sighed. "I was afraid of that. About this time every fall we put on the first play of the season. It's performed during the day and is only for the students. Later in the year we'll do two that are more demanding and the parents will be invited to those."

"I see."

"This play doesn't require much in the way of scenery, nothing elaborate, but we do need some trees and a house."

Just some trees and a house? Tess wondered what Janis would consider an elaborate set. "I haven't had much expertise in building sets."

"Oh, it doesn't have to be much. Mrs. Larson just had her students paint on cardboard. I've already checked and there's plenty in the supply room off the teacher's lounge."

"When do you need it?"

"Tomorrow, actually."

"Tomorrow? You've got to be kidding!" Tess stared at her in disbelief. "I can't have trees and a house painted that soon."

Janis looked perplexed. "Mrs. Larson didn't require any more time than this."

Tess managed to keep her temper in check. "Okay. Tell me exactly what you want." It was soon apparent that she would have to break her resolution not to stay late after school.

Although it bothered her to do so, Tess put her scheduled projects away and brought several sheets of cardboard from the supply room. If she had each class work on a tree or the house, they could have them almost finished by afternoon. She would ask for volunteers in each class to stay late and finish the scenery and put it in place.

By late afternoon, Tess's plan was resulting in significant progress, and she was beginning to believe she might finish the scenery on time. None of the students had been willing to stay after school, but several had agreed to return after dinner. Tess had accepted their offers. She couldn't afford to turn down any help, and they all told her that Mrs. Larson had always done it this way.

Knowing it would be at least seven that evening before the first of her volunteers returned to the school, Tess treated herself to a leisurely meal at Paulson's Family Restaurant. The food was good, the service adequate, and even though she preferred company when dining out, the break from routine was enjoyable. Or at least that was what she told herself. In reality, a growing sense of dread robbed her of any pleasure. Despite her efforts to keep her thoughts away from the traumatic events of Parents' Night, the shadowy figures that had frightened her by following her home drifted in and out of the dark recesses of her mind.

Logically, she knew that what had happened that night was an isolated incident, a prank played on her by students with too little to think about and too much idle time on their hands. Nevertheless, she had no intention of being the last one to leave the school building again.

Promptly at seven o'clock, she pulled into the school parking lot, glad it was still daylight. She knew the cleaning ladies and janitor had gone by now, and the empty parking lot suggested that all the faculty had gone as well. Wishing she'd had that option, she got out of her car and entered the building through the door closest to the parking lot. She left the door unlocked so the students who were coming to help her could get in, and after deactivating the burglar alarm system she headed for the auditorium.

The school was deadly quiet, and little of the dwindling daylight reached the interior halls, save that which came through the exterior doors' windows. She was glad the auditorium was relatively near the front of the building. As she passed the even darker stairs, she averted her eyes. Tess had never been fond of being alone in the dark and this building bothered her more than she would have thought possible.

The auditorium was unlocked just as she had been told it would be, but the cleaning ladies had turned off the lights. With no other choice, Tess propped open one of the auditorium doors and entered the cavernous space. Moving carefully in the darkness, she felt along the wall until she found the light switch. Hastily, she flipped it on, but only the lights along the back of the auditorium came on. The front seats and the stage remained in total darkness.

Tess told herself she was foolish to be so nervous. She had heard Hannah and some of the other teachers talk about working late and Hannah had said she even preferred to be in the building after everyone else was gone. Apparently Mrs. Larson had felt the same way. Tess knew she would simply have to get over her fears.

Lifting her chin and walking as purposely as if she did this every day, she started down the aisle.

The auditorium hadn't been remodeled in years.

The scarred, wooden seats looked as if they'd seen generations of use. The initials of numerous young lovers had been carved in the arm rests and seat backs for posterity, and here and there were the crude etchings that signaled assembly boredom. Tess found herself glancing up and down the rows of seats as if to be certain they were empty. She found that almost amusing. At the moment she would welcome company.

As she progressed toward the stage, her pace diminishing in inverse proportion to the increasing darkness, she tried to remember where Janis had told her the stage light control panel was located. Janis had been adamant that she not turn on the large lights, as the replacement bulbs were too expensive to use for scenery building. Instead, she was to use the smaller ones that were recessed into the ceiling above the stage. Unconsciously trying to repel the fear-provoking thoughts that threatened to seize her, she tried to recall from her high school drama classes mundane things such as which side of the room was stage right and whether the front of the stage was upstage or downstage. Drama had never been her best subject.

Suddenly, Tess stopped and cocked her head to one side. Had she actually heard something other than her own footsteps? She wasn't sure. The silence had become thicker, as if the auditorium were somehow isolated from everything outside. Again she thought she heard something, and she peered into the shadows on stage. It was a strange sound, like a rope rubbing and straining against something. "Is someone here?" she called out. Her voice was swallowed by the deadening silence.

No one answered. Tess told herself it was only her

121

nerves. No one could be in here, and if someone was, the lights would certainly have been turned on.

Drawing a deep breath to bolster her flagging courage, she went up the steps on one side of the stage and felt her way around the corner. When she brushed against the folds of the heavy stage curtain, she jumped, not knowing what it was. For a moment her mind raced through all the possible things it could be, then she concluded it must be the curtain. Tentatively, she reached out and touched the object, then breathed a deep sigh of relief that she had been correct. Resuming her search for the light switches, she slipped between the curtain and the wall, and cautiously edged forward, feeling her way along the dusty wall.

Much to her displeasure, she encountered several cobwebs, but persisted until she found the light-switch panel. With trembling fingers she located several switches that might have fit Janis's description of the ones she was supposed to use. She flipped the first two, but nothing happened. Tess again heard the creak of the rope. She pushed the curtain aside so she could look toward the stage. *Was that something hanging from the ceiling?* By now her eyes had adjusted to the darkness, and she thought she saw something a bit darker than the other shadows swaying, as if suspended, over the stage. She released the curtain and turned her attention back to the light switches. The third switch flooded the stage with light. The next one illuminated the wings and backstage areas. Wanting as much light as possible, she turned them all on, disregarding Janis's insistence that the larger lights be left off to save money.

Again Tess shoved the curtain aside so that she

could see the stage. It was empty. Where the dark shadow had been, there was nothing. Behind her, three sharp, metallic reports shattered the stillness. She flinched, then realized it was only someone knocking on the back door. It had to be one of the students who had agreed to help her. She went to open it and was relieved to see Mojo Conroe and Jason Cook.

"Are we the first ones?" Jason asked. "We came straight from football practice."

"Coach Hodges nearly ran us to death today," Mojo complained good-humoredly. "I thought he never was going to say we could go."

"You're the first. We may as well get started. The others must be running late."

With the boys' help, Tess carried the scenery out onto the stage. It wasn't heavy, but the pieces were large and unwieldy. Tess was glad the first to come were the ones with the most muscle. "Mrs. Denkle has marked where to put everything," Tess said to the boys. "I'm going to go out into the auditorium and see how they look."

She hurried down the steps and up the aisle. Halfway up the aisle she turned and studied the stage. It was a good thing that she had turned on all the lights, because without the ones out front which were aimed back at the stage, she wouldn't have been able to properly judge the scenery. The trees looked much better from this distance, and the class which had painted the house had even managed to do it with fairly decent perspective. She was pleased with the result.

Although she knew the boys couldn't see her, because of the lights shining toward them, she pointed to the larger of the trees. "We need to add some yellow to the one in front. It's not quite right with the others. And Mojo, will you touch up the chimney on the house? I can't see the mortar in the bricks."

"Should I make it wider?" he called to her.

"No, it needs to be lighter in color." She crossed between rows of seats to the other aisle so she could view the set from another angle. "Jason, could you bring the shorter tree forward and put the taller one in back?" Jason shaded his eyes and squinted, trying to see her as he pointed at the tree he thought she meant. "Yes, that's the one."

Soon the two girls she'd been expecting arrived, but they were obviously more interested in flirting with Mojo and Jason than in working on the set. Tess told them to go back stage and find the paint she had sent to the auditorium earlier in the day.

Keisha Dailey and Patty Sinclair exchanged an odd look, then turned back to their teacher. "I'm afraid to go back there," Keisha said.

Tess was so caught up in her work, she automatically said, "That's silly, Keisha. There's nothing back there that can hurt you."

Her friend spoke up, "She's scared of seeing Misty Traveno."

"Who? I don't know a student by that name."

Jason stopped what he was doing and frowned at the girls. "That's real funny, Patty. Misty was a friend of mine." To Tess he said, "Misty is one of the girls that died last summer."

"Oh." Tess had forgotten one of the suicide victims had been found on the stage, hanging by a rope. Refusing to dwell on the obvious connection between the tragic event and the sounds she thought she'd heard and the swaying shadow she thought she'd seen, Tess said, "I'll go with you and prove to you there's nothing to be afraid of. What happened last summer was a terrible thing, but there's no such thing as a ghost." She smiled at Jason. "Besides, why does everyone seem to think that if there were ghosts, that they would all be frightening? It could be comforting to see an old friend again." Jason didn't look convinced so Tess didn't press the subject.

As she swept behind the heavy black curtains that concealed the backstage area, she ran headlong into a baby grand piano. Keisha and Patty giggled nervously. Tess laughed as she rubbed her knee. By tomorrow she would have a bruise. The tension was broken, however, and the girls seemed to forget about their earlier apprehension.

When Tess had all four students again at work, she turned off the auditorium lights and went back out into the auditorium to see if the new colors were working. With the boys and girls laughing and jostling each other on the well-lighted stage, Tess's earlier fears seemed totally out of place. She had never been one to be superstitious, and while she had an active imagination, it had never run away with her as it had lately. Perhaps, she thought, her aberrations were a psychological response to the trauma of divorce and stress of a new job in a new town.

She strolled along the back wall from one side of the auditorium to the other, watching her students' progress and reflecting on her decision to move here. Maple Glen was a good school. It had a high scholastic average, an excellent football team, a principal interested in new teaching methods. She was certain she had made the right decision. When she thought about Lane Hodges, a broad smile spread across her face. He had started calling her after work just to talk, and they were routinely walking to and from school together. He had admitted to being lonely before she came to town, and she knew she wouldn't be as happy as she was without him. Maybe the affection she held for him was a rebound from the breakup of her marriage, but it felt genuine, and she preferred to believe it was.

As Tess moved back toward the stage, she saw Keisha shadowing her eyes and looking out into the audience toward the opposite side of the room from Tess. "Mrs. Bowen?" she called out.

"Over here."

The girl looked in her direction and seemed to be surprised to see her there, then pivoted her head back to the other side of the auditorium. Tess followed the girl's gaze. Because her eyes had adjusted to the brightly lit stage, she was having trouble seeing in the dark, but she thought she saw someone sitting in one of the seats. That, of course, was impossible. She had just come from over there, and no one was in the auditorium except for the four students on stage and herself. Apparently, Keisha had seen her on the other side of the room earlier and had assumed she was still there.

Keisha held up a paint can. "I need to put more water in this green paint."

"All right. You can use the girl's bathroom beside the band hall."

Keisha looked at Patty. "Can Patty come with me? I'm scared to go in there by myself."

Tess expected the boys to nudge each other and grin, but they seemed as ill-at-ease as the girls. "Okay, but don't take long. Let's get this finished so we can all go."

As the girls hurried out, she could hear their footsteps echoing in the hall that led to the restrooms.

"Mrs. Bowen?"

"Yes, Jason."

"I just remembered I let my brother take my car home. Is there some place I can call him to come back after me when we're through?"

"I'll drive you home."

"Are you sure you don't mind?"

"I don't mind at all." Tess didn't want to admit it, but she was grateful she would have Jason's reassuring bulk with her when she had to turn off the lights before leaving. She wondered if she should make an appointment of her own to talk with Dr. Hudson.

The girls came back with a minimum of giggles and squeals and the trees were soon finished. Tess was pleased with the results. Obviously the students had done scenery work before, and Tess felt a bit more kindly toward Janis Denkle and Mrs. Larson, who had set the precedent. Things were done differently here, but Tess could learn to flow with most of the school's idiosyncrasies.

When everything was set up for the play, she let the girls and Mojo out the back door. To keep Jason from following them and waiting for her by her car, she asked him to turn off the wing and backstage lights while she secured the door.

Jason did as she requested, and as quickly as she could, she joined him by the light control panel. He was looking up at the grid system over the stage and the ropes dangling there that were used for the suspension of scenery. Tess didn't have to be a mind reader to know he must wondering if Misty Traveno had hanged herself from one of those very ropes.

She flipped the switch that turned on the lights at the back of the auditorium, then said, "You go on ahead and I'll turn out the stage lights. There's no reason for both of us to flounder around in the dark." She waited until he had jumped off the stage and was striding up the aisle before she plunged the stage and front half of the auditorium into darkness.

Carefully she felt her way around the corner and toward the steps. With her toe, she found the first step and gingerly groped her way down. From in the darkness she heard the creak of a wooden seat as if someone had shifted his weight. She could see Jason look to one side nervously as he neared the dimly lit area in the back of the auditorium. Tess refused to think about it. No one was there. No one *could* be there.

Nevertheless she was relieved to leave the huge room, even if the rest of the school was equally dark. The halls stretched to either side, now in complete darkness. She almost ran into Jason. "Are you turned around, Jason? The outside door is this way," she said, pointing to the tiny square of light at the far end of the hall.

"I thought I saw . . . never mind." Side by side they walked the length of the hallway, neither venturing more than a few feet from the center where the light was better.

"I should have thought to leave a light on out here," she said. "It was still daylight when I came in, and it didn't occur to me." She hoped her voice didn't sound as panicky as she felt. What was it about this building that affected her so strongly? She could sense Jason trying as hard as she was to conceal his uneasiness, and she made a greater effort to walk with a measured stride.

She stopped at the alarm system and waited until Jason had reached the outside door and opened it before she activated the alarm. He was a good boy, and she was certain he was trustworthy, but she didn't want anyone knowing how to turn the alarm on and off. After a quick glance around, she followed Jason out of the building. He let the door close, and she pulled on the handle to be sure the lock had engaged.

"Do you come up here by yourself much?" he asked as they went down the sidewalk toward her car.

Tess glanced at him. At her old school, she wouldn't have answered such a question. Until she came to Maple Glen she hadn't realized how much she had been forced to remain on guard. "Sometimes, but I'm almost never here alone."

"I couldn't do it. I mean, I'm not saying I'd be scared," he put in quickly to protect his teenage ego, "but the building is creepy at night."

"I agree. Maybe it's because it's the only time the school is quiet. I've noticed that places that are usually noisy—a gym, factories, and so forth—seem strange when there's no noise."

"Mrs. Mitchell stays up here at all hours. Man, I don't see how she does it! Up there on the third floor all alone. I couldn't do that, for sure."

Tess knew she couldn't either, but she said, "There's nothing there in the dark that isn't there in the daylight. She probably prefers that to dragging papers home to grade and having to bring them back the next morning."

At her car, as Jason waited for her to get in, he looked up at the windows of Mrs. Mitchell's English room. "Hey! There's someone up there!"

Startled, Tess stepped back from the open car door and looked up to see what had caught his attention. "There are no lights on. No one can be up there. Where?"

"Mrs. Mitchell's room. The seventh window from the corner. See?"

Tess counted the windows until she found the seventh. "I don't see anything."

Jason frowned. "Neither do I now."

"Mrs. Mitchell wouldn't be up there looking out the window in the dark."

"It didn't look like Mrs. Mitchell."

"Was it a student?" She really didn't want to go back inside that building and investigate, but she felt an obligation to her new employer. "Maybe we should go up and see."

Jason quickly wagged his head from side to side. "I guess I imagined it. It must have been a shadow." Furtively, he glanced again at the upstairs windows.

Tess hid her relief. She knew no one could have gone into the building without setting off the alarm. Then she remembered she had turned off the alarm when she had come back to the school to work in the auditorium. For a minute she wavered. There could be someone up there bent on vandalism.

"Are you ready to go?" Jason asked. Already, he'd

gone around to the passenger side and was trying un-successfully to get into the car.

She realized she still hadn't unlocked his door. She pressed the release button and slid behind the steering wheel. Jason folded his long body into the passenger seat. As she backed away, Tess looked up at the third floor again and reassured herself that it was extremely unlikely that anyone was up there. She was glad to drive away.

Chapter Six

Kevin Donatello looked around the circle of faces seated around the fire. His new coven was almost complete. Darryl Watson sat on his right, Gary Valdes on his left. Darryl was new to the school and Kevin had been hesitant to include him at first, but Gary had been persuasive. Gary had said Darryl had a new stepfather, who had forced him to leave his old school his senior year and to come to Maple Glen where he knew no one. Furthermore, the stepfather was a stickler for obedience, and Darryl had tried to run away once already.

Kevin had known Gary Valdes for years and had almost invited him to be a member of the last group, but Kathy Alsop had come along at just the right time and Kevin liked the idea of an equal number of males and females. Gary had been smoking marijuana since the sixth grade and had been doing hard drugs since the eighth. To feed his habit he had started stealing and now had a criminal record impressive enough to land him in prison if he got caught again. It was only a question of time until his luck ran out completely, since crack was now life blood to him. Gary had been the first of the new group.

With his arms raised, Kevin started a chant, not unlike a mantra he had heard in a recent movie. "I call up my power. I call up my power. From the bowels of the earth I call up my power." His obedient followers repeated the words.

"I ask all the demons of darkness to fill me. I ask that I be given the sign." He waited for something to happen. A log on the fire broke, sending a shower of sparks spiraling upward. A murmur of appreciation from the group rose to his ears. "I demand that my followers be recognized by the demons and be kept safe to do my bidding."

The teenagers started to sway, almost imperceptibly at first but then with larger movements, as they followed the lead of a tall girl with thick glasses. Mona Dupree was a natural at this, Kevin thought with detachment. She had a fascination with demonology and had told him she once attended a real witch's coven before she moved to Maple Glen. Kevin wasn't so sure this was true, but it didn't really matter.

Bending toward the fire, Kevin passed his hand quickly through the flames. "I am one with the fire." He waited for his followers to do the same. Some seemed reluctant, but all did it. He was training them well. He had already started deciding on a date for the Grand Sacrifice. Naturally he hadn't told any of them what was to come. They weren't ready yet.

He had to chose the right moment for the ceremony. If he rushed into it, some might not be sufficiently brainwashed to do exactly as he said and it would ruin everything. If he waited too long, the group might fall apart. Kevin thought that was what had gone wrong in his earlier attempt to gain universal power. He had waited too long. The group had started to fray at the edges. Some had apparently had second thoughts and delayed their suicides until after midnight. The deaths all had to be as simultaneous as possible.

The last day of April was Beltane, a powerful night according to Mona. But that was months away. He didn't dare delay too long for fear of someone finding out they were meeting. None of his coven would even consider telling anyone about the meetings, but their parents might become suspicious. Now there were football games and other school related activities to help explain their absences from home in the evenings. By the end of April, everyone would be preparing for graduation and making plans for college. Kevin didn't want anything to usurp his power over them.

The second day of February might be the next best choice, but Kevin was impatient and not sure he could wait that long. On the other hand, Candlemas was one of the four witches sabbaths noted on the calendar he had hanging in his room. And February was such a dreary month, they might be willing to do anything to relieve the boredom.

This time, he resolved, he wouldn't tell them they were to die, and he wouldn't leave the choice of method by which they would die to them. He had been a bit surprised that the first group had agreed to kill themselves for him. Of course they hadn't thought they'd actually die. He had convinced them that in the act of suicide they would transcend death and become immortal. Kevin was frequently amazed what people would believe when they stopped thinking for themselves.

When the last of the followers finished passing her hand through the fire, Kevin nodded his approval. "I call on the powers of darkness to grant me my will. I ask that the rest of the group make themselves known to me by Friday, when the autumn moon will be full."

"May I ask a question?" Mona asked in reverent tones.

"Granted."

"How many of us will there be?"

"Twelve of you. And me."

"Thirteen. That's fitting." She lowered her eyes submissively. She had been raised in a strict religious household that demanded subservice of women, and she fell into obedience easily.

"Now each of you tell me why you've been chosen," Kevin commanded.

Gary said, "I'm one of the coven, because I'm a child of fire. I bring energy to the group."

Mona said, "I'm a child of water. I bring the strength of the ocean to the coven."

The boy beside her said, "I'm a child of the lion. I bring strength and daring."

Determining what each would bring had been the hardest part of his new organization. Kevin had done a great deal of reading before forming the first coven, and he had hit upon this idea. Now each of them saw themselves as integral to the coven and there was even less chance of them rejecting his brainwashing.

Darryl finished the circle by saying, "I'm a child of darkness. I bring the coven secrecy."

"So it is written. So it shall be done." Kevin looked

135

at each. "You're all to be vigilant the next few days. If you see a likely candidate, you're to tell me at once. Under no circumstances may you ask a person if they're interested or tell them anything about us." He waited for everyone to nod. "If we're discovered, we'll be forced to disband. None of us want that."

Mona's eyes seemed large behind her thick glasses. "Tell us, leader, what we'll become."

"You'll become all you desire. Together we'll call down so much power, you'll be able to choose whatever destiny you desire. Lovers will fall at your feet in passion, riches will come to you. But first we must purify ourselves to the point where we're worthy of all this power."

"How will we know when the time is right?" Darryl asked.

"You won't. I will. The power will speak through me." Kevin looked around the circle. This time it *had* to work. By next year they would all be graduated, and he would have more difficulty recruiting followers. Besides, it was too dangerous to risk a third suicide pact in such a small town. Eventually someone might link his name with the others. Like Kelly Nelson had. Of course, he'd taken care of Kelly, but he couldn't afford that kind of risk again. "When the time is right, we'll have a meeting such as you've never dreamed of. At that meeting, each of you will be invested with power and may use it to do your will forever."

Nods and smiles went around the circle. Kevin said, "The hour is growing late. It's time to disband for tonight. Gary, Darryl, you may stay behind and talk to me. I have a special task for you."

The others took a step back and snapped their

hands up in the Nazi salute. "Heil!" they said in one voice. Slowly they faded into the darkness as they headed toward their homes.

Gary and Darryl appeared impatient as they waited for Kevin to speak. Kevin let them wait. These two were the least obedient of the group. He had no intention of allowing a weak link this time. When the others were gone, Kevin said, "We're going to the school."

"The school? At this time of night?" Darryl frowned as if he might object.

"You got something better to do?" Gary challenged. "What are you going to do? Go home and watch TV with your old man?"

"I wouldn't watch crap with him."

Kevin said, "I've chosen the two of you because of all the others, you're the bravest. You're my fire and my darkness." The boys looked pleased. Kevin knew he had them. "Put out the summoning flame." He gestured at the low fire.

When the last ember was smothered Kevin led the way back through the woods to the dirt road. As they felt their way through underbrush, Darryl asked Kevin, "How did you find this place?"

"It was shown to me in a dream." Actually Kevin had spent weeks the year before scouring the countryside in search of a place where a fire at night would not likely be seen, and which was fairly accessible by a seldom-traveled road.

They reached the road and Kevin said, "When you get to the school, park your cars on the practice field behind the gym, in the shadows. If you see someone driving by, go around the block, then come back."

137

"Got you." Gary went to the battered pickup he drove.

"Wouldn't it be better to go in just one car?" Darryl asked. "We'd be less likely to be seen."

Kevin wished he had thought of that, but he couldn't allow anyone else to suggest ideas. "No, we'll be covered by your power of darkness." He went to his own car and started the engine.

Kevin arrived at the field first and was sitting on his fender when the other two boys drove up. Although he'd been there only a minute, he pretended he had been there longer. In the past Kevin had discovered his followers could be convinced easily of his powers by letting them think he could do things that went against natural laws. He had suggested more than once he could teleport himself from one spot to another. At times he wondered how they could be so gullible, but he was glad they were.

"Man, you must have flown," Gary said as he walked to Kevin.

Kevin only smiled. "I didn't come here by the usual way." Darryl looked unconvinced but he didn't argue.

"So what's our task?" Gary pushed his hands in the back pocket of his jeans and looked at the school.

"I want you to get my English book."

"What?" Darryl exclaimed.

Gary glared at Kevin. "Man, you've got to be kidding. You want us to risk our butts just to get your frigging book? What's so damned special about that book?"

"I left it in the English room on the shelf where Mrs. Mitchell has that ivy growing."

"The school must be locked tighter than Ft. Knox

by now," Darryl said. "Don't they have an alarm system or something?"

Gary put his head to one side and eyed Kevin suspiciously. "What's the catch? Why do you want us to do this?"

"I want proof of your loyalty and bravery. If you're to be given absolute power, I have to be convinced you're worthy of it. I'm not letting just any jerk in the coven."

"How are we supposed to get in? I've never broken into a place before." Darryl frowned at the building.

"There's not much of a trick to it." Gary studied the building with his practiced eye. "I've broken into harder ones."

Kevin gestured at the school. "Let's see you do it. Prove to me you're capable."

Darryl was reluctant but he wasn't about to admit that to the others. They had made him feel welcome in this new school, had given him an identity and a place to belong. Besides, his stepfather couldn't care less about where he was or what he was doing, and his mother didn't seem to care about anything but his stepfather. He followed Gary around the building to the band hall.

Gary squatted for a look into the band hall through the basement-level windows. "I don't see a wire. Do you?"

Darryl got down on his knees beside Gary to help look, but wasn't sure what he was looking for. He shook his head. "I don't see anything like a wire."

"When they put in the alarm system, I think they forgot the band room. I was back here one day last week and noticed it."

"Why would you notice something like that?"

"It pays to know about things like this," Gary said as if that were obvious. "Where would we be now, if I didn't know these rooms aren't wired to the alarm?"

Darryl wasn't convinced. "How do you know you just can't see the wires from out here? What if we get inside and the cops arrive?"

"Use your frigging power of darkness," Gary snapped. "I'm doing my part!"

Darryl didn't tell him he had no idea how to use the cloak of invisibility. He assumed he was the only in the coven who didn't know how to use the power Kevin had assigned to him. "So we're covered! Let's see you get us inside." He tried not to think about this being illegal. They were only after a text book.

Gary pushed on the window over the music cabinet. The hinges were rusty but they gave. Silently Gary lowered himself through the narrow opening and onto the cabinet. Darryl wished he could turn and run but that was impossible. He followed Gary into the building.

The room was almost completely dark. Darryl put out his hand and almost knocked over a music stand.

"Be quiet," Gary snapped.

"Who the hell can hear us?" Darryl retorted in a whisper. "There's nobody else here."

"I know that. Don't you think I know that?"

Darryl wondered if Gary was as fearless as he told others he was.

Together they moved around the edge of the room until they found the door that led up the steps to the first floor. Darryl liked this less and less all the time. He had never been in a place so dark and so frighten-

140

ing. All the familiar landmarks were swallowed up in the inky blackness. He turned toward what he thought must be the stairs and ran into the wall.

"Be quiet!" Gary grabbed Darryl's arm and jerked him upright. "Did you hear something?"

"I heard me running into a wall," Darryl said. His forehead was throbbing and already a bump was forming beneath the skin. "What's the matter? Getting scared?"

"Hell, no!" Gary moved toward the stairs and Darryl stayed close behind him.

Darryl bumped into something that proved to be the bannister and realized they were at the stairs. By the sounds of Gary's movements, he was already going up, but it was pitch black in the stairwell and Darryl couldn't see him. He wished their footsteps didn't echo so loudly. Why did it seem so noisy tonight when he had never noticed it during the day?

After what seemed to be hours they reached the third floor. Darryl said, "Why can't we turn on a light? We'll never find our way back down without falling."

"Is all your family brain dead? If we turn on a light, somebody might see it from outside. There's moonlight coming in from the window at the far end of the hall."

Darryl didn't point out the obvious. Moonlight or no moonlight, the hall was as black as a pit. "Let's just get the damned book and get out of here."

Gary chuckled. "What's wrong? Scared of the dark?"

They felt their way along the lockers until they reached Mrs. Mitchell's English room and slipped inside. The classroom was bathed in a silvery glow from the moonlight streaming through the wall of windows, and they could move about with greater ease.

Darryl went to the shelf beneath the window and felt in the ivy. "There's no book in here."

"Keep looking." Gary had stayed near the door and was leaning out as if he was listening for something.

The ivy was large and thick. It took several seconds before Darryl touched the spine of a text book. He pulled it out triumphantly. "I've got it!" he loudly exclaimed

"Why don't you yell it out the window?"

"Damn it, Gary, nobody can hear us. Why are you whispering like that?" Darryl was still scared and Gary wasn't helping any. He didn't relish the thought of having to feel their way down the stairs in the dark. One slip and he could break his leg or worse. Then how would he get out of the building?

"Come on," Gary urged as he eased out the door. "Close it behind you or Mrs. Mitchell will know some-one was in here."

"Hell no. Maybe you can see in the dark like some damned cat, but I can't. At least this way we can see where the stairs start."

In the ensuing silence, Darryl heard a noise of some sort that sounded as if it had come from across the hall where the lockers met an office door. Darryl's eyes darted about. "What was that?"

"I don't know. I heard it just before we went in the room. It's nothing."

Darryl strained to see but could only make out a shape a bit darker than the rest of the shadows. "Is that somebody standing there?"

"Don't talk crazy!" Gary's voice sounded scared.

142

"What do you think this is? A burglar convention? It's just a frigging shadow!"

"I think it just moved!"

"Come on. I've got more to do than stand here and listen to you." Gary moved toward the stairs at a faster pace than was prudent.

Darryl had no intention of being left behind. He hurried to catch up.

At the top of the stairs, Darryl stopped short. "Listen! There it is again!"

Gary paused. For a moment the silence was thick about them. Then a low sound came from no where in particular. "Someone else is in the building."

"But that can't be! Nobody's here but us."

Again the sound came. It was so soft Darryl couldn't be sure it wasn't his imagination. Then it grew louder. "That sounds like the chant Kevin uses around the fire."

"You don't think he's down there trying to scare us, do you?"

"If he is, the joke is going to be on him." Darryl hoped he sounded braver than he felt. "I'm going down." He glanced back at the moonlit hall and almost fell. "Gary! Look back there!"

He felt Gary turn. "What *is* that?"

"I think somebody's standing there." Darryl called out, "Kevin? Is that you? We see you. The game is over."

Although there was no answer, the dim silhouette turned slightly. A head and broad shoulders were touched by the moonlight. It was still silent.

"Kevin?" Gary growled. Fear was making him sound angry.

"Are you sure that's Kevin?" Darryl whispered. "Does it look like Kevin to you?"

The figure moved and again and seemed to be motioning for them to come back, though they heard no sound.

"Sure it's Kevin." Gary glared at Darryl. To the figure he called, "You scared this wimp half to death. I'll bet they'll have to mop up where he's standing." He punched Darryl in the shoulder. "Come on." He started walking toward the figure.

Darryl wasn't convinced, but he also didn't want to remain at the top of the black stairs alone. "Who's doing the chanting? Are the others here, too? How'd you manage that, Kevin?"

The figure went into the English room. Gary and Darryl followed him. They didn't realize their mistake until the moonlight shown on Troy Spaulding's gaunt face. "Hey," Gary said as he took a step backward and bumped into Darryl. "What's going on here?"

"They must be playing a trick on us," Darryl said uncertainly as he tried to disentangle himself from Gary. More of the shadowy figures were moving behind him and blocking his exit through the door. "Who are you?" he demanded.

"Shut up!" Gary commanded, almost as pale as the silent students. "Shut up! Can't you recognize them?"

Darryl glanced around the room. A girl was there with streaming red hair that looked dusty and matted. Another girl with frizzy brown hair stood beside her, her neck at an odd angle to her body. All of them seemed to have sunken cheeks and eyes that were deep in their sockets, as if they were wearing Halloween

144

makeup. None of them were familiar to Darryl. "Hell, no. Should I?"

"That's Troy Spaulding. And Brooke Wright. Joe Bob Renfro."

"Hey, wait a minute. Aren't those the names of the kids that died last summer?" Darryl was trying to remember. He had been new to town and hadn't known most of them. His eyes found the blank stare of Ellis Johnson. Darryl had met him because Ellis' dad and Darryl's stepfather worked together. He gripped Gary's arm and started to shake.

Slowly the shadowy figures moved closer, shutting off the path to the door and escape. Darryl and Gary were clinging to each other now and not caring that their fear showed. Darryl could hear Gary making choking sounds as if he were trying to shout but couldn't.

They backed away from the approaching ghosts until Darryl's back hit the wall of windows. His eyes darted around in terror. There was no place to go.

Joe Bob Renfro moved up beside Troy. "Jump," he commanded in a hollow tone.

For a moment Darryl thought he had mistaken the word. He looked fearfully at Gary who was climbing onto the narrow windowsill. "Hey, man! We can't jump from here! It's three stories down!"

Troy moved silently to Darryl and reached out his hand. In the moonlight Darryl could see the frayed edges of his cuffs and the sunken skin beneath Troy's eyes. He looked as if he had been dead for months. As he had been.

Darryl scrambled onto the sill next to Gary. "Don't make us jump," he pleaded. "Don't do this!"

"Kill," Joe Bob muttered, his eyes picking up twin points of light from the street lights outside.

"Die," Misty whispered. Brooke's gray lips moved with her. "Die. Like we did."

"Like we did," the others repeated.

Darryl heard a crashing sound as Gary's weight against the window broke the glass. Before he could react, Gary grabbed his arm, pulling Darryl out the window with him. Together they fell, their screams tearing the air. They landed in a heap on the concrete adjacent to the teachers' parking lot. For a moment Darryl remained alive and conscious, in spite of the pain. High above him in the English room, he saw faces fill the windows. As his eyes glazed over in death, they began to disappear.

Ross Wright sat in his den with his wife Lucy, pretending to watch TV. This was the part of day he had once liked best. At this hour on a school night both his daughters would be in bed, and he and Lucy would be winding down from their day's work. A deep sadness settled over him. Tracy was in the bedroom alone and while Lucy was here physically, mentally she was far away.

"What did you do today?" he said to her to make conversation during a commercial.

Lucy glanced at him as if she were surprised to find he was still in the room. "I went grocery shopping, washed some clothes. The usual."

"I saw Ed Hudson today. He was coming out of his downtown office. He said you haven't made an appointment to see him."

Lucy looked away. "I told you I don't want to talk to him. I'm not crazy."

"I never said you were. But I can see you're not happy."

"How can I be happy? I don't ever expect to be happy again." She glared at him as if she saw him as a traitor for even expressing the hope for happiness.

"Honey, we have to put our lives back together. We can't curl up and die. We have Tracy to live for."

Lucy grunted her disagreement.

"Why don't you take her shopping for a new dress or something? Lately I've noticed she's sinking back into that bad depression. She needs something to occupy her mind."

"I don't have time to go shopping with Brooke. This house doesn't clean itself, you know."

Ross tried not to frown. "Not Brooke. Tracy."

"I said Tracy."

He let it drop. "Maybe you ought to consider getting a part-time job. Something to get you out and around people more often."

Lucy looked at him in exasperation. "I stay busy. Most days I don't have time to do all the work that piles up around here."

"We could hire a cleaning woman."

"That would be silly. I can clean my own house."

Ross glanced around the room. Before Brooke's death Lucy had kept the house spotless. Now there was a fine layer of dust on the coffee table and the carpet hadn't been vacuumed in weeks. "I think all three of us should go see Dr. Hudson. We could go as a family."

"No."

"Lucy, you can't keep on like this!"

"The show is back on. Hush."

Ross fell silent, even though he wasn't interested in the show.

After a while he got up and went upstairs. As usual these days, he was exhausted and wanted only to take a hot shower and go to bed. When he passed Tracy's door, he was surprised to see a light under it. He knocked and she called out for him to come in. "What's wrong? Can't sleep?"

"Daddy, can I talk to you?"

"Sure." Ross had learned that Tracy only reverted to calling him 'daddy' when she had something important on her mind. He sat on Brooke's bed and waited.

Tracy was on her bed propped up on several pillows, her blond hair falling over the shoulders of her flannel nightgown. She looked the way she had when she was a little girl. "Something happened today that you ought to know about."

When she didn't go on he prompted, "What's that?"

"Mom came to school today."

"She did? Why did she do that? You aren't in trouble, are you?"

"No." Tracy's fingers twisted at the covers and she didn't meet his eyes. "She brought a jacket to Brooke."

Ross felt a chill settle deep inside him. "She did what?"

"It's not the first time she's done something like this. You know that a couple of weeks ago she found Brooke's old schoolbooks in the closet and brought them to her. Thank goodness I happened to see her in

148

the hall both times. I don't think she talked to anybody else."

"She must have meant to bring the jacket to you."

"No, she made a big deal out of me wearing a jacket when I left this morning. She even zipped it up for me like I was a little kid."

"Maybe she forgot."

"Dad, she said it was for Brooke and asked if I knew what class she had at that hour."

Ross sighed and leaned forward, resting his elbows on his knees. He buried his face in his hands and rubbed his eyes. All at once he was so tired he couldn't think. "I'm worried about her," he admitted. "She's not herself lately."

"I'm scared."

He looked at Tracy and tried to smile. "There's nothing for you to be scared of."

Tracy nodded and looked away. It was obvious she didn't believe him. Ross stood and said, "Let me worry about this. You just look after yourself."

She watched him leave and shut the door behind him. That was so typical of parents, she thought, as she pushed aside the extra pillows and lay down and stared at the ceiling. She needed to talk and he had brushed her off as if she didn't matter at all. As tears stung her eyes, Tracy wondered if everyone would be acting like this if she had died instead of Brooke.

Before Brooke died, Tracy and her father had been so close. He had often taken her places and asked her opinion about things as if she were an adult. They had been as close as Brooke had been with her mother. Since the deaths, her father had become distant and always seemed to have his thoughts somewhere else.

149

Tracy knew he was as worried about her mother as she was, but Tracy needed his attention, too. It was as if by dying, Brooke had turned him away from her, and she resented that.

Brooke had always been her mother's favorite. Lucy had tried to hide it, but Tracy had known. Her grades had never been as good as Brooke's and she certainly wasn't as popular. There was no way she would ever have as many dates as Brooke. She had tried out for cheerleading at the beginning of school, but she hadn't been surprised when she wasn't chosen.

Tracy turned onto her side and stared at the empty bed. She and Brooke had been close in spite of it all, and she missed her desperately. There were a dozen times a week when she wanted to ask Brooke's opinion or tell her some gossip she had heard at school. Sometimes it seemed as if Brooke wasn't gone at all, and at other times it was as if she had been gone forever.

No matter what her father had said, Tracy knew her mother was really sick. She hadn't noticed it at first, but now that she thought about it, her mother had been becoming vague and disconnected with reality even before Brooke died. There had been small things that hadn't meant much at the time. Times when she had seemed to be in a world of her own and times when she couldn't recall what day it was or what she had done the day before. Even Brooke had commented on it. For Brooke to notice it, it had to have been obvious.

Tracy curled into a ball, her pillow squeezed tightly against her middle. No one in the house knew Brooke had been drinking heavily. She hadn't been sure of it herself until she caught Brooke watering down the scotch to hide how much was missing. After that, she had been more observant and had noticed that Brooke often seemed spaced-out at supper and ready to go to bed early. Tracy assumed she must be drinking vodka since she never smelled of alcohol. But then, Brooke had worn a great deal of perfume and had used mouthwash religiously. The day Tracy confronted Brooke with what she suspected, they had fought, but Tracy convinced Brooke she would keep her sister's secret and they had made up.

In spite of her drinking, Brooke had stayed popular, and as far as Tracy knew, her grades hadn't dropped, though Brooke had often said she was afraid they would. Tracy had tried to convince Brooke to go to AA, but Brooke had only pointed out the obvious. If she went to Alcoholics Anonymous, her parents and half the town would know about it before she returned home. Maple Glen was small in population but big on gossip, and Brooke didn't dare risk it.

Tracy faithfully had kept Brooke's secret while she was alive because Brooke had asked her to and had kept it after she was dead because there was no reason to tell and spoil Brooke's image. But at times Tracy couldn't help but resent that even with this failing, Brooke had remained the golden girl while Tracy had to struggle in every class and pray for dates to the important events. It simply wasn't fair.

She let herself cry, her sobs muffled by her pillow. Her parents didn't care about her. They were both so destroyed over losing Brooke that they didn't seem to notice she was still alive and needing them. Instead of getting less depressed as time passed, Tracy had found herself becoming more so. For a while she had thought

151

she would make it through, but now she wasn't so sure. She had failed a history test that day, and had no hopes of passing the English test tomorrow. She couldn't get her mind on school and no one seemed to notice this, either.

She knew it wasn't healthy to lie around feeling sorry for herself, but Tracy didn't know what else to do. She had talked to Dr. Hudson off and on since Brooke died, but she didn't feel a connection with him. He seemed to always have more to do than he had time to do it in. Lately she had told her father she had gone to see him, when in reality she had gone to the movies with Amy.

No one noticed. No one cared. Tracy wondered why she was still trying.

Chapter Seven

The bodies of Gary Valdes and Darryl Watson were found by a passing patrol car. By then both boys had been dead for several hours. The cause of their deaths was evident. One of the large windows on the third floor was broken and their bodies lay in mangled heaps on the pavement below. Both were pronounced dead on the scene, Gary from massive head injuries, Darryl from a broken neck and shock.

Darryl's stepfather immediately granted permission for tests to be done to determine if his stepson had been drinking or was on drugs, but the results were negative.

The police had no trouble determining how the boys had gotten into the school; the window was still open in the band hall. The question of why they went up to the third floor English room and either jumped through or were pushed through a closed window was more difficult to answer. With no other indication of a struggle in the room, the authorities were inclined to believe that the deaths were either due to accident or suicide and not homicide, but assured the boys' parents and the school officials that a thorough investigation would be conducted and the answers would be found.

All the students were talking about it the next morning while they waited for classes to start. Some of their parents had scanners that picked up the local police radio communications and had quickly spread the word of the tragedy to many of those who didn't. Those students who had not been forewarned learned what had happened overnight immediately upon arrival at school. Almost everyone was either watching a local glass company replacing the broken window or staring at the pale stain that remained on the concrete below despite the janitor's best efforts to wash away the blood.

Even though only a few of the entire student body had liked Gary and Darryl was all but a stranger to most of them, the deaths of yet two more from among their midst was horrifying, and speculation as to why it had happened was running rampant. When the first bell rang, they all hurried into the school and away from the physical evidence that death had struck their school again.

Janis Denkle, too, was relieved that the school's routine had begun and in particular that this was the one day this week she did not have hall duty. She had been deeply struck by this new tragedy, as were virtually all the teachers, and she was in no mood to have to deal with any roughhousing or boisterousness from the students.

As she always did when she had a spare moment, she went to the auditorium. She wanted to be certain that the scenery was set up exactly right before assembly and felt that occupying her mind with the play would help her cope better. Even the darkness didn't bother her. She went down the aisle, up the steps and turned on the lights.

With her first glance at the stage, Janis gave a startled gasp, then she stared in horror for a long moment before running up the aisle to find Tess.

"What do you mean the set is ruined?" Tess asked.

Janis was actually wringing her hands. "Come and see for yourself. I keep telling myself it can't be true, but it is!"

Tess glanced at the clock in the hall. She had only a few minutes before her first period class was scheduled to begin, but from the look on Janis' face, this matter was of a greater priority. "Let's go."

As the they hurried to the stairs, Janis said, "I went into the auditorium to be sure everything was ready for assembly, today, and I couldn't believe my eyes. It's terrible!"

"Maybe it can be fixed. Paint can cover almost anything."

"You don't understand. It's *ruined.*"

Tess didn't argue with her. Everyone in the school was upset, and she assumed Janis was overreacting. True, the drama class was to put on the play today, but they had most of the morning to repair the set.

They went into the back of the auditorium and down the aisle. Long before they reached the stage, Tess could see that the cardboard trees and house were strewn about the area. As they got closer, she saw the scenery had not only been knocked over, but had been torn apart. She went to the nearest fragment of the house on the floor in front of the stage and started to pick it up.

"I wouldn't do that," Janis said quickly. "There's something smeared on the other side."

Tess nudged it aside with her toe, revealing a sticky, red substance on the floor where the piece of scenery had been. Looking around the stage, she saw that all the scenery had been smeared with the same red liquid. "What's that red stuff? It doesn't look like paint."

"I have no idea. I started to pick up the piece by your foot and whatever that is came off on my hand." Janis rubbed her fingers as if she could still feel it. "It looks like stage blood, but I haven't ordered any. I don't do plays that are gory."

Slowly Tess came up the steps. All the trees and the rest of the house lay about. The cardboard had been bent and twisted as if some maniac had tried to rip them to shreds. On everything she saw the red smear. "I can't believe it! This is heavy cardboard. It would take a lot of strength to do this."

"There must have been more than one pulling on it. See? Even the board supports have been broken."

Tess picked up a board, being careful to keep her hands clean. She was adverse to touching the mess that looked too much like blood. "It's snapped in two. I saw Mojo sawing these boards in the woodworking shop. They wouldn't break easy." She looked at Janis. "Have you told Mr. Crouthers?"

"He hasn't returned yet from the police station, so I came to you rather than wait for him." Janis ran her fingers through her cropped hair. "This is terrible. What on earth happened here last night?"

"I don't know. Gary and Darryl must have done it."

"This goes beyond mere vandalism. This looks more like hatred. And why would they both fall or jump through a window afterward?"

Tess had been thinking the same thing but was unwilling to put it into words. "I'm as stunned as you are."

"I'm not sure what to do. My students have practiced with this set in mind. Some of them have to hide behind the trees and house. I can't do the play without scenery."

"I guess you'll have to postpone it for a few days. Under the circumstances, Mr. Crouthers will probably not want the play done today, anyway. My classes have to finish projects today and tomorrow, but maybe I can have you another set by Monday. I didn't have anything planned for this weekend anyway." She kicked at a torn tree. She hadn't planned anything, but she didn't particularly want to spend her days off painting scenery at the school. "Can you come up Saturday?"

Janis shook her head. "My husband's family is coming down from Minnesota, and I have to stay at the house all weekend and entertain them. We almost never see them, and I don't dare not be there." She smiled ruefully. "My in-laws don't like me as it is."

"I understand."

"Besides, I'm not sure I can move the schedule around like that, even out of respect for Gary and Darryl. I had to schedule this assembly long before school started. None of the teachers will have made lesson plans for that hour." She looked as if she

157

wanted to cry. "And my class will be so disappointed that all their hard work has been ruined on top of everything else!"

"Let's go talk to Mr. Crouthers. Maybe he'll be in his office by now."

"He has to see this for himself or he won't understand why I'm so upset. Will you stay here while I go get him? I don't want any of the students wandering in and moving things about."

"I'll stay, but hurry. I have to get back to my room before the bell rings."

Janis jogged up the aisle and was gone.

Tess knelt and sniffed close to what was left of the roof of the house. The paint—she had to think of it like that—had an odd smell. She couldn't quite identify it. It had to be stage blood. Janis must have had a forgotten bottle of it on a back shelf. Or it wasn't completely impossible that a student hadn't bought it himself. Halloween was just around the corner, and fake blood in small quantities was available in many stores. But who would buy so much just to waste it like this?

In only a few minutes, Janis was back with the principal in tow. As they hurried down the aisle, she saw the shock on Mr. Crouthers' face. "This is just terrible!"

"I was in here yesterday evening with several of my students finishing up the scenery. We left about a quarter to nine, as I recall. Apparently Gary and Darryl did this when they broke into the school."

"I came down at seven when the police called me," Crouthers said. "We found an open window in the band hall, and I'm sure they entered the building there.

We looked in here, of course, when we checked the school out, but apparently we didn't look closely enough. I'm sure they must have done it."

Tess's thoughts jumped to the evening before in the parking lot when Jason Cook had reported that he thought he saw someone in Mrs. Mitchell's room. Guiltily, Tess said, "Mr. Crouthers, I just remembered something. Last night when Jason Cook and I were leaving the parking lot, Jason said he thought he saw someone in one of the upstairs windows. I looked, but didn't see anything. I really feel bad now that I didn't investigate, but—"

"And you didn't go up to investigate or call to report it?" He frowned at her."

"I know I should have, but when I looked, I didn't see anything suspicious. I thought Jason was mistaken."

"Well, it's done now. Don't blame yourself." He surveyed the damage again, then asked, "What's this on the cardboard? Red paint?"

"No, it's too runny and sticky. Janis thinks it's stage blood."

"I said it *looks* like stage blood. I have no idea where it could have come from. I never ordered any. You know I never put on shows that could frighten the students."

Tess thought it was probably impossible to frighten any high school student with a play, but she kept her opinion to herself.

"What are we going to do about the play? I can't put on a play without the scenery. That's an important part of the performance. Can we postpone it and my class still be allowed to perform?" Janis asked with concern.

"I was going to cancel the play for today anyway. It would be most inappropriate." Mr. Crouthers sighed and shook his head. "Let's go back to the office and call the police. They'll need to add this to their report. While we're waiting for them to get here, we can look at the schedule for next week, or perhaps the week after that."

"Everyone is so upset," Janis said. "We've all worked so hard on this play, and the art students did such a good job on the scenery, and now this! I just can't believe Gary and Darryl are actually dead! It just doesn't make any sense to me at all."

Tess glanced at her watch. "If you don't need me for anything else, I should get back to my class."

Mr. Crouthers seemed to have to rouse himself from his contemplation of the torn cardboard. "No, no. You go ahead. I'll take care of this."

Tess was relieved to escape the auditorium. Even with other adults on the stage and students in the building, she had felt uneasy being there. Had she not been reluctant to do something that would disappoint the students, she would have hoped the play was postponed indefinitely. She dreaded having to come to the empty school and work on more scenery over the weekend.

When her first period class was seated, Tess told them what had happened. "So we won't have assembly today and we may have to redo the set."

"We worked hard on that!" Mojo objected. He glared around the room as if he expected someone to explain. "I'd sure like to know why they did it!"

160

"We all would. Well, are any of you free to make a new one on Saturday?"

A few reluctantly held up their hands. Tess wrote down their names. If it was necessary, she decided, she would paint the sets in her backyard, not at the school. She didn't want to admit to anyone that she was afraid to go into the auditorium. "For now let's assume we won't have to rebuild it. I want you to work on your block prints today. Mary, will you and Susan hand them around?"

Hannah Mitchell was rather surprised to see Mr. Crouthers at her classroom door. He motioned for her to come into the hall and she said to her students, "Start reading on page 104, 'She Walks In Beauty.' We'll discuss it in a moment." She fixed the class with a look that said she would allow no nonsense even on a day such as this and went to the door.

When she was in the hall, Mr. Crouthers said, "I'm checking with all the teachers. Was there any evidence of vandalism in your room, aside from the broken window, that is?"

"No. I'd say that was enough." Hannah was deeply disturbed over the two deaths and was struggling hard to hide it.

"Someone—Gary and Darryl, I assume—also destroyed the scenery for the play Mrs. Denkle's class was to perform this morning."

Hannah drew back. "Why would they do something like that if they were planning on jumping to their deaths from my window?"

"We don't know that they came to the school with

that purpose in mind. Their primary intent may have been vandalism. Surely their deaths were accidental."

"I just wish I knew." Hannah tightened her lips and shook her head. "It's just awful!"

"I know. The police will be back here shortly to survey the damage in the auditorium, but I wanted to find out if anything else was harmed before they arrive."

Hannah went back to her class, carefully closing the hall door behind her. As they were still reading, she went to the window and looked out. This would have been the last thing Gary and Darryl saw before they fell or jumped. The thought was disturbing. Of all the nights for her not to have worked late! She might have been able to save the boys' lives had she been here! Hannah felt all the students were her children. It didn't matter that she hadn't particularly liked these two. With a puckered brow, Hannah went back to her desk and sat down facing the students.

All but one face was pouring over the text books. For a long moment Hannah couldn't think or move. The girl staring back at her was Brooke Wright.

Brooke didn't move or blink. Except that she was paler and her cheeks were sunken and gaunt, she looked exactly as she had the last time Hannah had seen her. It was as if time was suspended. Hannah wasn't aware of her own breathing and she was frozen in place.

As suddenly as she had appeared, Brooke vanished. Hannah tried but failed to stifle a gasp and several of her students on the front row glanced up. Slowly she stood and braced herself on her desk.

162

"Mrs. Mitchell?" Keisha Dailey asked. "Are you okay?"

Hannah couldn't answer. The desk where Brooke had been sitting was empty. The boy who should have been sitting there was absent that day. Hadn't that been the desk Brooke had occupied last year? Hannah couldn't remember.

Weak-kneed, she crossed to the door and opened it so she could look out into the hall. As she had known it would be, the hall was empty, well-lit and normal. Yet, the girl she just had seen was Brooke, and Hannah knew she wasn't mistaken. Even if she had been wrong about the girl's identity, she wasn't wrong about her vanishing.

Hannah knotted her hand against her stomach. She prided herself on never being shocked and almost never frightened. Now she was both.

She turned to go back to her desk and found most of the class was watching her. Trying to move naturally and hide her apprehension, she crossed to her chair and sat down. She knew they would assume she was upset over the deaths.

"Mrs. Mitchell? Should I go get the school nurse?" Keisha asked, her voice anxious and her face showing her concern.

"No. No, I'm fine," she said, but she felt as if she would never be all right again. "Have you all finished reading?"

A few of them nodded. Most avoided her eyes. Hannah drew in a deep breath. "Let's read it together. Randy, you take the first stanza." Her mind was so preoccupied with what she'd just witnessed that she was only barely aware that the boy had done as she'd asked.

The impossible had happened. She had seen Brooke Wright, and she knew there was no mistake about it. A cold sweat broke out on her forehead, but she ignored it. This panicky feeling was much worse than she had ever experienced before, but she couldn't give in to it. This was only the first of five classes she had to teach today. She couldn't give in. She didn't want to give Crouthers any reason to insist that she take the retirement she was eligible for. As she knotted her hands in her lap to keep them from shaking, Hannah noticed the boy had finished. "Keisha, you take the next stanza." She wished she had chosen a longer poem for them to read—she wasn't sure she would be able to pull herself together so quickly.

Tracy had never liked gym. She was neither athletic by nature nor particularly competitive. Unlike Brooke, she was usually among the last chosen for any team, and this embarrassed her even if she hadn't wanted to play in the first place.

She also disliked the showers. Tracy's body hadn't developed the way Brooke's had, and she was ashamed of the way she looked. It didn't matter that there were other flat-chested girls in the school or that the showers were a necessary ritual. She always hung back until the others were finished before she showered, even though it made her habitually late to her next class.

She stayed at her gym locker, pretending to be unable to untie the knot in her shoelace until she heard the last shower cut off. As the other girls dressed and gossiped, Tracy went into the tiled room and shucked off the last of her clothes just before she turned on the water.

As always, she washed as quickly as possible, being careful not to mess up her makeup since she never had time to reapply it. The locker room grew steadily quieter as the other girls finished dressing and went to their next class. This was a relief to Tracy, as it meant she would also have the lockers more or less to herself.

She turned off the water, and as she wrapped a white towel around her body, she heard a noise coming from the direction of the lockers which was neither surprising nor unusual. Someone else was late in dressing.

Tracy dried off quickly and, still wrapped in the towel, picked up her gym clothes and went back into the locker room. The muffled sounds she'd heard before were somewhat clearer now, as if someone was whispering. Tracy was immediately suspicious. Was someone playing a prank on her? If so, it was in particularly bad taste, since everyone in the school was tiptoeing around due to Darryl Watson and Gary Valdes's deaths the night before.

"Patty? Is that you?" she called out. Patty Sinclair and Keisha Dailey did things like this from time to time. Both girls were good at sports, and that made Tracy a natural target for their pranks. She yanked open her locker, expecting to see something pop out, but nothing had been tampered with. As quickly as possible, she tossed the towel aside, pulled on her panties and snapped her bra.

Again she heard the noise. This time it sounded as if someone were walking slowly down the row of lock-

165

ers. She heard only one set of footsteps. A shiver ran up her back as she thrust her feet into her jeans, yanked them on and buttoned them. "Quit trying to scare me, Patty. I know it's you." She reached into her locker and pulled out her red blouse.

When Patty still didn't answer, Tracy peeped around the locker door. As she did, Brooke stepped into the alley formed by the rows of lockers.

Tracy froze. Brooke didn't move for a long time. Her hair wasn't as shiny as it had been and looked dusty. Her skin had a gray pallor and her unfocused eyes were dull. But it was unmistakably Brooke.

"Brooke?" Tracy whispered. "No, it can't be!"

Brooke's eyes met Tracy's. Something like the old spark she'd seen there before lit them. "You're alive," Brooke said in a whispery monotone. "Still alive."

Tracy felt her entire body go cold, and she shivered. She wanted to run or to call out, but she couldn't seem to move or speak. All she could do was stand there, her blouse clutched to her chest, and stare at the impossible sight. Finally she was able to say. "How can you be here?"

"Cheated," Brooke said. "I was cheated. You're still alive. Cheated."

Tracy couldn't make any sense of this. "You feel cheated? Is that what you mean? Because you're dead?"

Brooke's face began changing ever so slowly and subtly until it was a mask of rage. She raised her eyes and glared at the lockers nearest her. To Tracy's amazement, the lockers began to teeter. She whipped her eyes back to Brooke.

166

"Cheated," Brooke whispered again in that hollow voice so unlike her natural one. "Dead!"

The lockers began to fall and Tracy watched them as if they were moving in slow motion. Then realization dawned on her and she dived under the wooden bench between the rows of lockers.

The crash brought shouts and the sound of running feet. Tracy was too stunned to realize help was coming. She found herself screaming again and again, her eyes screwed shut to block out any sight of Brooke.

She heard the voice of her gym teacher asking if she was all right. Tracy opened her eyes and saw the woman kneeling where Brooke had stood and looking under the bench. Tracy crawled to her. She was still shaking all over and had trouble standing.

"What happened?" Mrs. Jeffereys demanded as she helped Tracy to the bench in the next aisle. "Are you hurt?"

At first Tracy couldn't speak. Her eyes darted around in search of Brooke. There was no sign of her. "No," she said. "I'm not hurt."

"You have a bump on your head. Here. Put your blouse on and come into my office."

Tracy stared down at her blouse a long moment before she recognized it as her own. Automatically she dressed and was doing the last button when Lane Hodges ran into the room.

"I was coming into the gym and heard a crash. Is anyone hurt?"

Mrs. Jeffereys said, "I'm not sure. Tracy, can you tell me what day it is?"

Tracy thought for a minute. "Tuesday. Is it Tuesday?"

"How many fingers am I holding up?"

She looked at Mrs. Jeffereys' hand. "Two."

Lacy Jeffereys bent closer to look at the bump on Tracy's head. "It doesn't look too bad. How do you feel?"

Tracy shook her head. How could she possibly explain to anyone how she felt after the experience of having her dead sister try to crush her with a row of lockers? "Okay, I guess."

"She sounds vague." Mrs. Jeffereys frowned at her, then turned back to Lane. "Does she sound vague to you? Could be a concussion."

"I think she should have the nurse look at it." Lane was watching her carefully. "What class do you have next period?"

The knot on her head was starting to throb. Tracy touched it tenderly. "English."

"I think she should go straight to the nurse," Mrs. Jeffereys said in a concerned voice. "It pays to be safe."

Lane was looking back at the fallen lockers. "How did that happen? Were some of you roughhousing?"

Mrs. Jeffereys gave him a disgusted look. "Have you ever seen girls get that rowdy? I saw what happened. The lockers just fell."

"That's impossible," Lane said with conviction.

"You saw what happened?" Tracy gasped. "You saw Brooke?"

Both teachers stared at her. "What did you say?" Mrs. Jeffereys asked.

Tracy shook her head. She didn't want them to think she had lost her mind. "My books. My books are in my gym locker. I can't get to them."

168

"I'll write a note to your teacher. Are you sure you feel like going to class?"

Tracy nodded as the tardy bell rang. How had so much happened in such a short time? "I'll be in trouble if I don't hurry."

Mrs. Jeffereys scribbled a note for her explaining her tardiness and lack of books. Tracy took it and walked away as Lane and Mrs. Jeffereys started arguing about how a row of lockers could have fallen over without having been pulled out of the floor.

Tracy started running when she reached the gym and raced across the echoing floor as if devils were after her. She didn't feel safe until she had made it up the stairs and into the English room. As she handed the note to Mrs. Mitchell, she gasped for breath. Mrs. Mitchell nodded for her to take her seat, and as Tracy sank into her desk, she was relieved to hear the woman resume reading the poem Tracy's late entrance had interrupted. Although the normalcy around her was somewhat reassuring, she couldn't stop thinking about having seen Brooke and the fact that her dead sister had tried to kill her.

Immediately after his last history class on the following day, Lane Hodges gathered up the homework papers he had to grade and took them with him to his office in the gym. It always took the boys a few minutes to change into their gym shorts, and during that time he could grade several papers, reducing the work he'd have to do at home that evening.

He quickly shifted his concentration to the students' papers, relying on the tardy bell as his signal to quit.

After several minutes, he realized it was too quiet. The boys should be pouring in, laughing and talking and jostling each other.

He looked at his watch and discovered it had stopped, but that didn't explain where the students were. It felt as if ten minutes must have passed since time for the last bell. He stood and went to the door of his office. Through the wire-reinforced windows, he could see the locker area. Overnight a maintenance crew had come in and put the lockers back up and had resecured them to the floor. If he had been thinking, he would have asked them to rearrange the lockers so he could see down the aisles, but with all that had been going on, he hadn't thought of it in time. With this arrangement, he couldn't tell at a glance who was in the locker room.

He opened the door to investigate but stopped to listen. Was that a voice whispering just beyond the first row of lockers? Lane called, "Who's there?" No one answered.

With a sense of deja vu, he walked down the rows, not seeing any students at all. This had happened before, that time he had found Troy's football jersey folded on the bench exactly as he had left it there at the end of the last school year. Although Lane knew the jersey was locked away in a drawer in his office, he had the uneasy feeling that he might find it on the bench again.

Lane wasn't one to let his imagination run away with him, but he had an eerie feeling, as if he were dreaming.

The locker room was empty, and he was about to go

back to his office and check the time on the wall clock when he heard a shout in the gym. The fine hairs on the back of his neck bristled. It was a yell he had thought never to hear again. Whenever Troy made a score, whether it was on the football field or basketball court, he celebrated with a war whoop of his own invention.

Running, Lane burst through the door and into the gym. No one was there. But at the free-throw line, a basketball bounced to a stop, then rolled to center court.

For a long moment Lane couldn't move. No one else was in the gym, and there was no way a person could have left it so fast as not to be seen. Slowly he walked onto the basketball court and picked up the ball. He recognized it as one from the equipment closet. The school initials were stamped on its pebbly surface.

Again Lane looked around the gym, but it was obvious he was alone. Troy's war whoop still echoed in his ears. No one else ever made that particular sound, nor would they now, under the circumstances.

The door at the far end of the gym opened and the students started wandering in. Lane looked at his watch and the second hand was moving again. He didn't move until he heard one of the boys say, "What's wrong with him? He never lets us walk out there with regular shoes on."

Lane ignored the comment and slowly walked back to the locker area and went to the storage closet. He unlocked it and put the ball away, then locked the door again. There was no explanation for any of this,

171

and he wasn't sure he wanted anyone to know what he must have imagined.

As they left the movie theater, Lane took Tess's hand. She smiled up at him. "I'm sorry I'm not good company tonight. I'm still upset over someone ruining the scenery my class and I worked so hard on."

"Do the police have any idea who could have done it?"

"Not a clue. Hannah told me they found a window open in the band hall. Apparently that's where they got in. The security system wasn't wired properly when it was installed."

"That figures. It's probably the only one Terry Stubbs ever put in." He smiled at her. "Crime isn't big business here in Maple Glen. A lot of people thought it was a bad idea to buy a security system in the first place. I don't look forward to the next parent-teacher meeting."

"At least no valuable property was destroyed."

They walked in silence for a block. Finally Tess said, "Is something bothering you? It's not like you to be so quiet."

"It's nothing." He sighed. "That's not true. This morning someone took a basketball out of a locked closet."

"You mean it was stolen?"

"No, it was in the gym. You're going to think I've gone crazy, but I have to tell someone about this. I sure can't go to Crouthers. He'll think I've taken to drinking."

Tess smiled at him reassuringly. "What happened?"

172

"I was in my office in the locker room and noticed my watch had stopped. The place should have been filling up for my first boys gym class, but they weren't coming in. Then I heard a noise and went to investigate. No one was in the locker room, but I heard someone yell out in the gym." He paused as if he were considering whether or not to tell her any more. "It sounded like Troy Spaulding's war whoop, the one he always let out when he scored a point. It wasn't a sound that would be easy to imitate. When I went to see who was on the court, I saw the basketball bouncing along as if someone had tossed it."

Tess didn't know what to say. "Someone must have been playing a trick on you."

"Yeah. That must be it." He didn't sound convinced.

"What else could it have been?"

"I don't know. When I looked back at my watch, it had started running again."

Tess put her arm around him. "You've been under a strain. I know you were close to Troy, and you must miss him a great deal."

"Not so much that I'd hallucinate that he's come back."

"Then how do you explain it?"

"I can't. That's why I'm not going to tell anyone but you about this. It was eerie, Tess. I knew I was alone, but I didn't *feel* as if I were. And the boys didn't start coming into the gym until after it was over. You know how students are—they hurry everywhere. Even if they're not late, they seem to be rushing."

"But things like this don't happen." She was thinking of the strange feelings she had experienced in the school when she was alone. "I can't believe in ghosts. They don't exist."

"I know that."

"On the other hand, I have to admit, I don't like being alone in the school."

"Speaking of strange happenings, have you caught sight of any of the students who followed you home that night?"

"No, I haven't, but I'm still looking." She matched her steps to his. "And since we're talking about strange things, has anyone found an explanation as to how the row of lockers in the gym fell on Tracy Wright?"

"No. The bolts holding them to the floor had been pulled out of the concrete. I can't see how it could have happened. I had new concrete anchors installed. It won't happen again. Thankfully her parents are willing to accept that it was an accident and are not going to sue the school."

"Well that's good. I mean since it wasn't the fault of the school and since she wasn't hurt. Incidentally, the play has been rescheduled for Monday. It's only fair, I suppose. Janis can't disappoint her students and life does go on. So I'm going to spend my Saturday painting trees and a house."

"By yourself?"

"A few students have offered to help, but they weren't enthusiastic. I doubt all of them will show up."

"I don't think it's a good idea for you to be in the school alone."

She nodded. "Don't worry. I won't be. This time I'm painting in my backyard. Just between you and me, that auditorium gives me the creeps."

"I know. I've often wondered why anyone would wire lights so they can only be turned on in the wings where it's so dark. It doesn't seem safe."

Tess was glad to hear she wasn't the only one who had wondered about this. Was Lane equally nervous in the auditorium? It didn't seem to affect Janis at all. "I guess when they were wiring it, they had temporary lighting rigged up and didn't realize how inconvenient it would be until it was too late to change it."

"I can come over on Saturday and help you paint."

"You'd do that?"

"What are friends for?"

"I'd really appreciate it. I'm not looking forward to it. I'll make sandwiches for whoever shows up."

"And I'll help you take the scenery to the auditorium when it's finished. There's no point in you having to do it alone. Besides, those flats can be heavy."

"Thanks. I appreciate it."

"Tess? Don't mention what I told you about the basketball in the gym. Okay?"

"Of course. I wouldn't say anything about that." She heard the concern in his voice and realized he was really worried about what had happened.

"Would you like to come to my house for dinner tomorrow night after the junior varsity game?" He smiled down at her.

"I'd love to. Should I bring anything?"

"Just yourself. I'll make my killer chili. The weather is finally cold enough to justify it."

"It sounds fiery," she said with a smile.

"I have to register it as a lethal weapon."

Ahead Tess saw her house, and for the first time it

looked like home. She was adjusting to her new life. "I'm glad I came to Maple Glen."

"So am I." He put his arm around her and gave her a hug as she walked.

Tracy found Amy after school and said, "I've got to talk to you."

"Okay. Want me to drive you home? Mom actually let me have the car today. Can you believe it?"

Tracy wasn't interested. "I want to tell you what really happened in gym last Tuesday."

"I was wondering if you were ever going to tell me. Everybody's been asking, and I didn't know what to tell them." Amy shifted her books to her other arm as they left the school and headed for the parking lot. "Was it Keisha and Patty? I'll bet anything it was."

Tracy waited until no one was nearby. "It wasn't either of them. It was Brooke."

Amy stopped abruptly. "What?"

Tracy glanced nervously around. "I said it was Brooke. I saw her as clearly as I'm seeing you."

"Yeah, right." Amy looked at her with skepticism. "Like I really believe that."

"You don't believe me?" Tracy frowned and touched the bruise on her forehead. "I'm telling you, Brooke did it!"

"Give me a break. Even if Brooke could come back, why would she want to hurt you? You two were always close."

Tracy frowned. "It was Brooke, but it wasn't like her. I mean, she'd changed. She said something about being cheated."

Amy looked as if she didn't believe a word she was hearing. "Brooke is cheating? That doesn't make any sense at all."

"I said cheat*ed*. I think she means she was cheated out of being alive, and she was mad about it."

"Tracy Wright, I'm your best friend, and I can't believe you're standing here and trying to tell me stuff like this!" Amy strode toward her car.

"I'm not lying! I don't lie to you. I sure wouldn't lie about something like this!" Tracy hurried to catch up with her. "Haven't you heard everybody saying the lockers couldn't have fallen over like that? Coach Hodges told Jason Cook and he told Britanny Sinclair and she told me that the bolts were pulled out of the concrete floor! Pulled out! Not unscrewed!"

"Since when do you talk to Britanny? You know I don't like her since she started going steady with Jason."

"Aren't you listening to me?"

"Sure, I am!" Amy turned to face her. "And you're talking crazy. If you ask me, that bump on your head did something to your brain."

"That's a fine thing to say!" Tracy frowned at Amy and made no attempt to get into the car. "It seems to me that my own best friend ought to believe me."

"That you saw Brooke's ghost and she tried to kill you? Have you told anybody else about this?"

"No. I'm afraid to."

"Well, I guess so! It's crazy."

"No, it's not! But the teachers wouldn't believe me. You know how they are. I can't tell my parents a thing like this. You're the only one I can tell!"

"You're weird, Tracy. If you want me to drive you home, get in the car."

Tracy jerked her chin up angrily. "No thanks. I'll walk."

"Suit yourself. But stay out of the sun. You're already talking weird."

"Stop saying that!"

Amy opened her car door and tossed her books inside. Turning to Tracy she said, "If I can't tell you, who can? We've been friends practically forever. If you keep talking like this, somebody is going to think you're crazy." Amy dropped her gaze. "I have to go."

"Crazy like my Mom? Is that what you're saying?" Tracy felt angry and hurt at the same time. She wanted to cry, but didn't.

Amy looked back at her. "I didn't say that."

"Is it what you meant? Answer me, Amy!"

For a long time Amy was silent. "No. I don't think you're really crazy. Maybe you have a concussion or something. Did you go to the doctor?"

"No. I'm not hurt that bad." Tracy noticed Amy retracted her accusation of her being crazy but she was avoiding the same retraction about Tracy's mother. She stepped back from the car. "I guess I don't want a ride home after all."

"Okay." Amy started to get behind the wheel but paused to say, "I'm sorry, Tracy. I shouldn't have said I don't believe you."

"Are you saying you do believe me?" Tracy challenged.

"How can I?"

Tracy turned away so Amy couldn't see her tears.

"I'll see you around." She walked away as briskly as possible.

When Kevin fell into step beside her at the corner, Tracy made no objections to him walking her the rest of the way home.

Chapter Eight

"Is something wrong?" Tess asked as she put her lunch tray on the table beside Hannah.

Hannah jumped, not realizing anyone was near her. "I'm fine," she said almost defensively. "I haven't been sleeping well. That's all."

Tess looked troubled. "I didn't mean to be prying. I was only concerned about you."

Hannah sighed. "I'm sorry. I didn't mean to snap your head off. I'm having some personal problems and didn't realize it showed, and then there were the deaths." Since seeing Brooke Wright appear and vanish in her class, Hannah hadn't been able to put the incident out of her head. She had even considered calling in sick that morning.

"Do you mind if I sit with you?"

"No, no. Of course you're welcome."

"I guess you heard that the police have no clue as to why Gary and Darryl fell."

"Yes, I heard Mr. Crouthers say that yesterday. Was anything disturbed in your room?"

"No."

"I've thought about it so much, but I can't make sense of it. Why *my* window? Do you think it had something to do with me personally?" Her voice dwindled as she remembered Brooke's pale face.

"No, no, I'm sure it was only a coincidence." Tess put sugar in her tea and stirred it. "I guess we'll never know what was in their minds. Are you going to be staying late tonight?"

"No!" Hannah snapped, then saw Tess's startled expression and realized she was revealing too much of her true feelings. "That is, I don't have any papers to grade tonight. No, I'll be leaving with everyone else." She couldn't tell anyone she was afraid to be alone in her room in the top of the building. She wasn't sure she could ever be in the building alone again. "Why do you ask?"

"I have to redo the scenery for Janis' play. I'm going to paint it at home, but I was thinking it might speed things up if I took the cardboard to the art room after school and use the opaque projector to enlarge the drawings we made last time."

"You don't want to be alone in the building?"

Tess avoided her eyes. "It's not that," she said a bit too quickly.

Watching her face, Hannah said, "May I ask you something?"

"Of course."

"Have you noticed anything peculiar about the school?"

Tess shrugged. "I haven't been here long enough to be able to answer that. Peculiar in what way?"

Hannah was almost positive Tess was evading the

question but decided not to press. "Never mind. It's nothing."

"Are you talking about Gary and Darryl?"

Hannah nodded. Let her believe whatever she might. She couldn't risk asking if Tess or anyone else had seen ghosts about. That would be too ludicrous. Surely if anyone else had seen anything of that nature, Hannah would have heard about it through the grapevine. Maple Glen High was usually a hot bed of gossip. "I wish today was Friday. This has been a long week."

"I agree."

As she had done often since seeing Brooke, Hannah wondered if she were having a nervous breakdown. She didn't know what else to call it. She had decided that was all it could be. Brooke, along with the other eleven poor souls, had been buried for almost three months now. She couldn't possibly have been in the English room. Hannah felt absurdly like crying.

"Are you sure there's nothing you want to talk about?" Tess was watching her again with concern. "You seem so upset."

"As I said, it's been a long week, and this has been a particularly hard day." Hannah almost laughed at the understatement. "And it's only half over."

"If you're not feeling well, maybe you should go by the nurse's office."

Hannah shook her head. "I'm never sick. As I said, I have some personal problems that are keeping me awake at night." She stood, even though she had only half-eaten her meal. "Excuse me, but I have some work I need to do before the next class period."

"Of course." Tess continued eating as if she had no reason not to believe her.

Hannah put her lunch tray on the conveyer belt and walked out into the hall. A number of the students were milling about. The cheerleaders had worn their matching outfits in order to be ready for the junior varsity pep rally that afternoon and were huddled beside the water fountain giggling. Some of the couples were awkwardly holding hands in the bloom of puppy love. Occasionally a football player jostled against a teammate as if he were pretending to tackle him. The students were behaving normally.

Surely, Hannah thought as she went toward the stairs, if anyone else had seen anything, the students would all know about it and be talking of nothing else. That meant she must be the only one who had seen Brooke, and therefore, it had been an hallucination.

This explanation wasn't comforting. Hannah wasn't taking any new medication. Other than the hormones she had taken for years and an occasional aspirin, she wasn't taking any medicine at all. So why had she seen Brooke?

Hannah had known Brooke almost since the girl was born and would have been able to recognize her under any circumstances. It wasn't a case of mistaken identity. She didn't believe in ghosts—at least she hadn't until she'd seen Brooke in her class—and she had always thought people who did were either fooling themselves or not connected to reality.

She climbed the stairs and her steps slowed as she neared the top floor. No students were allowed above the first floor during lunch hour, so the top floor was quiet. Occasionally she could hear a burst of giggling or a shout from below, but nothing else.

For a long moment she stood at the top of the stairs, deliberating whether she really wanted to be up here alone.

She knew she couldn't afford to be afraid to be alone in her classroom, so she forced herself to head on down the hall. Not for the first time, she wished there were more classes on this floor. The offices here were seldom used anymore, the ones on the first floor being more convenient, and as the student body was not growing, there was little reason for the unused space up here to be made into classrooms.

Hannah paused at her door, then opened it. The room was empty, just as it should have been, but she still felt tiny pulses of fear coursing through her nervous system. She wasn't sure what she had expected to find here, but seeing nothing unusual didn't reassure her. Hannah sat behind her desk, facing the empty seats. Had there been a trick of the light that had made her think she saw Brooke? That seemed highly unlikely. Nor had Brooke been on her mind at the time.

Hannah put her face in her hands and rubbed her eyes. There must be something wrong with her, or with her mind, to be exact. She remembered an aunt, now long deceased, who had professed to have "seen things." Everyone in the family had thought she was mentally off-kilter. Now Hannah was displaying the same symptoms. She decided to give serious thought to retiring after this year. In most school systems she would have been retired several years before now, and she didn't want to drag out her career until the students laughed about her behind her back.

She heard a faint noise from out in the hall, and she looked toward the open door. No one was there, of course. She took out the test she was preparing for the following Monday and tried to work on it.

Tracy and Amy hadn't spoken since the day Tracy tried to tell Amy about seeing Brooke. Before this semester started, Tracy would have said she and Amy would be friends for life and that nothing could have ruined the trust they shared. Now she didn't want to see or talk to Amy at all.

Between her fourth and fifth period classes, she saw Amy talking with several girls at the door of the drama classroom, and when Amy saw her, she deliberately turned her head. Tracy knew Amy was pretending not to have seen her; she had seen Amy do that to other people on many occasions. With flaming cheeks, Tracy went on to her class and tried to pretend she didn't care that she no longer had a best friend.

Her grades were starting to slide, though her parents didn't know it yet. Since seeing Brooke, she had no interest in her lessons. She didn't even care if she flunked out of school. The depression that had begun with Brooke's suicide had grown until it now encompassed her. She didn't even care about her clothes anymore. She wore black almost altogether now, brightened only occasionally with crimson, and she let her hair hang straight without even trying to curl it. Just getting through the days and nights took all her energy.

On top of everything else, her mother's mental condition was eroding. Lucy had started calling Tracy by

Brooke's name nearly all the time, and the evening before, she had asked Tracy if Brooke was in from cheerleading practice yet. Tracy was embarrassed for her mother's sake, and whenever she found that her mother had put a plate at Brooke's former place at the table or had left a new blue blouse lying on Brooke's bed, she removed them before her father had a chance to notice. If her mother was aware that she was covering up for her, she made no comment.

That morning before leaving for school, Tracy saw her mother sitting on the foot of her parents' bed, just sitting and staring straight ahead, not moving or even seeming to breathe. Tracy had spoken to her, but Lucy had not responded. It had been so creepy that Tracy had come to school early. Numerous times during the day, she had thought about how strange it was to see her mother sitting on the bed so perfectly still and wondered if she was still there, staring at nothing. She had no idea why her mother was behaving that way. It was just another of the many unanswered questions that plagued all her waking hours.

She had, however, figured out an explanation for her having seen Brooke. It was stress. She had heard someone on TV say that stress could cause a person to do or see almost anything, and Tracy had grabbed the excuse like a lifeline. Anything to keep from having to believe Brooke had come back from the dead to try and kill her.

Of course that didn't explain how something as heavy as a row of lockers could have fallen, but Tracy was the first to admit that she knew nothing about physics. Maybe there had been some sort of earth tremor or some quirk of natural phenomenon that could have caused something that unlikely to occur. She couldn't deny that the event actually happened, but surely the cause hadn't been her dead sister. Besides, she had told herself on many occasions, Brooke had only *looked* at the lockers. She hadn't even touched them.

She had almost managed to convince herself that Brooke had somehow come there to warn her not to be hurt by the lockers, that she had somehow confused what Brooke had said and the look on Brooke's face. After all, Brooke would have tried to save her in real life.

After school Kevin met Tracy and began walking with her even before she left the school grounds. "Where's Mona?" Tracy asked. "I thought you were going steady with her by now."

"I'm not going steady with anybody. Mona's only a friend. I just wanted to tell you that tonight's the night."

"What are you talking about? The night for what?"

"For you to be admitted to our group."

Tracy frowned. "I don't know if I still want to. I've got homework." She didn't intend to do the homework. It was just too difficult to decide to go back out once she reached home. It was so much easier to just stay in her room or watch TV.

"Come on. Everybody's expecting you. It's great."

"I just don't feel like it."

"It's not like you and Amy have something planned."

"What's that supposed to mean?"

"I've heard she's giving you the cold shoulder these days. That's why it's so great for us to have each other.

187

A lot of the others are having trouble, too. Take me, for instance. My mom doesn't care anything about me except as somebody to boss around. My dad's gone— he just walked off and left us. Mom seems to think I ought to step into his shoes and do all the work around there."

Tracy looked at him with growing interest. "You never told me about yourself before."

"I don't like for it to sound like I'm feeling sorry for myself. So I found a way to be powerful without having to count on parents. You can do it, too."

"Me? Powerful?" She let out a humorless laugh.

"I promise. We've learned how to do a lot of things. Secret things. I want you to be a part of it."

"Is Mona one of your bunch?"

"We don't tell. You'll have to come and see for yourself."

"What if I don't like it? Can I drop out again?"

"No one has ever wanted to drop out. We're closer than family. Everybody else may give us trouble and we may lose friends or parents, but in the group—we call it a coven—we're all important."

Tracy listened thoughtfully. "It's been a long time since I really felt like I was a part of anything."

"I had a feeling you'd say that. Come tonight."

"I don't know, Kevin."

He smiled as if he already knew she would give in. "I hope you'll change your mind." As usual he walked away without so much as a good-bye.

Tracy went home and put her schoolbooks on the kitchen table. There was no point in carrying them upstairs when she had no intention of opening them. "Mom?" she called out.

There was no answer. Tracy knew Lucy was home. The car was in the driveway. The breakfast dishes were still in the sink, the countertop still had coffee circles from her father's morning coffee and the newspaper from the day before was still on the floor in the den. Tracy would have to clean the house before her father came home from work. She went upstairs to change clothes.

As she passed her parents' bedroom she stopped short. Her mother was still sitting there on the bed, just as she had been when Tracy had left for school that morning. She was still wearing the robe and she hadn't even combed her hair. A cold chill ran down Tracy's back. "Mom?"

Lucy turned her head and looked at her daughter, but she gave no sign of recognition.

Fighting against the anger that was rising in her, Tracy went back downstairs. It was so unfair, she thought as tears stung her eyes. She shouldn't have to come home from school and do all the housework so no one would know her mother no longer did it. She would also have to convince her mother to get dressed and comb her hair so she would appear more normal. Tracy was tired of it all. And she no longer even had Amy to commiserate with her.

She went to the phone and dialed Kevin's number. It took him several rings to answer. "I'll be there tonight. What time and where do I go?"

"Great! I'll come by and pick you up at seven."

Tracy hung up and went to the sink and started washing the breakfast dishes.

* * *

"That was great chili," Tess said as she helped Lane clear the table. "You cooked. I'll wash."

Lane took a clean cup towel from the drawer and watched as Tess ran hot water in the sink.

"How well do you know Hannah Mitchell?" she asked as she added soap to the water.

"We aren't close friends, but I've known her ever since I moved here. Why?"

"I've noticed she's been acting strangely lately. I asked her if she felt sick, and she seemed to get even more upset. I don't know her well, either, but she doesn't usually snap at me."

"That doesn't sound like Hannah."

Tess washed a dish and handed it to him to dry. "I'm not the only one who's wondering. Janis apparently knows Hannah quite well, and Janis mentioned the same thing to me. Hannah said it's some personal problem."

"That must be it then."

"I suppose. I just feel sorry for her. She lives by herself, and Janis has told me she seems to have no close friends outside of school. If she were sick, who'd take care of her?"

"I believe she has family not far from here. There are several nieces and nephews, I understand. She's not as alone as it might seem."

"Good. That makes me feel better."

"You really care about people, don't you?"

"Of course. Don't you?"

"Yes, but not everyone does. My ex-wife, for instance. Unless Hannah had been one of her circle of close friends, she wouldn't have cared or even have noticed if Hannah was unhappy or not." He shook his head. "I still wonder why we ever decided to get married. It was a mistake from the start."

"My marriage started off just fine, but it died a slow death. Looking back on it, I can't recall when it started drifting down hill, but by the time we called it quits, neither of us gave any thought to a reconciliation." She hesitated. "Even so, it was a surprise to me. I guess I had become so accustomed to us going our separate ways that I thought it would always be like that." She picked up the pot in which Lane had cooked the chili and dunked it beneath the sudsy water.

"No regrets?"

"No. I have to admit it's been an adjustment learning to live alone after nearly fourteen years, but I'm getting the hang of it."

"Do you think you'll ever decide to remarry?"

"Maybe. It all depends. I know now what I don't want, but I'm not sure if the reverse is true. What about you?"

"I've had more time to adjust. Yes, I think I will some day. When the time is right." He gave her a long look and smiled.

Tess smiled back as she felt the warmth of his gaze spread through her. She was also having to relearn how to let a man know she was interested. A lot of things had changed during the years she had been married. She handed the clean pot to Lane. "When this is dry, we're all done."

Fifteen minutes later they went into the den and Lane put on some music. Tess sat on the couch and leaned back. "I like that one. Isn't that something? We seem to have all the same music."

"It must be fate." Lane sat beside her and held her hand. "I'm glad you came to Maple Glen."

"So am I." Feeling uneasy with the growing intimacy, she asked, "How is the football team shaping up?"

"We're improving. We should have gone to state this year but the boys are still upset over losing Troy Spaulding and Jimmy Frye. I knew they'd be affected, but I didn't expect them to have this much trouble. We have a lot of seniors on the team who'd known Troy and Jimmy all their lives. They can't seem to shake their deaths."

"I guess that's to be expected."

"I never expected something like this to happen in a small town like Maple Glen. In a city maybe, but not here."

"I suppose everyone feels it can only happen to someone else."

"I think the reason no one can put it behind them is the mystery of why it happened in the first place. These kids had nothing in common."

"They must have. That's too great a coincidence."

"I know. The police are baffled. Everyone is relatively sure all the kids died by their own hands, but it's not necessarily fact. Misty Traveno, for instance, hung herself in the auditorium, and Troy Spaulding was also found in the building on the third floor. It's possible he helped Misty rig up the rope, then killed himself."

"If that was true, why would he go all the way up to the third floor?"

"That's just it. It makes no sense. I would have

expected him to go to the gym. It's much nearer the auditorium, and he spent most of his time there."

Tess laced her fingers through his. She could sense he needed to talk this out.

"Then there was Toni Fay Randall. Someone could have drowned her in the pond by her house, then left. By the time the deaths were reported and the police could start investigating, clues might have been obliterated. Maple Glen doesn't have a large police force. Other than giving tickets to speeders and investigating an occasional traffic accident, the police here don't have much to do. They might have overlooked a clue that a more sophisticated force would have noticed."

"Didn't they ask for help from the surrounding towns?"

"Yes, but by then the bodies had been moved. You can't expect parents to leave their daughter floating face down in their pond until the police arrive to take pictures. If there had been telltale footprints in the mud, the family had walked all over them."

"It seems unbelievable to me. Twelve children!"

"The police reports say they all probably died right around midnight."

"And there was no connection with their locations?"

"None. Some were at home, some miles from home. The only two who were even in the same building were Troy and Misty." He absentmindedly rubbed his thumb over her hand. "And none of them were friends as far as anyone knew. Brooke and Troy had dated, but they had broken up, and she had driven her car into a tree several miles out of town."

"I suppose the suicides coupled with the last two deaths are what's troubling Hannah. I don't know much about psychology, but I've heard that shock sometimes hits with a delayed response to tragedy. I've heard her say she was quite close to a couple of the students. I guess it's possible she's only now realizing they're actually gone."

"I'm sure that's it. I know she thinks of her favorite students almost as if they were her family. She takes a personal interest in all of them. And then there was the runaway, Kelly Nelson. That was a shock, too."

"I feel sorry for Hannah. I wish there was something I could do for her."

"Time will fix it. In the meantime, thank goodness Ed Hudson is there for anyone who needs him. I've been told he's even waived his fee in some cases, especially for the parents who can't afford counseling. I'm sure he's including the Valdes and Watson families, too."

"Not many people would do that for free. Not even under these circumstances."

"We watch after each other here. I'm glad it's like that."

Tess closed her eyes and lay her head on Lane's shoulder. Yes, she was glad she had chosen Maple Glen.

When the appointed hour for the meeting arrived, Kevin was waiting, the fire crackling and hot. Behind him in an isolated part of the woods, Tracy was waiting. They had talked for the past several hours. It was nearing ten o'clock. In the time since he had picked her up, he had explained everything to her. How he and the others had discovered a way of using demonic power to get what they wanted and how her entrance into the group would increase the power considerably. As he had expected, Tracy had grown more and more interested until she was eager to be a member of the coven. She was there now, mediating as he had instructed her, and waiting for him to return for her.

The first of the already established members to arrive was Mona. "Heil," she said as she approached.

He made the customary response, and she sat beside him instead of in her usual place. "I saw you with Tracy this afternoon," she said angrily. "I thought I was your girlfriend."

"You are. I was talking to Tracy about joining the coven."

"I don't want her here."

Kevin grimaced. He had hoped to bring Mona to heel by pretending to be her boyfriend, but it was backfiring on him. "You don't have a say in who joins. I'm the leader."

"You just want her around because she's prettier than I am."

It was true that Tracy was prettier, though that had nothing to do with Kevin's invitation to her. He couldn't have cared less if either of them were pretty. "I was given a sign that Tracy will be one of us. The last one," he added.

"I don't want her. If she joins, I'm out of here."

"Mona, you don't mean that. Now quit talking to me like this. You know when we're here it's not the same as when we're out together." He was tired of placating Mona. "You're a necessary part of our

195

coven. You're our water element." He drew himself up and tried to become remote to put distance between them. He hadn't foreseen jealousy when he starting taking Mona out.

He heard a sound from the woods. "The others are coming. Go to your regular place."

For a moment it looked as if Mona would refuse. Then she got up and went to a place farther from him. Kevin closed his eyes as if he were meditating, but he could feel her watching him. One by one he welcomed the other members of the coven.

"Heil," Rocky Mancelli said as he sat beside Mona. Kevin returned the salute. "What are we to do tonight?"

Kevin smiled. "Tonight I have a special meeting in mind. After tonight, our circle will be complete."

"It will? Who else have you asked to join?"

"No questions." Kevin waited in silence for the others to arrive.

At last everyone was seated in a circle with one place empty. Kevin stood and raised his arms to the night sky. "I thank you, dark spirits for sending us the last of our circle." He could feel the interest. With an enigmatic smile he stepped into the darkness and went to where he had told the initiate to wait. Taking her cold hand, he led her to the others. "I bring you your sister."

When Tracy Wright stepped into the firelight, Kevin saw surprise on the faces of several of the others. Tracy held back as if she were shy, but she made no effort to run away.

As he had done with all the others, Kevin faced

Tracy and said, "Do you swear loyalty to us and to all we stand for?"

"Yes," she said waveringly. "What do you stand for?"

"We are the chosen. As with the others, I am not the agent that chose you. Your name was given to me by inspiration. It was because of this inspiration that I spoke to you."

Tracy glanced at the others.

"Look only at me," Kevin said. "I'm your leader and the leader of the group. It's through me that the powers are translated, and it's through me that you will receive your own power."

"I don't understand. What power are you talking about?"

"We aren't allowed to say his name. I'm the only one who knows it for certain. When the time comes and you all are purified, I'll give you his name."

Kevin put his hands on Tracy's head and closed his eyes. "I consecrate this girl into our group. I welcome her into our coven."

"We welcome you," the others said in unison as they had been taught to do.

"You will be our sister."

"You are our sister," the others echoed.

"Your strength will become our strength and ours will become yours."

"So it is written," the group intoned.

"Alone we are weak. As a group we are invincible."

"So it is written."

"With you as our sister, our group is complete. Your special powers and talents have given us the final element to attain perfection. Our coven is complete."

"Our coven is complete."

Tracy glanced at the others as if she were bursting with questions but she kept her silence.

"I give you the secret name ordained for you. Kevin leaned forward and whispered in her ear. "Omega." He straightened. "Tell no one of your name, but hold it in your heart. When you become weak—and in the first days of initiation you may—repeat it silently to yourself and you'll be given strength."

Kevin turned from Tracy to the others and motioned for them to rise. As they formed a double line beside the fire, Kevin said, "You will now be born into our circle." The opposite sides joined hands overhead to form a tunnel, and Kevin led Tracy to the nearest end. Bending, he walked with her through the center of the line. As they passed, each member whispered their special service to the group.

"I am fire," the first boy murmured. "Fire cleans and destroys." Tracy recognized him as Matthew Greenway from her English class.

"Darkness," Billy Joe Robertson was saying as the first words died away. "I conceal us."

"Know me as water," Mona said in her turn. "Water is the first mother, strong but yielding."

Rocky Mancelli whispered, "I am the lion. I give the coven my strength and daring."

When they reached the far end, Kevin turned to Tracy and took both her hands in his. "You are quicksilver, ever changing, never changing." He wasn't too sure what this meant, but it was pretty and sounded mystical. Tracy looked pleased. He stood her in the empty place and joined her hands with Rocky's. "Now we are complete. We have born ourselves and are whole."

"We are whole," the others repeated.

"Together we will be invincible."

"We are invincible because we are one," Mona said.

Kevin made a mental note to be firmer with Mona. She was developing a tendency to interject her own thoughts during the meetings. He had to be the undisputed leader, or he wouldn't have their blind and unswerving obedience. He motioned for them to sit around the fire.

Tracy looked as if she were afraid of doing or saying the wrong thing, but she also appeared to be excited. It had been an inspiration to recruit her and Kevin was quite proud of himself. Brooke had been an integral part of the first coven and it was only fitting that her only sister be a part of this one.

"May I ask a question?" Mona said as she sat crosslegged on the ground.

"Yes, sister." Kevin gave her a benevolent smile as if she were a precocious two-year-old.

"Now that we are complete, what is our mission?"

"Most of you know we have joined together to multiply our power, to become the leaders and shapers of a new world."

"How can this be, Leader? We are but children in the eyes of the world."

He wondered why Mona always talked during the meetings like she was a character out of some myth. "Does anyone here feel like a child?"

Everyone quickly shook his head, Mona included.

"There is your answer. In the eyes of the world, we

are young. In the ways of the spirit we will become strong."

"How?" Billy Joe didn't mince words.

"I am guided by strong spirit forces, and you will be guided by me as their spokesman. I've told you before that you'll know this spirit's name when I'm told to speak it."

"How did they pick you?" Matthew seemed concerned. "How did this happen?"

"I was chosen while I was deep in the Sword Meditation." This was true. Kevin had discovered he could focus his energy more if he stared at a shiny surface. He had an old calvary sword his father had given him one Christmas, and he often gazed into it as he would have used a crystal ball if he'd had one. "A voice came to me and told me to gather a group, to be called a coven, and to meet where we now are. I was instructed to have six males and six females and was told that I would be in charge of your obedience."

"I still don't understand what you—we—are doing here," Tracy said. "Is this like some sort of club?"

"We're far more than that. As I told you when I contacted you, all we do here must be kept secret. If even the smallest detail is told, it will bring ruin on us all. Did you not tell me you would welcome anything that would change your life?"

"Yes, but—"

"Believe me, sister, this will change all our lives as nothing else ever has or ever will." Kevin met each pair of eyes in the circle. "It is written that twelve is the perfect and complete number for a coven as it encompasses all the abilities and strengths we need. As we become more and more a part of each other, so will our strengths increase. When the time is right, we will have a meeting and transform ourselves into rulers of the earth."

"The whole earth?" Rocky asked doubtfully.

"I'm speaking figuratively," Kevin said in exasperation. At times Rocky could be thick-headed. "Not the entire earth. At least not immediately. In ten, twelve years, who knows? I've not been led that far yet." He looked at Mona. "I'm perfectly obedient as you all must become."

"What about Gary and Darryl?" Billy Joe asked bluntly. "Weren't they chosen like we were? They're dead now."

Kevin frowned for a moment, then remembered he should appear to be aloof. Squaring his shoulders, he said, "Gary and Darryl became weak and were disposed of. The one I serve purified the coven by ridding us of weak and untrue elements. In order to be strong, we must be obedient and trustworthy to the coven.

"But they're *dead,*" Billy Joe persisted.

"Does that cause your faith in us, in me, to waver?" Kevin questioned, meeting Billy Joe's eyes squarely until the boy looked away.

Sheepishly and without making eye contact, Billy Joe said, "No. I believe in what we're doing."

"Good. How about the rest of you?" He looked to each of them in turn. If they had any doubts, he needed to know. No one spoke up or looked as if he had any ideas of rebellion. "Good," Kevin repeated. "The new brothers and sister have been sent to us and we're now stronger than ever. Our circle is complete."

No one else seemed to have any questions, so Kevin straightened his spine and rested his hands on his

201

thighs, one palm up and the other down. He waited until the others assumed similar positions and closed their eyes. Kevin shut his eyes and started the low hum that would lead them into a meditation. He would teach them to be totally loyal to him. This time it would work. He had no doubt about it.

In the dark and empty school, a murmuring swept through the halls and up the stairs. "Again!" it whispered. "Again!" The sound was so soft as to be almost no more than a wafting of air, but there was no one in the old building to hear.

"Complete!" The word was whispered from the auditorium and was answered in the blackness of the hall outside the English room. "Complete!"

The sound gathered and rushed through the building as if looking for a way out through the locked doors and closed windows. "Complete! Again!"

Two blocks away Hannah stirred restlessly in her sleep. In her nightmare, Brooke had come to her, her body mangled and bloody as it had been in the wreck of her car. Brooke reached out her hands imploringly and her haunted eyes demanded that Hannah help her. Hannah turned her head on her pillow.

Behind Brooke she saw Troy Spaulding and the others. All of them were staring at her and reaching out toward her. Brooke was trying to speak, but no words were coming from her mouth.

Hannah awoke with a cry. She looked frantically around the room, not sure if she was alone or not. The familiar shape of dresser, chair and night stand reassured her.

She turned on the light beside her bed and looked around again. The dream had seemed so real!

Her German shepherd, Rommel, raised his large head from the rug closest to her bed and whined softly. Hannah reached down and patted him. Willard hadn't liked animals in the house, but Rommel was a comfort to her, and Hannah did things her own way now. Even though she was wide awake, she couldn't shake the nightmare. She had never dreamed anything quite like this before. Was it possible Brooke's spirit was trying to tell her something? But what?

She got out of bed and went into the kitchen, turning on lights as she went. Rommel padded after her, his movements sleepy but loyal. Hannah poured herself a glass of milk and opened the back door. Rommel reluctantly went out, and she stood in the doorway to wait for his return.

The night was still and unusually dark. The air felt heavy, as if a storm was building. Hannah shivered as she drank the milk. What had her dream meant? She firmly believed there was hidden meaning in dreams, though she never breathed a word of this to anybody for fear of being ridiculed. Troy and the others had been standing behind Brooke. Could it be they were trying to tell her why those twelve had chosen to end their lives on the same night?

"If that's it," Hannah whispered to the night, "I want to know. We all want to know what happened to you that night."

There was no answer but she hadn't expected one. Rommel trotted back into the house and Hannah closed and locked the door. She felt better once the night was fastened out and wondered again if she was turning senile. "Next I'll be checking under the bed for burglars," she confided to the dog as she ran water in her glass and set it in the sink.

Rommel thumped his tail on the floor and waited for her to go back to bed.

Hannah was reluctant to risk another nightmare as vivid as that one had been, but she was tired and too logical to sit up the rest of the night. Her classes were to tackle Chaucer the next day, and she wanted to be rested for that. All the same, sleep was late in returning.

Chapter Nine

"Oh, no, that won't work at all," Janis said as she and Tess waited for Tess's art students to get settled at their tables. "You have to paint the scenery here."

"Why? I can do a better job at home." She didn't want to admit to anyone that she was afraid of the auditorium. "Several of the students have volunteered to help, and we can paint on the grass. I won't have to be so careful of spilled paint."

"Mr. Crouthers discourages having the students come to our houses. Several years ago there was a bit of a scandal over one of the girls visiting a bachelor teacher at his house. He swore he did nothing but tutor her, but her story was different, and we had lots of parents who were up in arms. He quit because of the uproar, and although it's not school policy yet, allowing the students to see us outside of school functions and off school property is risky."

"But we're only going to paint scenery and there will be several there. Lane Hodges said he'd help out, too."

Janis shook her head. "Doesn't matter. No, you'd be well-advised to do the work here."

Tess thought the risk would be worth it to avoid working in the school on a Saturday. "I'll think about it. Okay?"

"Please do. And bear in mind that it's supposed to rain tomorrow. Eighty percent chance."

"Eighty percent? I guess that settles that. We can't paint outside in the rain."

"You know I'd be there to help if I could. Having a house full of in-laws for the weekend is no treat in my book. I'd much rather be painting scenery. I'm sorry it has to be redone."

Tess sighed. "That's all right. I'll take care of it."

Janis smiled and went back to her room.

Tess went into the art room and closed the door behind her. "There has been a change of plans for tomorrow. Because it's supposed to rain, we'll work on the scenery here instead of at my house. Hold up your hand if you'll be here to help." She counted the few volunteers and tried not to be discouraged. Mojo was dependable and talented. He had said he would be there, and that meant she could probably count on Keisha being there as well, since they had recently started going steady.

Soon the students were all busy working on the chalk drawings she had assigned. This was one of her smaller groups, and they required less attention than some of the others. Tess went to the back of the room and started selecting the tempera paint they would need for the scenery.

"Mrs. Bowen?" Mary Reynolds said. "There's someone to see you."

206

Tess straightened and came around the partition to find Lucy Wright standing among the tables looking bewildered. The students were curiously eyeing her and restlessly shifting in their seats as if they were wondering what would happen next. Tess went to her. "Hello, Mrs. Wright. Are you looking for Tracy? She's not in art this period."

"Tracy?" Lucy looked confused. "No, I'm here to see Brooke."

Tess took the woman's elbow and steered her out of the room. Behind her, she could hear the murmur of voices and knew it would soon be all over school that Tracy's mother was behaving strangely again. At the door Tess hesitated. She shouldn't leave her class unsupervised. "Keep on working," she said firmly. "Mojo, that means you. Leave Jerry alone. I'm going to be right out here listening so keep on drawing."

She shut the door and said, "Mrs. Wright, surely you mean you came to see Tracy."

"No, this is Brooke's," she said, holding up a white Angora sweater. "I walked over here to give it to her in case she got cold." Lucy stroked the sweater. "Do you know where I can find her?"

"Come with me." Tess led her down the hall to the teacher's lounge. She was relieved to find only Hannah Mitchell there at the coffee pot.

Hannah looked at them in surprise. "Hello, Lucy. What are you doing here?"

"I came to bring Brooke's sweater to her. I thought she had art this period but I guess I was wrong."

Hannah and Tess exchanged a glance. Tess said, "I'm going to call Mr. Wright and have him give her a ride home."

"Come have some coffee with me," Hannah said to Lucy. "It's a cold day out there."

"I know. That's why I thought Brooke might be cold. Tracy has a jacket."

Tess went to the phone. "What's Mr. Wright's number?"

Lucy gave it to her and turned back to Hannah. "I wanted to see you Parents' Night, but those stairs are so hard on a body. Don't you get tired climbing those stairs?"

"I do for a fact." Hannah poured Lucy a cup of coffee and gave it to her.

Tess dialed the number and said, "Mr. Wright, this is Mrs. Bowen at the school. No, no, there's nothing wrong with Tracy. Mrs. Wright is here and needs a ride home."

"Lucy is at the school?" Ross asked. "What's she doing there?"

Tess had hoped he wouldn't ask. "She came to bring Brooke's sweater to her." She waited for a response but got nothing but silence. "Hello?"

"I'm on my way." The line disconnected.

"He'll be here soon," Tess said to Lucy. "I have to get back to my class. Mrs. Mitchell, will you be able to stay with her until Mr. Wright gets here?"

"I certainly will." Hannah settled in the chair beside Lucy. "Let me tell you how well Tracy is doing in my class."

Tess was confidant that Hannah could take care of the situation, and she didn't dare be gone from her class any longer. She hurried down the hall and back to her room. The students had stopped drawing as soon as she'd left as she had known they would, but they weren't being loud enough to disturb the other classes. She gave them all a firm look that sent them back to the chalk and paper. She sat at her desk pretending to grade previous drawings, but her mind was on the Wright family.

She leafed through the stack of drawings until she found Tracy's. She pulled it out for a closer look. The girl had drawn a picture of a dead tree with stark limbs reaching out threateningly toward a small figure. The subject didn't disturb Tess—the assignment had been to depict Halloween. The size of the girl in comparison to the tree did, however, as did the slashing lines of black. Closer examination showed the girl had red hair, and Tess knew it was meant to represent Brooke.

Concerned, she graded the paper and put it with the others to be returned later that day. Tracy had seemed withdrawn lately, and in conjunction with her mother's latest visit to the school, Tess figured she was under great stress. She wished there were some way to get the students not to mention having seen Lucy Wright at school, but she knew any admonition would only make their tongues wag faster.

Tess's eyes kept going back to Tracy's drawing. It seemed more sinister than most of the others. She wondered if she should talk to Mr. Hudson about Tracy or if it would be more prudent to mind her own business. Being new to the school she couldn't decide what course to take. She decided to do nothing until she had thought about it more carefully.

All day Tracy had been able to think of nothing but the meeting the night before. The trepidation she had

had about attending Kevin's secret meeting had faded during the meeting, and by the time it was over, she was elated, filled with the fire of adventure, powerful. She had barely slept the entire night, only occasionally dozing, then suddenly awakening with some part of the strange ceremony running through her head. Once she had seen what went on during those meetings, she understood why Kevin had been so adamant that the meetings and what transpired there be kept secret. No parent would be happy about them.

In the morning light, though, she was beginning to have some doubts. After all, some of the things Kevin and the others had said were pretty weird. It was ridiculous to think of Matthew Greenway as the personification of fire. He was a rather dull, studious boy who wore thick, dark-rimmed glasses and had pimples. Why had Kevin given him charge of such an unlikely quality? And what did those qualities mean anyway? "Quicksilver, changing, never changing" didn't mean anything.

As she had been told to do, Tracy closed her eyes and silently repeated to herself, "Omega, Omega, Omega." Magically her doubts faded.

She opened her eyes and glanced around the classroom to see if anyone had noticed. No one had. Maybe, she thought, that was what Billy Joe's property of darkness did—it concealed the members of the coven from prying eyes. Some of the sensation of power she'd felt the night before flowed back into her.

Tracy had never been a part of anything like this. Her first instinct was to tell Amy. That was impossible, of course. If she still had had Amy as a friend, she wouldn't have gone to the meeting in the first place. Again she sensed a bond with the others.

Across the room she saw Matthew bent over his book, straining to follow the teacher. Why Matthew as fire? she wondered again. But nevertheless, she felt a certain kinship to him, a link. As if he had heard her thoughts, he looked over at her and gave her a faint smile. Kevin was the leader, and he had guidance of a sort that Tracy couldn't comprehend. Kevin must have known what he was doing.

For the next few minutes, Tracy listened to Hannah Mitchell explain what Tennyson had meant to convey in "The Palace of Art," then her attention wandered again. Last year, somewhere in this very room, Brooke had sat and listened to Mrs. Mitchell explain about Tennyson and "The Palace of Art." How many years had the woman given this very same lecture, used the same words, explained the same symbolism? The sheer boredom of it all pressed down on Tracy.

She wished she hadn't thought about Brooke. These past hours had been the first since last July that her sister hadn't lingered somewhere in her mind. Being without her for a while had been a relief.

A nagging thought was trying to surface. Something about Brooke. Hadn't Brooke once mentioned something about being like fire?

Tracy blinked and stared down at a blank place on her desk in her effort to remember. They had been in their bedroom and were having a pillow fight. Brooke had fallen between the bed and the wall and had gotten stuck for a minute. She had giggled something about trapping fire. At the time it hadn't made any sense. Later Tracy had thought Brooke was only referring to the color of her hair, though that had seemed like an odd thing to do. But what if she had been referring to fire in a different sense?

Tracy thought back on the people she had seen around the campfire the night before. They had nothing in common except for their interest in what Kevin was giving them. Mona Dupree was intelligent and studious. Matthew Greenway probably had a learning disability, given his often incorrect and sometimes nonsensical responses in class. Rocky Mancelli was wild; Billy Joe Robertson was a loner—he never even dated, as far as Tracy knew.

The students who died that same night as Brooke had had nothing in common either.

Tracy's mouth dropped open. Had Brooke been in a coven like the one she had visited last night? And didn't Tracy remember that there had been times when Brooke had come home late and her hair and clothes had smelled of wood smoke?

"Tracy, what do you think Tennyson is trying to tell us in the last stanza?" Mrs. Mitchell asked.

For a moment Tracy had no idea what her teacher was talking about. Frantically she read the last lines. "I believe he's saying that she doesn't want to move away from her palace forever."

Hannah gave Tracy a lingering look that meant she knew the girl had been grasping at straws and been lucky. "It might also be referring to a nobler art toward the service of humanity."

Tracy tried to look thoughtful, as though her teacher's last statement had triggered an intriguing new curiosity for her, but her real curiosity was over the question of whether Brooke might have been in a

212

coven. *Impossible.* Brooke had been popular and beautiful. What could she possibly have been looking for?

But then Tracy recalled the times Brooke had come to bed drunk and how she had frequently watered down her parents' bottles of bourbon in order to disguise the fact she was drinking it. If Brooke had been so happy, why had she drunk so heavily?

Tracy felt someone watching her, and she lifted her eyes to see Matthew regarding her thoughtfully. She looked away before anyone could notice. Matthew's carelessness would be sure to give them all away, if they weren't careful. Or was that carelessness on his part? Couldn't he also be perceptive enough to intuit that she had suddenly entertained doubts? Tracy decided to stay alert and see if she could find any other clues that might link Brooke to the coven.

Saturday was a gray day, and even though it was ten o'clock and the rain hadn't begun, it was definitely threatening. Tess resented having to repaint the set at school, but had to admit it would have been foolhardy for her to have insisted they do the work in her backyard.

She let herself into the building, and as she deactivated the alarm, she wished that Lane hadn't called that morning to tell her he was having car trouble and would have to spend the afternoon trying to repair it. She'd counted on him being with her so she wouldn't be doing this alone again. But it wasn't his fault, and she *was* an adult and perfectly capable of handling this by herself. Or at least she should be. A big part of her new independence was proving to herself that she didn't have to have someone else to help her with things like this. Besides, she reasoned, she had no valid reason to be afraid. A few odd things had happened for which she had no logical explanation, but that was the stuff scary movies were made from. She had a job to do here, and, alone or not, it had to be done.

Shivering against the relatively cool and decidedly clammy air in the old building, she went up to her room, turning on lights at every opportunity. She wanted to hurry and finish the job so she could salvage as much of the weekend as possible.

She tapped tempera powder into the empty coffee cans she used for mixing the paint and added water. Taking a brush from the can where they stood ready for the next class, she stirred the paint until frothy bubbles formed on the top. Usually she enjoyed mixing paint. Today she only wanted to be finished with the job.

From in the hall she heard a rushing sound, like a whisper, and she paused. Were the students arriving already? They had been told to go directly to the auditorium and not to roam about in the school. Mr. Crouthers had stressed that when she reminded him she was to paint the scenery once again. He had hesitated to allow the students in at all, but she had told him flatly that she wasn't going to do the work alone, and the only other choice was for the students to come to her house, a situation that he strongly advised against.

"Mojo? Is that you? Keisha?" There was no answer. Tess went to the door to look out. Although the hall was empty, she could still hear the sounds.

Warily she stepped out into the hall and listened. Had someone gone up to the third floor? She walked to the stairs and looked up. It was dark but that might not matter to a teenager bent on adventure. The whispering sounded nearer from the stairs. "Keisha? If you're up there, answer me. I can use some help carrying the paint down to the auditorium." *Was that a smothered giggle?*

Tess couldn't ignore the sounds. She was the adult in charge, and she was still suffering from guilt for not having investigated on the night Gary Valdes and Darryl Watson died. Cautiously, she climbed the stairs and looked down the hall. It was shadowy and still, but the window at the far end let in enough light to show that it was empty. "Keisha? Mojo?"

The voices sounded again, this time from below her. Tess jumped and looked back down the stairs. Was someone playing tricks on her? Mojo wouldn't be beyond doing that if he knew she was nervous. She made herself go back down the stairs and listened again. The soft giggle this time was accompanied with the click of a locker shutting on the third floor. Tess backed away from the stairs. She wasn't going back up there.

She bumped into something solid and gasped. Whirling, she found Jason Cook behind her. She almost collapsed. "Jason, you scared me half to death!"

"I'm sorry. I thought you heard me calling you."

"No, I didn't." She tried not to sound angry. Jason hadn't struck her as a prankster. "Who else is here?"

"Mojo and Keisha are in the auditorium. I turned on the lights."

"Thank you. I was just about to carry the paint

down." She glanced at the stairs. "You're sure they're in the auditorium?"

"I'm positive. I just left them. Why?"

"No reason." She went back to her room with Jason following behind. It was comforting knowing the three students were in the building. Apparently, the building had some odd echo factor that made it sound as if their voices were coming from a different place.

·When she and Jason entered the auditorium with the cans of paint, she saw that Mojo and Keisha were indeed there. She smiled at them. "I didn't hear you come in."

"You didn't?" Keisha tilted her head to one side. "When we didn't find you in the auditorium, we thought you were probably upstairs. We hollered up the stairs to tell you we were here. I thought I heard you answer."

Tess decided to let it go. "I've already drawn the trees and house onto the cardboard and some of the shop students put the supports on the back. All we have to do is paint. Again." She pushed up the sleeves of her old sweater and knelt on the floor with Jason. "I hope this won't take long."

"So do I," Mojo said. "I have to pick up my sisters at noon."

Tess glanced at the clock on the auditorium wall. That left a little less than two hours. She didn't doubt that when Mojo left, Keisha would, too. Jason wasn't likely to want to stay behind and work with just her, and she wasn't sure it would be a good idea if he did. The school was already sensitive to students being alone with teachers of the opposite sex.

They worked at a fevered pace. The trees weren't as

well done as the first batch had been, but in two hours' time they were recognizable as trees. Keisha had been working on the house, and it needed more effort put into it. She tended to be a perfectionist and had worked more slowly than the others.

Mojo stood and propped his tree on its stand. "How's that?"

"It looks good. Do you have time to help Keisha with the house?" Tess held her breath.

He checked his watch. "No, I've got to go and get my sisters, or my Mom will be mad at me. She likes us there at meal time, and it's already getting late."

"I understand."

Keisha added quickly. "I guess I'm going to have to leave as well. Mojo gave me a ride over here."

Tess nodded. "Thank you for helping. I'll see you Monday."

Mojo looped his arm around Keisha's shoulder and they strolled out.

Jason stepped back and eyed the cardboard house. "I can finish the windows pretty quick. Keisha's roof looks good, and she's put in some bushes around the bottom. Will that be good enough?"

"Yes. We don't want to do too much to the house or the trees will look unfinished. If you can paint the windows, I'll carry the rest of the paint upstairs and start cleaning the brushes."

Jason nodded. "It shouldn't take long."

Tess was reluctant to leave him in the auditorium alone, but there seemed to be no other choice. Perhaps, she told herself, it didn't frighten him as much as it did her. She loaded her arms with cans of paint and started up the aisle.

217

She didn't allow herself to think about her apprehensions as she went to the art room and into the storage area in the back. The building seemed empty again, although she knew Jason was still painting. The almost inaudible sounds had to be her imagination. No one could possibly be moving along the hall, bumping softly into the lockers. There was no reason to go and see for herself.

She washed out the brushes and put the plastic lids back on the coffee cans of paint. In the distance she heard a rumble of thunder. She had never liked storms, and she blamed her uneasiness on its approach. The area had been under a severe thunderstorm watch when she left her house. If she hurried she might make it home before the storm arrived in full force.

She went back down to the auditorium and from the doorway called out, "Jason? Are you finished?" She didn't see him anywhere. "Jason?"

When she was halfway down the aisle the lights went out. Thunder roared loudly. For her to hear it in the auditorium she knew lightning must have struck close by. That did nothing to ease her mind. Blackness crowded all around her, and she was overwhelmed by a sense of panic. "Jason? Answer me!"

She had lost her bearings and was afraid to move. In her panic she couldn't remember having closed the auditorium doors behind her, but if she hadn't, shouldn't she be able to see at least a rectangle of light? And where was Jason?

The lights flickered on and off again. Tess almost screamed. Was that someone on the other aisle? In the strobelike effect, she hadn't been able to recognize the

218

girl, but she was positive it wasn't Keisha. "Who's in here?" she demanded, making her voice sound angry to cover her fear. Only a half-heard whisper answered.

Tess reached out through the blackness and found the row of seats closest to her. Feeling from one seat back to the next, and aware she was going up the gentle slope of the floor, she started back the way she had come. Whether Jason was on the stage or not, she had to get out of the auditorium. Was that someone bumping against the seats behind her? She quickened her pace.

By the time she reached the doors to the hall, she was almost running. She shoved against them with all her strength. To her vast relief they opened, and she stumbled into the gray light of the hall. For a moment Tess could only lean against the opposite wall as she stared back at the open doors she'd just come through and tried to catch her breath and steady her breathing. The school was silent again. Whoever or whatever had been behind her had not followed her out. She tried hard to tell herself that the flickering lights had jangled her nerves, causing her to think she had seen a girl where no one had been.

"Mrs. Bowen?" called a voice from deep inside the auditorium.

Tess forced herself to step back into the doorway. "Yes?"

At the far end of the room she saw a dim light. Jason was by the other exit, holding the door open. "Is the electricity off?" he called to her.

"Yes." She felt relief wash over her. He had only stepped out the back door. "I think the lightning knocked it off. There's not any point in us waiting for

219

it to come back on, but we shouldn't leave the building without turning the light switches off."

"Okay." He propped the door open, then disappeared into the inky darkness. She could hear him moving about on stage, crossing to the switch panel. An instant later, the lights came on. "That's funny. The switches were turned off," he said as he came back onto the stage.

Tess stared at him. "That's impossible. There's no one here but you and me, and neither of us touched them. It was the storm."

"No, ma'am. The switch was down."

Tess looked around the auditorium. There was no one here but Jason and herself and no way anyone could have left without going out one of the two doors. "Did you turn the lights off as a joke?"

"No, ma'am." He sounded surprised that she would ask such a thing.

She forced herself to smile. "Of course not. It's just that storms make me edgy."

He nodded as if he didn't question it. "I painted two windows and the door. Is that good enough?"

"It looks fine to me. There's no need to paint window boxes. Let's call it quits. What do you say?"

"That suits me. Can I go now?"

"Help me clean up the rest of the paint and brushes first." Tess didn't care if she was breaking a school rule by being alone in the school with a student. At the moment, she couldn't force herself to go back upstairs alone and she couldn't leave the paint open and the brushes to dry out until Monday.

He gathered up the brushes as Tess took the cans. Together they went up to the art room and the building stayed quiet. "Do you need a ride home?" she asked as she capped the last of the paint.

"I brought my car."

She was glad to shut the art room door and go downstairs. Although she listened for it, she couldn't hear the whispering sound. She could almost convince herself that it had been her imagination.

Tracy slashed red paint across the paper. She had always before liked art, but this year her heart wasn't in it. There was so much else to think about.

Kevin was constantly on her mind. Up until this year she hadn't known him all that well. He was the sort of person who most people wouldn't notice. But now that she knew him, she found him fascinating. Not Kevin personally, but his ideas. Kevin had a way of thinking about things that was unique and compelling. She had never thought of herself as having occult powers, but when she was sitting around the fire with the others, she didn't doubt it at all. It was only after she left the meetings and returned to normal life that she had doubts. She wondered what there was about Kevin that affected her—and apparently the others as well—in that way.

She still felt silly claiming to be the child of quicksilver. Mercury had an elusive and mysterious quality that she found appealing, and it was a quality that fit well with her eclectic style of dressing, but the words made no sense to her. If Brooke had been involved in something like Kevin's coven, had she had such doubts? The others didn't seem to have any.

Her father had been giving her a hard time lately

221

about her grades and her unexplained disappearances after supper. He hadn't fully bought her lie about having a new boyfriend. He had said he expected her dates to pick her up from her house, not to meet her at the Burger Shack as she had told him. She tried to cut him slack since she knew he was worried about her mother, but lately she wished he would simply leave her alone. She thought she might be on the track of learning why Brooke had died. But naturally, she couldn't tell him that yet. Before she left for school that day, he had lambasted her again for dating someone who wouldn't meet her parents or conform to their rules. Tracy wished he would simply leave her alone. He hadn't watched over Brooke so closely.

From the corner of her eye she saw Mrs. Bowen coming down the row of tables checking on progress. Tracy bent lower over her paper. She was tired from the late hours she was keeping. Her father had no idea that she frequently slipped out of the house after they had gone to bed. He would be furious and would ground her forever if he caught her, even though she was doing this for Brooke, for all of them. He just wouldn't understand.

Mrs. Bowen stopped next to Tracy. Tracy didn't look up.

"What are you painting?"

"Fire. What does it look like?" Tracy had discovered that most people let her get by with rudeness since Brooke had died.

"The assignment was to paint your idea of hope."

Tracy shrugged. She thought that was a stupid assignment. "Fire makes me feel hopeful." This sounded good, she thought, though it wasn't what she'd had in mind when she started. She had been thinking about the meetings around the "summoning fire" and the mysteries of the coven.

Mrs. Bowen didn't comment, but she also didn't move away. Tracy risked looking up at her. She was frowning the way teachers did when they were thinking she wasn't doing her best.

In a low voice, her teacher asked her, "Are you all right?"

"Of course," Tracy responded, not bothering to speak softly. According to Kevin, she was one of the chosen few. For a moment she could feel her power strong within her, as strong as it was when she was in the group. "Why wouldn't I be doing all right?" Her level gaze dared her teacher to challenge her. Before joining the coven she would never have had the nerve to speak to a teacher like that.

Tracy waited until Mrs. Bowen's gaze wavered, then she looked down with a secret smile. Maybe Kevin was right. Maybe she did have the power. She had only had to realize it. She added more scarlet to the fire she was drawing. Now that the teacher seemed uneasy, she was determined to make the picture more flamboyant. Tracy found she enjoyed pushing the limits. It was something Brooke had never done.

When Mrs. Bowen turned and walked away, Tracy felt the power growing within her like a flame that was being fanned. Brooke might have been popular and pretty and smart, but Tracy was willing to bet Brooke had never felt this dangerous sense of omnipotence within her. If she had, she wouldn't have killed herself by driving her car into a tree. Maybe she was wrong about Brooke being in the coven.

As she added black to the fiery painting, Tracy wondered exactly how Kevin intended to build the power within them as he claimed he could. He was always so sure of himself. She had, on several occasions seen him command that a sign be given, and in response the wind had lifted or an owl had called. Once he had even called down a shooting star. No one but Mona had been looking in the right direction to see it, but Tracy had no doubts that Mona had witnessed it. How was this possible? At the time his power had seemed so real!

Kevin forbid speculation outside the group meetings, but she had risked asking Rocky Mancelli what he thought the final ceremony would be, the ceremony that Kevin said would purify them so they could reach his heights. Rocky had been nervous about discussing it, but he said he thought it must involve a sacrifice of some sort. Tracy was afraid Rocky might be right. Several times Kevin had alluded to a "supreme sacrifice." She hoped it wouldn't involve an animal. She liked animals and was too softhearted to allow one to be killed.

She bent over the picture and added a face to the flames. She liked the result, so she added several more. Once she had seen a book of surrealistic art, and she had been fascinated by the artist's interpretation of everyday subjects in fanciful ways. Above the fire she added the moon. At the last meeting the moon had been full, and she remembered seeing it over the tops of the flames. She smiled at the thought that no one else would ever understand the picture the way she had intended it. Perhaps after it was graded, she would give it to Kevin. It might make him believe she was a wholehearted believer in his doctrine.

At the front of the room, Tess was watching Tracy while pretending to be busy on the next week's assignments. Tracy was engrossed in her strange picture, and Tess was worried. At the start of school Tracy had been shy, introverted and depressed. Tess had been concerned that she was bottling up her grief over Brooke rather than releasing it. Now the girl's personality seemed to be changing.

Tess had thought she was imagining it, until she overheard Jason talking to Amy Dennis. After all, Tess hadn't known Tracy before Brooke's death. Amy and Tracy were best friends, or had been, but Amy told Jason she seldom saw her anymore. After years of teaching, Tess knew teenage best friends came and went as friendships changed or faded, but Amy seemed more worried than angry.

Since that time, Tess had paid closer attention to Tracy, and she could see the change was remarkable. When Tracy started drawing such odd pictures and being overtly rude in class, Tess had become more concerned.

She had considered calling Ross Wright and discussing it with him, but decided that would be overreacting. After all, Tracy wasn't cutting school, and she was completing her assignments. Her artwork typically ranged from chilling to threatening, but Tess didn't know her all that well. Maybe this was the sort of art Tracy had always done.

All in all, Tess had resolved to keep a close watch

over the girl, for her own peace of mind, if nothing else. Tracy would never know.

Hannah Mitchell stuck to her routine as never before in hopes that her jangled nerves would return to normal by habit, if nothing else. After working her way through the cafeteria line, she carried her tray to the long table where the teachers ate lunch, nodded to those already there, and sat down at the only available place. "Pass the salt, please," she said. The woman to her left passed both the salt and pepper.

"This stuff tastes like library paste today," Tess said as Hannah salted her potatoes and gravy. "I'll never know what the cooks do to it."

Hannah smiled. "It's probably best that we not know. Cafeteria food is always notorious."

"I guess it's like that everywhere," Lane said. He was looking at Tess with more than a casual interest.

Hannah saw Tess meet his eyes and smile. The moment held a bit too long. Hannah looked away before they saw her interest. Could it be that Lane and Tess were falling in love? She had never been a romantic, but she would like to see that happen. Hannah liked Lane and knew he had been lonely since he came to Maple Glen. Hannah wanted him to be happy, and Tess would be a good choice for him.

"Catsup, please?" This was why Hannah disliked sitting on the end of a table. Everything she needed always seemed to be at the other end and she had to ask for everything to be passed to her.

"The play went well," Tess said. "I had no idea the drama department was so good."

"We do seem to have a good one this year," Hannah said. "Janis told me she thinks they have a good chance in the regional competition."

"For a relatively small school we do quite well," Lane agreed.

"It was too bad we lost the first scenery we painted," Tess said. "It was so much better than the ones we ended up with. But we did the best we could under the circumstances. My art students are capable of better work than that."

"I'm sure they are." Hannah tried her potatoes. "This really does taste like paste." Her attention wandered over the roomful of students as she ate.

Tracy Wright was seated by herself two tables away, her black clothes a sharp contrast from the regular clothing of the other girls. Lately Hannah had noticed that Tracy had changed, and she wasn't pleased. There was the matter of her choice of clothes for one thing. Always before, Tracy had dressed as if she shopped at a gypsy camp, and Hannah was accustomed to this. But these days she frequently wore nothing but black, and she seldom wore the jangling bracelets and dangling earrings that were irritating to a teacher but that were a part of who Tracy was. She knew as well as anyone that girls' tastes in clothing were subject to change, but Tracy's current style, if you could call it a style, didn't seem to fit her personality as Hannah knew it.

Not far from Tracy sat Kevin Donatello. Hannah normally would have overlooked him, as he wasn't one of the troublemakers in class, nor a gifted student, but it struck her as odd that he was also dressed in black. Was this some new fad that was catching on?

She hoped not. In view of the deaths, Hannah didn't think this was appropriate. Kevin and Tracy weren't sitting together, but several times Hannah saw them glance at each other, and once Tracy nodded as if to acknowledge something Hannah had missed. Hannah would have said Kevin wasn't Tracy's type at all.

As she chewed another mouthful of potatoes, she surveyed the other students. None of the others were dressed in black. Maybe this was only a coincidence. Her eyes fell on a girl across the room with long, red hair, and she swallowed hastily and blinked.

There was no mistaking that hair. Brooke Wright was sitting there near the back of the room, looking as real as any of the other students. Hannah dropped her fork with a clatter.

"Hannah? Are you okay?" she heard Lane ask. It sounded as if his voice came from far away.

"Look! Do you see her?" Hannah hissed, not daring to take her eyes off Brooke.

Lane lifted his head to look in the direction Hannah was staring. Tess did the same. "See who?" he asked.

Hannah slowly stood, holding onto the edge of the table until she was certain her legs would support her. Brooke continued to sit perfectly still, her face in profile to Hannah. "Are you saying you can't see her?" Hannah demanded to Lane. "Look!"

"I *am* looking. Who are you talking about?"

Hannah started walking toward Brooke. She knew she was moving forward, but she felt numb, as if she were in a dream. Or a nightmare.

As she neared Brooke, the girl slowly turned to face her. For a moment their eyes met, and Hannah couldn't breathe. Then as silently and as suddenly as if she had never been there at all, Brooke vanished.

Hannah sagged against a table. Dimly, she heard someone asking if she was all right. She couldn't answer. No one else had seen Brooke, but Brooke had looked straight into her eyes.

Time and space and reality had lost all meaning for Hannah Mitchell. She found herself sitting down and staring at the empty chair where Brooke had been. All around her students were whispering and acting concerned. She felt hands on her arm and heard Tess say, "Come on. I'll take you to the nurse's office." Hannah went without argument. There was no way to explain what she had seen. There was no explanation at all.

Chapter Ten

Tess worried aloud about Hannah as she and Lane walked to school the following morning. "You say she's never done this before?"

"Not to my knowledge. She's always quick to say she's never sick."

"She was so pale! I thought she was getting up to get more tea. Where do you suppose she thought she was going? There's no exit at the back of the cafeteria."

"I guess she became disoriented. You saw how she was staring at the back of the room."

"She kept asking if we saw someone. What could she have meant?" Tess shifted the papers she was carrying to the other arm.

"Who knows? If you ask me, she had a blood sugar drop. I've seen that happen to boys who try to work out after a lunch of candy bars. They can pass right out."

"At the time I was sure she saw someone and was going to them. But there was no one sitting at the back table. Was there?" Now that she'd voiced it, Tess wasn't so sure what she'd said was true. Didn't she have a vague memory of seeing someone at that back table just before Hannah had started acting so strange?

"There was no one there. She was about to faint and must have been dizzy. You saw how she held to the table when she stood up. No, I'm betting on blood sugar."

"I'm just glad she didn't break anything. When I was in college, my grandmother fell and broke her hip and we thought it would never mend properly. I'd never say this to Hannah, but she *is* getting along in years. I wonder if she's given any thought to retiring."

"I can't imagine this school without her. She's teaching her second generation of students and my assistant coach says she's practically part of the school. None of the other teachers can remember a time when she wasn't here."

"She does love her job."

They went up the walk to the front door of the school and Lane reached past her to open it for her. Tess smiled. "Would you like to come over for dinner tonight? I'm cooking hamburgers, nothing fancy."

"Sounds good."

As they walked past the principal's office, a pretty, young woman approached them. "Pardon me, but could you tell me where room 317 is? I'm new here and I seem to be turned around. I tried the stairs down there, but they only led to some offices."

"You didn't go far enough down the hall," Lane said. "Room 317 is almost at the other end. It's the only classroom up there. The kids say it was designed that way for inconvenience."

"Isn't 317 the English room?" Tess asked.

231

"Yes, Mrs. Mitchell called in sick today." The young woman shifted the books she carried. "She marked the lesson plan but I have to admit I'm nervous. By the way, my name is Laurie Alexander."

"I'm Tess Bowen and this is Lane Hodges."

"I just moved to Maple Glen. I registered to substitute teach, but I never expected to be called the next day."

"You'll do fine. Did Mr. Crouthers happen to mention what might be wrong with Mrs. Mitchell?"

"No, when he called, he only said a teacher was too sick to come to school and that I should come right down."

Tess said to Lane, "I'm going to call and check on her before going up. I'll see you at lunch."

Lane nodded. "Come on, Miss Alexander. I'll show you where to find the English room."

Tess went into the principal's office and reached over the counter for the phone. The secretary smiled in greeting. Tess dialed Hannah's number and waited for her to answer. After a long wait, Hannah said, "Hello?"

"Hannah? You don't sound like yourself."

"Hello, Tess. I'll be okay. I just . . . couldn't face coming in today." Her voice was weak and trembling.

"Do you have anyone to stay with you? Are you going in to see the doctor?"

"No, there's no reason to do that."

Tess wasn't so sure she agreed. "Is it okay if I come by after school to see about you?"

Hannah paused, then said, "I'd like that."

"I'll see you as soon as I can get away. You take care of yourself now."

"I will."

Tess hung up, still concerned about her fellow teacher, but the direction of her concern had shifted. Hannah had sounded more frightened than ill. Tess had known other people who reacted to even minor illnesses with panic, and since Hannah was rarely sick, she might be worrying about her health more than was warranted and scaring herself needlessly. Tess concluded that a large dose of reassurance might be just what Hannah needed most, and after school, she'd see to it that it was delivered.

She went up the stairs to her room and put her purse in the desk drawer. Her watch told her that the doors would soon be unlocked and the first students would be arriving within minutes. She had intended to get to her classroom earlier and have the ink pads ready for the students to use the block printers they had made.

She went to the back area and got the metal boxes from the top shelf. When she turned to the sink, she gasped and almost dropped them.

The sink was full of paint that, at first glance, Tess had thought to be blood. Above the sink in large letters was scrawled the words, "Help us."

Tess put down the boxes and went to the sink. Gingerly she touched the writing on the wall. The paint was already dry, so whoever had written it hadn't done so recently. "Help us," she read again. Help who? This seemed to be an odd choice of words for someone to write as a prank.

All at once Tess had the feeling she wasn't alone. She jerked her head around and looked over her shoulder. Behind her in the doorway was the red-haired girl she'd seen the first day of class. Tess turned around, her eyes never leaving the girl. The girl didn't smile or speak; she only stared at Tess. For a moment Tess couldn't speak. "Who are you?" she finally managed to ask in a choked voice.

The girl's eyes grew sad, and she turned silently and left the room.

Tess ran after her. "Wait! Don't go! There's something I want to ask you!" When Tess reached the hall, she saw Janis Denkle opening her door across the hall. The girl was gone. Tess went to Janis. "Did you see that girl with the long red hair?"

"No. I just arrived."

"You must have seen her! If you just came up the stairs, you had to have passed her as she was going down."

"Is something wrong?"

"There certainly is. Come and look." Tess led Janis to the sink.

" 'Help us.' Who wrote that?"

"That's what I want to know. That girl was standing in my door and watching me. She must know something about this. Are you sure you didn't see her?"

"Long red hair, you say? A student? I don't think we have anyone in the school who'd fit that description. Except maybe Amy Dennis. She has long hair."

"Yes, but I know Amy and her hair is brown. It wasn't Amy."

Janis stared at the words. "Why would anyone write this? Does it make sense to you? It doesn't to me."

"It makes no sense at all. If someone was in trouble, why would they ask for help in this way? There's no name or any other information."

"Maybe they were in a hurry. It says 'us.' That implies there's more than one."

"If someone was in a hurry, why not just use a pencil? I have pencils all over the room. Or chalk?" Tess frowned at the pool of red paint in the sink. "Whoever did this must have used a whole can of red paint!"

"It looks awful, doesn't it? It reminds me of blood."

"That's what I thought at first, too." She picked up a can that was laying on its side. "It came out of this. It's empty now."

"Such a waste! Do you know what I think? I think those vandals must have broken into the school. I don't know what's going on with kids these days. I've never seen a year where so much bad has happened!"

Tess nodded as she put the empty paint can back on the counter. "This makes no sense at all."

"I'll go get Mr. Crouthers. He should see this."

"Okay, but please tell him to hurry. I don't want any of my students to see this." Tess started checking the shelves to see if anything else had been disturbed. Everything else was exactly as she had left it. Again she went back to the sink. It simply didn't make sense that someone would go to this much trouble in order to leave such a message.

Mr. Crouthers bustled into the room, his round face already fixed in a scowl. "What's this about more vandalism?" he asked as he neared the work area.

Tess stepped aside so he could see for himself. Crouthers faltered, then came closer. He picked up the paint can and peered into it as if he thought it might contain the answers. "Do you have any idea who did this?"

"Not really." Tess shook her head. "I saw a girl in the doorway, but she's not anyone I know."

"Is she a student here?"

"She must be. I've seen her more than once." Tess didn't want to tell him she had seen this same girl vanish. She had managed to convince herself that that had been a mistake on her part. "She's a bit taller than average and has long red hair and unusually pale skin."

Crouthers looked as if the description reminded him of someone he knew. "We no longer have a student here that looks like that. You must be mistaken."

"I may be wrong about her having anything to do with this, but I certainly know I saw her." Tess was getting tired of having people tell her there was no student who looked like this in the entire school. "Is there any way a student could have come in early enough for the paint to have had time to dry? This is mixed thick. It wouldn't dry instantly."

"That's impossible. I was the first one here this morning, and I'm certain the doors were locked. The cleaning staff would have noticed if it was here when they came around to sweep the room yesterday evening."

At the sound of the first bell, Tess said, "I have to clean this up. It wouldn't do to have my class see this."

"Yes. Yes, you're right." Crouthers nodded but he continued to frown. "That wouldn't do at all. I'll call the police and tell them someone has broken in again." He shook his large head. "This beats all!"

Tess found it difficult to put her hand into the red paint to open the drain plug, but she did it, nevertheless. As the paint drained, she ran water over her hand

and arm and scrubbed them clean before attacking the writing on the wall. The words were chilling, and she was glad when they were gone.

Lane was in his office when he heard a knock on the door. Through the glass he saw Jason Cook and motioned for him to come in. Jason opened the door and sat on the worn chair by the desk. Lane smiled. "What's up?"

"Can I talk to you?" Jason seemed upset and nervous.

"Sure. Is something wrong?"

"I don't know. Coach, something happened last period that really upset me."

Lane waited and when Jason didn't continue, he said, "What happened?"

"I thought I saw something. Coach, I swear I don't do drugs. I never have."

"Who's saying you do?"

"Nobody, but that's what I'd think if somebody besides me saw what I saw between classes."

Lane put down his pen and said, "I don't have any idea what you're talking about."

"I saw something I couldn't have seen." Jason shifted uncomfortably in the chair. "Maybe I shouldn't tell you."

"If you don't, I can't help you."

"Okay. It was like this. I was coming out of English and going to geometry."

"Yes?"

"This isn't easy to say." Jason ran his fingers through his hair. "I saw Troy Spaulding."

237

Lane leaned forward. "Excuse me?"

"Yes, sir, I know that's not possible, but I did! Coach, he was as near to me as that file cabinet there!"

Lane leaned back in his chair and studied Jason. The boy was clearly upset, and he had never known Jason to be the dramatic type.

"I knew you wouldn't believe me." Jason rose and started to leave.

"No, wait a minute. You said yourself that Troy couldn't possibly have been there. Let's talk about this." Lane was remembering the time he had found Troy's football jersey folded on the bench in front of the locker he had used the year before. And the time he was positive he had heard Troy's war whoop and found the basketball bouncing in the middle of the court.

"You're humoring me. Right?"

"No, I'm trying to hear the whole story."

Jason sat back down. "I came out of English. Mrs. Mitchell isn't in school today, and we had a substitute teacher." He made a face to show his low opinion of the substitute.

"I know. I met her."

"I was wondering if the sub would be here tomorrow as well and whether or not I could catch Brittany Sinclair before she went to biology. Troy Spaulding was the farthest thing from my mind. I swear it!"

Lane nodded. He could tell Jason wasn't lying. The boy was too upset.

"I looked up as I was leaving the room, and there he was! He was standing there and looking straight at me."

"You must be mistaken."

238

"Coach, I've known Troy all my life. We were co-captains of the football team last year. There's no way I could be wrong about this!"

Lane didn't know what to say. He knew Jason couldn't be mistaken. "That's impossible."

"I know! That's why I'm so upset!" Jason frowned at him and his fingers picked at his dog-eared book covers. "Do you think I'm going crazy?" he mumbled.

"No." Lane smiled at the boy. "No, you're not crazy. Your eyes must have been playing tricks on you."

Jason regarded him doubtfully. "How could that happen?"

"I have no idea."

"We just stood there and stared at each other. He looked just like he always did. He was even wearing his letter jacket! For a minute I thought his dying had been some kind of bad joke. You know? Like he was gone on a long vacation and had just come back to town.

"Then Kevin Donatello bumped into me, and I looked away to tell him what I was seeing, and when I looked back, Troy was gone." He glanced back at Lane. "I guess that sounds like I'm lying, but I'm not. Troy was my friend. I wouldn't lie about this."

"I know. Jason, it's no mistake that Troy is dead. You were at his funeral."

Jason's frown deepened. "I know that."

"He's gone, and he won't be back."

"So how did I see him in the hall outside the English room?"

Lane had no answer.

* * *

Janis had already started her classes on the Christmas play. At Tess's instigation, she was also involving the art department early in the preparations. "This is so much better," Janis said as Tess helped her move a flat forward. "Mrs. Larson never wanted to be bothered this early."

"This is better for my schedule. It's hard to find kids who will agree to spend extra time painting sets at the last minute." This was Tess's free period, and she was more than willing to give it up and not have to be in the auditorium after hours.

"Brittany, watch your fingers. That window is tricky." Janis gestured to a boy. "Chet, go help Brittany."

Tess watched the boy saunter over to where Brittany Sinclair was wrestling with a fake window. It had been Tess's idea to do actual theatrical flats. Janis had been so excited, she had gone to Mr. Crouthers with the idea between second and third period. It had taken a week to build them, but as Janis said, they would last for years.

"We should have done this long ago. You just can't imagine, Tess, what it's like to teach drama in a small town. All the people think about here is sports, sports, sports."

"I think it's like that everywhere."

"At first Mr. Crouthers said we didn't need flats to put on a play. He pointed out that we'd never had any, and we'd done just fine with cardboard cutouts."

"How did you convince him?"

"I didn't. I called some of my students' parents and mentioned we'd like to have flats. Since I've lived here all my life, I knew exactly which ones to call. Sure

240

enough, the PTO meeting that Friday addressed the suggestion and here are the flats!" Janis looked back at Brittany. "No, no! You'll break your fingers that way!" She hurried over to show the girl the proper way to place the window into the opening in the flat.

Tess went to the wings to look at the diagram of the set that Janis had taped to the wall. The angle of the last flat was wrong, and if she didn't change it now the whole set would be off-center. Tess hurried out to make the change.

The students had been more exuberant than knowledgeable and the boys had piled far more sandbags than necessary on the board that supported the flat. "Don't tie that one in place yet," Tess called out to the boys who were about to lash the next flat in place. She tugged at one of the sandbags and found them heavier than she had expected.

Glancing up she saw a girl standing in the wings, watching all that was going on. "Come help," Tess said. "These are heavy."

The girl didn't move or show any sign she had heard. Tess frowned and said, "Didn't you hear me? Help me move these bags before we run out of time." She wanted to have the flats in place so her next day's classes could start painting them, and she was short of time.

The girl finally looked at Tess. For a long moment the girl met Tess's eyes, then she turned and walked away.

Tess wasn't used to such blatant disobedience, let alone a stare with such open hatred, so she dropped the end of the sand bag and hurried after the girl. When she reached the wings, she looked about. The girl wasn't there, and there was no door she could have used to leave.

"Is something wrong?" Janis asked as she passed to check the design sketch.

"Do you have a student who's about this tall"—Tess held her hand in the air to indicate a girl smaller than average—"who has short, frizzy brown hair?"

"Not in this class. Come to think of it, no one this year has hair like that."

"I guess that's why she didn't come and help when I called to her." Tess frowned at the stage wings. "I wonder where she went. By the time I got across the stage, she was gone."

"I don't know. I didn't see anyone."

"Maybe I've started seeing things," Tess said with a perplexed laugh. "Will you help me move these sandbags? The wall is angled wrong."

"Those things are heavy. Chet, you and Brady come help us move sand bags."

Tess went back to work but she found herself wondering more than once about the girl with the curly hair.

In spite of their efforts, the set wasn't complete by the end of school. As Tess had feared, Janis asked her to stay behind and help her finish. Reluctantly, Tess agreed. She didn't feel comfortable leaving Janis to do the work alone. Especially not in the auditorium.

Janis was waiting for Tess already in the auditorium when Tess arrived. She was holding the set sketch and comparing it to the arrangement of the flats on stage. "Something about this doesn't look right."

Tess looked over her shoulder. "Shouldn't the door be closer to the front?"

"Of course. That's it. I should have been watching Chet more closely. That boy seems to have his head in the clouds all the time."

"That's an apt description of most teenagers," Tess said with a laugh.

"You're right about that. Let's move it back. Between the two of us, we can do it."

Tess followed Janis up onto the stage and started untying the ropes that held the flats together. "I'm glad our classes are working together on this. Mary Reynolds told me this morning that she has always been afraid to take drama, but she really likes painting the set."

"Mary Reynolds? Is she the girl with the brownish hair? The bashful one?" Janis frowned slightly as she tried to place the girl.

"That's her. She's really started to bloom this year. She even said she might be interested in taking a class in set design. Do you think Mr. Crouthers would let us teach that next summer as an extra class? Neither of us will have regular classes then to interfere."

"He might. We can ask him."

Tess loosened the last rope and held the flat up while Janis maneuvered the one containing the door to the other side. Tess dragged her flat down a space. "I don't know that much about set design myself, but I know about painting large canvases, and it's not much different. That's why I'm suggesting we both teach it. You could teach the theatrical aspect, and I could address the art. Have any of your other students expressed an interest in extra courses?"

"You know how kids are about going to school, especially in the summer. But I have several who are planning to major in drama when they start college, and they may be interested."

Tess finished tying the flats together and went to help Janis drag sandbags onto the supports to secure them to the floor. Janis went out into the audience and called back, "That's much better. Would it be possible to make a rock wall out of Styrofoam? We've always painted cardboard before, but I've never been happy with the way that looks."

"Where can we find Styrofoam in large blocks?" Tess sat on the edge of the stage where she could see the set and Janis as well.

"I have an uncle who's in the shipping business. Maybe he'd know." Janis put her head to one side as she planned aloud. "It would have to be cheap. Or better yet, free. Mr. Crouthers would never allow extra in my budget."

"I'm surprised he let you buy canvas and wood for the flats."

Janis came toward the stage. "It's supposed to be confidential, but the money was donated by Britanny's parents. It seems her mother is a frustrated thespian. She majored in drama but chose marriage over a career under the lights." Janis laughed. "At least that's the way she explained it to me." She went up the steps and sat opposite Tess.

Putting the drawing between them, Tess said, "We can put the rock wall here and use one of the trees from the last play where it meets the curtain. I'll have someone paint it more realistically."

"I need that space between the flats on stage left to look like an alley."

"No problem. I've already started teaching perspective to the juniors. They can block it out and the sophomores can paint it. That way every class feels they've contributed."

"I've given a lot of thought to storage. Between plays I have to put the flats away. The band director is already giving me dirty looks, and the Christmas concert is two months away!"

"I know. He really has an attitude." Tess was already planning what colors to use for the street scene.

"Tell me about it! He seems to think this stage is his own exclusive property. We've been battling him over it for years."

Tess lifted her head and looked out into the auditorium. "Did you hear something?"

"No." Janis paused to listen, then shrugged. "Maybe it's the band director sneaking around to spy on us and blow up our set." She laughed and looked back at the sketch. "I hope that doorway will do. If only we had a real door to hang in the opening."

"We can add to the sets over the years." Tess pointed at the drawing. "If I cut up the cardboard we used for the house last time, we can stand it at an angle here and it'll look as if the door is open. We just can't close it."

"That's better than using an opening in the curtain like we've done all this time. Mrs. Larson had no interest in drama at all. She only had her class paint cardboard for my class because she didn't want to have to think up new projects for them. I really believe that."

Tess turned her head back toward the seats. "Are you sure you don't hear anything?"

Janis shaded her eyes against the stage lighting. "What does it sound like?"

"I thought I heard the doors open and close."

"If they had, we would have seen light from the hallway."

"That's true." Tess rubbed her arms as if she were cold. "I must be mistaken."

"One year Mrs. Larson refused to do the scenery for the senior play! Can you imagine that? We had to make do with props. I told my students it was improvisational theater."

Tess smiled. She was certain she was hearing something in the shadows at the back of the seating area. "Are the front doors of the school locked?"

"I'm sure they must be." Janis glanced back at the room behind her. "Now you have me hearing it."

Tess shaded her eyes and felt the pulse quicken in her throat. "Is that someone sitting back there?"

"It can't be." Janis squinted trying harder to see better. "I think I see several shapes." Raising her voice she said, "Chet, is that you? Brittany?" No one answered.

"Maybe we should go," Tess said uneasily.

"It could be the cleaning ladies. I'm not sure what time they arrive and school has been out nearly two hours."

"Then why aren't they answering us?" Tess found herself whispering.

Janis stood and dusted the back of her skirt. Her forehead puckered in concern. "Who's back there? Answer me!"

Tess hopped off the stage apron onto the auditorium floor and walked a few steps up the aisle. "It

246

must have just been shadows. I don't see anyone from here."

"Neither do I now." Janis didn't seem eager to walk back there to be certain. To Tess she said, "Is there anything else we need to do today?"

"No. No, I'm finished with my plans. How about you?"

"I'm through." Janis was still frowning out at the audience. "Let's lock up and leave."

Tess went up the aisle to the double doors and held one open while Janis turned off the stage lights. She heard Janis move quickly back to the stage and down the side steps, but she was uneasy until Janis jogged into the dim light and they stepped out into the hall. Neither wanted to talk about what they thought they had seen.

Hannah Mitchell finished washing her supper dishes and went into the den and turned on her TV. Her house was quiet and cozy, and she thought again how glad she was that she had resisted the urge to move after her husband Willard had died. The house was larger than one person needed, but it was filled with memories. Rommel looked up as she settled onto the couch, his tail thumping the floor in greeting.

With the remote control, she changed from one channel to another. Nothing particularly good was on. She didn't care much for the current trend in sitcoms. They seemed silly and juvenile. Didn't anyone write comedy for adults anymore? "I guess I'm getting old," she commented to Rommel. The dog wagged his tail again, loyally agreeing with anything his mistress said.

The phone on the table at the end of her couch rang, and Hannah grimaced as she looked at the clock. Nine o'clock. She hated for the phone to ring so late at night. Until she answered it, she always thought something terrible must have happened to one of her nieces or nephews. She picked up the receiver and put it to her ear. "Hello?"

"Hello, Mrs. Mitchell? This is Lucy Wright."

Hannah released her pent up breath. "Yes, Lucy. How are you doing tonight?" Hannah had taught Lucy in school and still couldn't bring herself to call the woman by her more formal title. "How's Ross these days?"

"Ross?" Lucy asked, then momentarily paused before saying, "He's fine."

Hannah didn't talk with Lucy often, but thought her voice sounded odd, as if she were distracted or her mind had wandered. "Was there something you wanted?" she prompted.

After another moment of silence, Lucy said, "I'm calling for Brooke's assignment. Is she supposed to read 'Lady of Shalott' for tomorrow?"

"Tracy's class is reading 'The Eve of Saint Agnes.' " She didn't point out to Lucy that she had used the wrong daughter's name.

"Tracy's class?" Lucy sounded confused.

"Are you all right?"

"Yes. Of course. Why wouldn't I be?" Lucy defensively snapped.

"Is Ross there with you?"

There was another long silence. Hannah was on the verge of concluding that Lucy wasn't going to answer her or that she had hung up when Lucy finally said,

248

"He's here." Then her voice became querulous. "I don't see why everyone is trying to keep Brooke a secret. No one wants to talk about her anymore."

"I know her death must have been hard on you," Hannah said. "I miss her, too."

"Death?"

Hannah couldn't miss the question in Lucy's voice. "Could I speak to Ross?"

"No. That is, he isn't home."

"But you just said he was."

"I have to go." The line went dead.

Hannah sat there for a while, holding the receiver and wondering if she should call Ross. Slowly she put the phone back on its cradle. Lucy had never had all her ducks in a row, so to speak, but Hannah hadn't realized how disconnected she had become.

Her thoughts turned to Tracy—a sweet girl, but one who would never be as popular or as outgoing as her older sister had been. Hannah had frequently thought it must be difficult for Tracy to grow up in Brooke's shadow. It must be doubly difficult now that Brooke was dead. Tracy almost certainly had entertained jealous thoughts that would come back to haunt her with guilt, and Hannah would be much surprised if Lucy hadn't practically deified her lost child.

Hannah stood up and Rommel rose expectantly. "Okay. We'll go for a walk. You're getting spoiled rotten, you know."

As if he understood every word, Rommel trotted to the kitchen and waited at the broom closet where his leash was kept. Hannah soon caught up with him, snapped his leash onto his collar and out they went.

Rommel was her constant companion when she

wasn't in school. If the truth were known, he often accompanied her when she was grading papers late at night. Hannah wasn't sure how the school would view this, so she never had told anyone. Rommel was sweet by nature, but she had no doubts that he would fight a dragon if one threatened her.

The nights had turned cool, but Hannah didn't want to go back after a sweater. She knew she would warm up as she walked. Lately, she had felt her age catching up with her, and she was battling it all the way. Rommel set the pace, and they turned automatically in the direction of the school.

As she walked, Hannah wondered what, if anything, she should do about Lucy. Ross was no fool, and he must know his wife was acting more than slightly peculiar. Hannah had no connection to that family except for having taught them all in high school, but she felt a certain kinship to all her students past and present. It troubled her to see Lucy going off the deep end, as Willard would have colorfully put it. Still, families seldom welcomed interference, and Hannah wasn't sure that the Wrights wouldn't see it in that light.

She decided the best course would be to wait and see if Lucy did anything else out of the way. It would be better to err on the side of conservatism.

Just ahead was the high school, a dark bulk in the night, its walls lit only dimly by the streetlights. That was another thing that bothered Hannah. Nearly every street in town had new, brighter lights, except for the one the school was on, and in her opinion, that was the very place lights were most needed. Children were frequently here after ball games or band trips or whatever, and the current lights offered practically no security. Not that Maple Glen had ever been troubled by a high crime rate, but Hannah saw that as no reason to be slack.

Rommel's ears pricked and he stopped walking. Hannah almost tripped over him. "You silly dog. I need to get you some brake lights," she grumbled good-naturedly. She rested her hand on his head and was surprised to find him trembling ever so slightly.

She looked in the direction Rommel was staring but could see nothing. Was someone trying to break into the school? The front doors were in shadow from this angle. She led Rommel across the street and up the walk, but uncharacteristically, he lagged behind rather than leading or staying abreast of her. He followed her reluctantly.

"I've never seen you act this way," Hannah said to the dog. "What's the matter with you?" Rommel was walking slower and slower.

She looked up at her windows, then stepped back for a better look. Had she seen someone at the window? She squinted for a better look and wished she had brought her glasses. The window seemed vacant now—but she was sure she had seen a movement and a glimpse of a face.

Tess and Janis Denkle had been here tonight. She remembered Tess saying they were going to work on scenery. Had they forgotten to lock up?

She went to the doors and tried them. They were securely locked. It was barely possible that someone could have sneaked in while Tess and Janis were working and hidden until they had gone. Hannah had heard stories of vandals going to extreme lengths to ravage a building. The security system was somewhat difficult to operate. Perhaps Tess hadn't thought to reactivate it when she left. She stepped back from the building and looked again at her windows on the third floor. With a sigh she said, "I guess I ought to go up and investigate."

Rommel whined softly and looked toward home before snapping his head back around. Hannah knew something was bothering him. "I'm going to have to teach you to talk."

She took her keys from her pocket and put the correct one in the door lock. She had done this so many times she was as familiar with it as with her door at home. From the time the door opened she had five minutes to turn off the alarm before the siren would go off. She started toward the alarm control box, but Rommel refused to budge.

"Rommel! What's gotten into you? Come on!"

The dog did as she commanded, but he was trembling visibly now and was carrying both his tail and his head down low. His apparent cowardice bothered Hannah more than anything. She would have said he was fearless.

She bent down and petted him, but he wasn't reassured. Suddenly the school seemed too large and too silent for comfort. Hannah had rarely been frightened of being here at night, but she found herself at the moment almost paralysed with an unexpected fear. Hannah had never allowed herself flights of fantasy, so she left Rommel at the door and felt her way to the alarm switch. The familiar metal door was cold under her fingers. She opened it and pressed the proper sequence of buttons.

From somewhere high overhead in the school she heard a faint sound. Was someone whispering up there? The acoustics in the old building were such that if someone whispered even from as high as the third floor stairway, it could be clearly heard on the lower floors. Not many people knew that, and because of that unusual phenomenon, she had once caught students sneaking in to steal tests.

Hannah moved silently to the foot of the stairs and listened again. She could hear voices, and although she couldn't make out what they were saying, she was reasonably sure there were several of them. She looked back at the door. Rommel had come a few steps into the building, but he was still slinking along with his tail between his legs.

Uncertainly she wondered what to do. It would be more prudent to go to a nearby house and call the police, but she had never been afraid of students and she wasn't prepared to be frightened by them now. It was only the echoes that made their voices seem so strange. She started up the stairwell.

Hannah didn't turn on the lights as she went. She wanted to catch the students red-handed in whatever they were doing. She was very protective of her school and would personally see to it that they were expelled for breaking into it.

She found the second floor silent and empty and frowned in the darkness. That meant they had to be on the third floor and that also meant they were breaking into the only classroom on that floor—hers. She had told the students she was giving a test tomorrow. Were some of them trying to steal it?

Tiptoeing so she would make no sound, she climbed

the last flight of stairs. The voices were louder. At the head of the stairs she paused. She could see the dim silhouettes of students in the hall, but they didn't seem to be doing anything but standing there. Hannah squinted to try and see them better. Why weren't they moving about?

She fumbled for the light switch and flooded the hall with brilliance. They were all there. Troy with his mouth slack and his eyes empty, Brooke with her red hair dusty and dull. Misty Traveno moved behind her, her arms dangling at her side, her head at an odd angle to her body.

For a moment Hannah could only stare in shocked disbelief. She knew them all, or had known them in life. When they started to move toward her, she took a step back. "No," she whispered. "I can't be seeing this. It's not real." Far below her she heard Rommel start to howl and the sound raised the hairs on the back of her neck.

"Alone," Misty whispered, her voice sounding hollow.

Joe Bob Renfro edged forward, his dull eyes on Hannah. She had last seen him when she told him he wouldn't be passing English that year. He had been furious but had been afraid to act on his anger. Now he stepped away from the others. "Kill," he said.

As Joe Bob and the others began to move toward her, Hannah began to shake. She took another step back and cried out as her foot found only air. For a moment she teetered, her arms flailing the air. She heard Rommel racing up the steps, his snarls resounding off the walls. As the dog leaped past her, she lost her precarious balance. She screamed as she fell backward down the stairs, tumbling head first over the railing to the steps on the lower flight.

The next morning the janitor found her body when he came in to open the school. An ambulance was called, but she was pronounced dead on the scene and taken away before any of the students arrived. Everyone assumed it had been an accident. After all, Hannah often worked at the school late at night, and she had often said the stairs seemed to be steeper than they had been when she was younger.

Rommel's death was more difficult to explain. He wasn't found until the first student went up the third floor. His mutilated body lay in the hall in front of the English room, and the top floor had to be closed off until the police returned to take pictures and ask more questions. After they were finished, they gave the janitor permission to scrub the blood from the walls and floor.

"It was awful!" Amy told Tracy. "I got up there before they closed the floor and blood was everywhere!"

"What happened to him?" Tracy asked. "Had he been shot?"

"I heard Miss Bowen tell Coach Hodges that it looked as if he had been torn apart." Amy glanced around fearfully. "You've seen that dog. He was huge! What could do that to him?"

"Maybe she was exaggerating."

Amy shook her head, her eyes large and frightened. "I thought I was going to be sick. Mrs. Bowen looked as if she felt the same way, and so did the janitor." She leaned closer and clutched her school books to her chest. "Do you know what I think? I think Mrs.

Mitchell came to the school and found somebody robbing it or something. She could have fallen down the stairs and the burglar could have killed the dog."

Tracy gave her a disbelieving look. "Why would a burglar tear a dog apart? That's gross! Besides, that dog would have ripped anybody to pieces before he could be hurt."

"I don't know. But you should have seen the mess. It was *awful.*" She hurried away toward her next class.

Tracy wondered what had really happened in the school the previous night. She didn't believe for a single minute that a burglar had killed Rommel. And if one had, didn't that mean he had also murdered Mrs. Mitchell? She hadn't been one of the most popular teachers with the students, but no one hated her.

Against her will, Tracy thought of the coven and wondered if there was any tie-in. If Brooke's death—and the others—were connected, wasn't it likely that Mrs. Mitchell's was as well? Tracy felt chilled. Gary Valdes and Darryl Watson had also been members, though that was before she was initiated. Kelly Nelson was missing, but Tracy knew she wasn't a member of the coven—or had she died, been replaced, and simply wasn't mentioned anymore? No, if Kelly was dead, everyone would know and would have talked about it.

Tracy rubbed her forehead as she told herself she was letting her imagination run away with her. No one in the coven was a killer! The idea of Matthew Greenway or Mona Dupree killing someone was ridiculous. Even Rocky Mancelli, the wildest one in the coven, wasn't capable of murder. She had just seen too many horror movies or something. This was real life and that sort of thing only happened in fiction.

All the same, Tracy was uneasy for the rest of the day. By the last period, she had almost convinced herself that Brooke and the others, especially Mrs. Mitchell and her dog, had no connection with the coven. Otherwise, as Brooke's sister, she wouldn't have been allowed to attend the meetings. The truth she couldn't acknowledge was that she was afraid to stop going. So she told herself she would continue for a little longer.

Chapter Eleven

Kevin was always careful not to be publicly associated with anyone in his coven. His followers didn't understand why that was necessary, but Kevin knew that after the Grand Sacrifice he would be the only one left alive, and he didn't want to be implicated in the deaths. His power to bring money and women to himself would be useless if he were locked away in prison.

Every day he believed more and more in the power he was to create for himself. He took the worn black book from its hiding place behind his dresser, then lay on his bed before opening it. As he inhaled the familiar scent of moldering paper and musty attics, he marveled that anyone could have parted with it. Its previous owner almost certainly hadn't known the secrets it possessed.

The television was on in the other room, and from the canned laughter he heard at intervals, he concluded that his mother was watching a sitcom. He rolled over onto his stomach. In a few short months he would graduate and then would never have to see this house again. All he was waiting for was his diploma.

He was envious that his father had been able to simply walk away from a situation he didn't like, and he longed for that freedom for himself. But Kevin had invested twelve years of schoolwork in that diploma and wasn't so stupid as to cheat himself out of it. Besides, he didn't dare do anything that might draw attention to himself with the Grand Sacrifice pending.

There was, however, the matter of Mona. She seemed determined to become the mouthpiece of the coven. At times it was almost as if she were living in a real world of Dungeons and Dragons. She had that way of asking questions, as if she were following some previously written script. At times it was rather eerie.

Worst, she was beginning to insist on being a part of his daily life. Today she had even intercepted him in the hall and tried to make him walk her to biology class. He knew now he had made a mistake in taking in Mona into the coven, but what was he to do about it?

He could kill her. There had been a furor for a while about Kelly Nelson's disappearance, but when no body was found or any sign of a disturbance, it had been generally accepted that she had run away. Would he be able to do the same with Mona?

She was a loner, but she was also better known around the school than Kelly had been, even if Mona was relatively new to the school and Kelly had gone there all her life. More people might question the disappearance of a girl whose life seemed to be bounded by studies.

Not long ago she had even gone so far as to hint that she wouldn't be adverse to having sex with him. She told him she had read that the act of sex built powers and that they could rule the coven together. Kevin had been appalled. All the books he had read had said exactly the opposite—that the release of sexual needs would sap his power and tie him to earth. As for Mona becoming a co-leader of the coven, that was out of the question. Kevin had formed the coven for one purpose, and that was to use the Grand Sacrifice to make himself into the most powerful warlock in history.

Even if he was successful in killing Mona, her absence would present a problem. Without her, there would be only eleven followers. The book he used as a "bible" was adamant that there be twelve followers and a leader to make the number the magical thirteen. Some of the others might start to drift away or become troublesome if there were more deaths or disappearances. Besides, it would take too much time finding another person to round out the circle. Finding Tracy and the boys to replace Gary and Darryl had been pure luck. No, Mona would have to stay in the coven.

For a moment Kevin paused and thought about Gary and Darryl's deaths. He was the only one who knew why they had gone into the school that night. That made him even more perplexed. He had told the others that the two had died because they had been weak and untrustworthy, but Kevin knew he had made that up. Gary Valdes hadn't been afraid of anything and he assumed the same was true for Darryl, too. Certainly neither of them would have jumped willingly from the third floor window. Nor would they have pushed each other. So why had they fallen?

For that matter, what had happened to Mrs. Mitchell and her dog? No one seemed to be connecting their deaths with Gary and Darryl, but all four had happened on the third floor. How long would it be before someone—even someone in his coven—put the facts together and became suspicious?

There was only one option as he saw it. He had to plan the Grand Sacrifice as soon as possible. There was a rap on the door and his mother pushed it open. "Kevin? Will you take out the trash?"

"Later." He didn't bother to look at her. He could smell her cigarette smoke and she wasn't even in the room.

"I asked you to do it after supper. And look at this room! How do you live in such a mess?"

Kevin let the book drop onto his pillow and rolled his eyes. "I said I'll take out the trash. Now get off my back!"

Becky Donatello didn't leave. "Please don't talk to me like that. I love you so much. You're all I have left in the world."

Kevin hated it when she talked that way. "Have you been drinking again?" he demanded, swiveling his head around to look at her. In disgust he answered his own question. "You have."

"I can't help it. You don't know what it's like to lose a husband."

"No, Mom. Of course I don't. I doubt I'll ever have a husband." His words dripped sarcasm. "Why do you always put it like that? It sounds like he's dead."

"He might as well be, as far and you and I are concerned." Becky's words were slurred from several hours of drinking.

"Would you get of here and leave me alone?" He went back to reading.

Becky came to the bed. "What are you reading? I

remember when you were little and I used to read you 'Winnie the Pooh.' Do you remember that?"

He groaned. "Yeah, right. That's what I'm reading. 'Winnie the Pooh.' " When his mother drank she became morose and stickily sentimental.

She leaned closer and tried to focus on the page. "Where did you get such an old book? Why, it's practically falling apart."

Kevin slammed it shut and glared at her. "I told you to leave."

Large tears gathered in Becky's eyes. "I only wanted to talk to you. I get so lonesome." She reached out as if she would touch his cheek.

Kevin jerked away. "Get out! Now!"

With resignation Becky stood and went back to the door. "Will you come out after awhile? I just want you to talk to me for a little bit."

"Yeah. Close the door behind you." He opened the book. This was a familiar pattern. In an hour's time she would be passed out on the sofa, the empty rum bottle nearby.

When he heard the door close, Kevin rolled over onto his back and stared up at the stained ceiling. He wished she had never come in. She reminded him of how much his life had changed since his father had left them. True, she had never been any prize, and he had always wondered why his father married her in the first place, but she hadn't drank so heavily then.

He rubbed his eyes. Where was his father and why had he deserted them the way he had? Kevin had come home from school one day and found his mother crying. His father had left work early, packed, and driven away without even waiting to tell him good-bye. His mother said there was another woman, but Kevin wasn't sure he believed her. It seemed more likely to him that his father simply couldn't stand being married to her another day.

A commercial came on TV and the first strains of a familiar jingle advertising laundry detergent were interrupted as his mother began changing channels, over and over. Nothing ever seemed to hold her interest.

Kevin looked around his room. Where did she get off telling him his room was dirty? It was no worse than the rest of the house, in his opinion. Becky had never been strong on housecleaning and now that she had to work, she seldom bothered at all. What was he supposed to do? Go to school and clean house, too? He felt the hate building, and he nurtured it. If she wanted the garbage taken out, she could do it herself.

He picked up the book and started to read. It was of vital importance for him to pick the best date for the Grand Sacrifice. Although he had thought his previous date of midsummer's eve had been inspirational, the sacrifice hadn't worked. Besides, he had already decided he couldn't wait until summer.

One of the preferred days for casting spells, according to the book, was Candlemas. February 3, Groundhog day. Kevin counted up the months. Could he hold the coven together four more months? He was running out of ways to keep them interested and loyal. If he gave them too much time, his followers would become bored and leave. His other coven had been together only three months and some of them had started to waver. The earliest recruits for this group had been meeting with him for six weeks already. February was too far away.

The next best choice of dates was All Hallows Eve—Halloween. Kevin sat up and tossed his black hair out of his eyes. It seemed terribly obvious, but that could work in his favor. The coven would be expecting something spectacular on that date. They might be willing to do as he told them if he worked particularly hard with them in the intervening week. And as far as they would know, the Grand Sacrifice would be no more than some of the other rituals Kevin had led them through during the past few weeks. They wouldn't realize *they* were the sacrifice until it was too late.

As he had done many times before, Kevin planned the sacrificial ritual. There could be no more mistakes. Everyone would gather together and this time all would die at once, or as close to it as he could manage. But how to do it?

He knew he couldn't depend on everyone shooting themselves or cutting their wrists at once. Girls were afraid of blood and they might rebel at the last minute. Besides, he had heard of people surviving suicide attempts involving guns and knives. Taking aspirin or some other drug was also unreliable. It might work faster on the smaller followers and not at all on the larger ones.

Poison. The word came to him like an inspiration. He could use poison.

Kevin sat up and his black eyes darted about as he thought. Suddenly it came to him. He could mix wood alcohol with something and have them drink it as a part of the ritual. Even ingested in small quantities, wood alcohol was lethal. A moderate amount would give him additional insurance. He'd studied destructive distillation in chemistry and was sure he could make the methanol himself. Starting now, he'd have plenty of time to produce enough for the ceremony without anyone being suspicious of his absences. It would be simple to hide it in his bedroom. No one, especially his mother, was allowed in his room when he wasn't there.

What did methyl alcohol taste like? Would they be able to tell they were drinking it and not the safer ethyl alcohol? To be sure, he would mix it with something with a strong taste, like grapefruit juice. Surely the taste of grapefruit juice would hide anything.

He went to his desk and opened his school notebook. Propping the black book of spells beside him, he started writing the incantation. It had to be impressive and he would have to memorize the words. At exactly the right moment, the instant they started actually to die, he would begin saying the incantation to call to himself the power of their souls.

Kevin worked feverishly.

Tess had found it difficult to get ready for Halloween. While she and Hannah hadn't been long-time friends, she had known her well. Hannah's death, on the heals of that of Gary and Darryl, seemed almost insurmountable.

"If I were Mr. Crouthers," Tess said as she got into Lane's car, "I would have canceled all Halloween activities for this year, and possibly forever."

"So would I. I just can't get over what happened to Hannah."

"It was an accident. It had to be."

"Her dog, too?"

Tess hesitated. "Did you see him? Or I should say, what was left of him?"

"No."

"I did. I heard a girl screaming, and I went up to investigate. Just thinking about it makes me sick. It was as if he had exploded!"

"That's why I don't see how anyone can say Hannah's death was an accident." He frowned as he turned his car down the street that led to the stadium.

"The police sergeant I spoke with said it was ruled accidental because she died as a result of the fall. Her neck was broken, and she had a massive skull injury. Aside from the dog, there was no other sign of violence."

Lane shook his head in exasperation. "I'd have said that would have been enough."

"So would I."

First the stadium came into view, then the field house. Several cars were already parked in the lot. "We aren't the first, I see."

Tess nodded. "That's Janis's car. I don't recognize the others. Do you think we'll have any customers? I'm afraid everyone will stay away because of Hannah's death. I would, if I hadn't made a commitment to help out."

"We'll see soon enough. Morbid curiosity may make the crowd larger than usual."

"Sad, but true."

They parked in Lane's reserved space next to the building, and as they were getting the supplies they had brought out of Lane's trunk, the field house doors burst open and two boys came running out, pushing and tumbling against each other and laughing so hard they could hardly see where they were going. As they hurried on past Tess and Lane, she heard one of them say something about being haunted by Mrs. Mitchell's ghost. Tess's first instinct was to be angry with them for being so frivolous about the death of one of their teachers, but before she said anything, she remembered that Ed Hudson had said that everyone dealt with tragedy that touched their lives in different ways. Perhaps the boys' making light of Hannah's passing was their way of coping. If that was true and if it was a prevalent attitude among the students, this was going to be a long and difficult evening for Tess.

"Are you sure this is a good idea?" Tess asked Lane again as they went into the field house. "I'd have thought that after all that's been going on these past few months, no one would have wanted a haunted house on Halloween."

"It's a school tradition," he explained. "Each class tries to outdo the previous one. The money raised will fund the senior trip. I'm just glad we have an out-of-town game Friday so the field house can be decorated ahead of time. Last year we had to work on it all day to have it ready to open that night. At least this year we can spread it out over a couple of days."

Several of the art students were draping fake cobwebs in the area partitioned off in the front of the building. A drama student was hanging black string in a doorway in such a way that it would tickle faces as people walked by.

Lane went over to Jason and Mojo, who were nailing some cheap paneling onto frames to make temporary walls. "Be sure none of the nails pokes through. We don't want anyone to be hurt."

Mojo grinned at him. "Aw, come on, coach. Just a little blood?"

"Only if it comes out of a bottle."

Tess liked watching Lane interacting with the students. He genuinely liked them and they all knew it. She went to oversee the table that was being set up as the "operating room."

Tracy was helping Keisha push the table into place near a wall. A sheet was stapled to the top in such a way that it would hide the buckets of "entrails" and "brains." One of the drama students would be the victim, another the mad surgeon.

Keisha said, "Can you see the buckets from there?"

Tess looked at it critically. "No, not all."

Pretending she was the surgeon, Keisha reached into one of the buckets and pulled out imaginary body parts as she cackled wildly. Tracy gave her a long-suffering look. Keisha nodded her acceptance of the set-up. "Do we know what we'll use for brains and guts?"

"I'm going to cook cauliflower and put tomato sauce over it," Tess said. "We'll have the usual spaghetti 'veins'. I think if I put red food coloring on some and blue on the rest, it will look like veins and arteries."

Keisha made a face at Tracy and tried to pull her into the fun. Tracy ignored her and put some more staples in the sheet. "I'm not sure I'd want to be the surgeon," Keisha said. "Yuk!"

"It's only spaghetti," Tracy said in a bored voice.

Keisha wasn't daunted. "What about boiling some of the kind of pasta you can use in chicken and dumplings? It might look like pieces of skin."

"That's a good idea. And I'll peel grapes for 'eyeballs.'"

"Everybody does that," Tracy said with a sigh. "Grapes don't fool anybody."

"Mrs. Denkle suggested plastic tubing for the intestines," Tess told Keisha. "She says she can bring some from home."

"Mojo gets to be the chain saw murderer," Keisha said, her black eyes sparkling. "He's going to bring his daddy's chain saw from home. Without the chain on it, of course."

"Won't that be too much?" Tess had never participated in setting up a haunted house before and she was constantly amazed at the students ideas on how to frighten the wits out of their peers.

"We *have* to have a chain saw murderer," Keisha said as if she were shocked. "Everybody's seen that movie a thousand times."

"Not me," Tracy told her.

"Yes, you have. We checked it out at the video store last year at Amy's slumber party."

Tracy shrugged. "I forgot."

Tess watched Tracy's languid movements. What was wrong with the girl? She had expected this project to liven up even Tracy. The girl looked as if she were already dressing for the event. She wore black as always, here lately, this time tights and a blouse that covered her almost like a dress. Her hair was pulled back and tied with a black ribbon and she wore spider earrings. The makeup was heavy on her eyes but her lips were pale. "Tracy, are you going to work in the haunted house?"

"I suppose so."

Keisha nodded. "Mrs. Denkle says the drama students will do most of it. The girls like to scream. There aren't many boys in the class so she says she may have to recruit some of the art students. That's how Mojo gets to be the chain saw murderer."

Tess already knew all this but she nodded. "Are you going to be in it?"

"I get to be one of the living dead."

"Which reminds me. I need to go see how the tombstones are coming along." She left the two girls and went out to the parking lot where several of her students were painting wooden boards to look as if they were covered with lichen.

Chet Dawson was painting a name on one while his friend, Brady, nailed another to a support in such a way as to make it seem to be leaning with age. Tess looked over Chet's shoulder. " 'Mrs. Bowen.' Thanks."

"It's just a joke, Mrs. Bowen," Chet said hastily. "We didn't think you'd mind."

"I don't."

"We put Coach Hodges on one, too," Brady said. "This one will be Mrs. Denkle."

Tess was secretly pleased that the students accepted her enough to include her name on one of the stones. Although it was startling at first, it meant they liked her enough to want to tease her. "We'll set up the graveyard out here," she said to Chet. We need enough stones to fill this corner of the fenced area."

"Won't people knock them over as they go by?" he asked.

"Not if we put them back from the door and make the victims stay on a path to the gate. Remember, the living dead will be out here, too. They can scare people into the right direction."

"This is going to be the best spook house ever," Chet said. "A lot of kids are already talking about it."

"Coach Hodges has sent out advertising to the newspaper and radio," Tess said. "My art classes are going to make posters to put around town."

"We'll scare everybody to death," Brady put in.

Tess stepped back. She still wasn't sure this was a good idea. "Just remember to keep it safe."

"Sure. Nobody ever gets hurt at one of these." Chet grinned at the very idea and exchanged a look with Brady.

Tess made a mental note to keep an eye on those two. They might have something cooked up that wasn't in the teachers' plans.

Lane came to the field house door and called her. "Will you come look at this?"

She went inside and found the partitions were in place. "This is great!" The inside of the building had become a maze leading from one arena to the next.

"We start here with the gross-out room," Lane said. "This is where they will be asked to taste the eyeballs and so forth. Then they go through here and walk over these mattresses. In darkness, of course."

"Of course." She found it surprisingly difficult to walk on the yielding surfaces even with the lights on.

"To make it more interesting, Amy Dennis and Tracy will be here with hair dryers to blow hot air at them." He tested the walls to be sure they were sturdy enough to withstand a falling student. "Hey, Jason! Let's put a few more screws in this wall."

"Okay, Coach," Jason's voice called from the other side of the wall.

"Next we come to the vampire room."

"I'm going to put arrangements of dead flowers in here tomorrow morning," Tess told him.

"I've already arranged with the funeral home to borrow their transport casket. In the dim light it will look like a real coffin. Jason will be the vampire."

"He'll be perfect." She laughed to think of the antics Jason could perform in this role.

"Then we come to the mad doctor." He grinned at Keisha, who was still arranging buckets behind the table. Tracy stood to one side, not doing anything.

They turned the next corner and Tess saw a table painted to look as if blood were dripping from it. "The chain saw murderer, I presume?"

"The same. Mojo will chase them out with the chain saw and they'll find themselves in the graveyard." Lane pushed open the back door and daylight rushed in.

"Perfect!"

"The living dead will be walking around out here. The crowd will be sent out the gate and into the parking lot."

"You've worked hard on planning all this."

"I've been on this committee before. We try to change it every year, of course. The kids like being scared and part of that is the element of surprise."

"I assume someone has arranged for security."

"Janis did that. We have several policemen lined up who won't be on duty that night, and some of the firemen." He smiled down at her. "Quit worrying. I can see it in your eyes."

272

"I guess Halloween just isn't my favorite time of the year."

"Last year we made almost enough to fund the senior trip, but we ran it two weekends. Everyone was exhausted, especially the kids that had to perform in it. This year it will be only on Halloween night."

"I've told Janis I'll be here all night to help with security."

"So will I. Would you like to ride down with me?"

"I'd like that." She glanced around to be sure none of the students were within hearing distance. She could remember from her own school days how interested students were in their teachers' social lives. "I could cook us an early dinner."

"That sounds good. I'm not sure I want to encounter eyeballs and intestines on an empty stomach."

Tess wrinkled her nose. "You make it sound so fascinating. By the way, let's keep an eye on Chet and Brady. I have a feeling they're up to something."

Lane glanced over to where the boys were painting and whispering together. "Probably. I'm watching Mojo, too. He's not beyond a practical joke or two."

"I hope this goes over without incident."

"It will. You'll see."

Tess didn't feel any more confidant.

Chapter Twelve

"I hear Laurie Alexander has been hired to fill Hannah's place," Tess told Lane as they checked the final preparations for the haunted house.

"She seems competent." Lane straightened a black curtain that would hide the chain saw murderer from his "victims" until the last minute. "She hasn't been out of college very long, but that could be in her favor. The kids seem to relate to her." He paused to look back toward the main school building. "I guess it'll be a long time before any of us thinks of the English classes and doesn't associate them with Hannah."

"Yes, I haven't been here long, but I can see how that will be true. I miss her a great deal, and I didn't know her all that long. I wonder what she'd say about us doing the haunted house this year."

"She'd probably say that life goes on. Hannah was one of the most logical people I've ever known. She'd have understood." Lane adjusted his brown monk's robe. "I don't know how you women get around in skirts. My feet keep tangling."

Tess laughed. "Now you know why you never see

monks in athletic events. How on earth did you happen to pick that costume?"

"I didn't. It was a costume in the senior play last year. Janis loaned it to me." He glanced at her appraisingly. "Your costume doesn't match your personality either."

"I guess half the people here will come as witches, but I didn't have time to be very creative. This black bathrobe is one I haven't used in years. I'm surprised I kept it. I cut the moon and stars out of sticky-backed shelf liner and just stuck them on." She gave the curtain a final pull. "Stand over there and see if you can still see the table."

Lane backed away. "Pull it a little farther to the left. Perfect."

Tess tugged on the curtain then pushed up her sleeve and looked at her watch. "Shouldn't the students who are to work in the haunted house be here by now?"

"Any minute now. I just hope the rain holds off."

"So do I. We've worked hard to put all this together so quickly."

They went to the first room and Tess started pouring the "veins" into a clear jar. "These look really disgusting."

"I agree. They look a lot more like veins and arteries than I expected. How did you come up with the idea of red and blue cake coloring to get the right effect?"

"I have a devious mind. And I made good grades in biology."

"Did you see this?" He held out a box that contained what appeared to be a severed finger. When Tess looked closer, he wiggled it at her.

She flinched. "Now that's really gross!" she said with a nervous laugh.

"Gotcha!" Lane said as he pulled his finger out of the hole in the bottom of the box. "This is Chet's creation." He looked up when he heard a car door slam. "Sounds like they're starting to arrive."

"I'm so uneasy about this. I don't even like spook houses."

"I think next year I'll suggest we have it somewhere else. The field house really isn't large enough to do it right. Maybe we could take over the cafeteria. That way if it rains, the people waiting in line won't get wet."

"Let's just get through this one first."

Chet and Brady were the first of the student participants to come into the building. Both were dressed like the living dead. "Where's everybody else?" Chet asked.

"The others will be here soon." Lane propped open the door allowing a cool breeze into the room. "That looks like Amy's car now," he said.

Amy came in carrying an armload of hair dryers, plastic gloves, and masks. "My brother sent these masks. He said anyone is welcome to use them, but he'd like them back before you leave."

"Just put them over there," Tess said. "I'm going out back to finish setting up the headstones."

"I'll help you," Lane offered.

They went around the building to where a makeshift cemetery had been built. The headstones had been tilted at odd angles and green funeral grass had been used to hide the wooden supports. In the fading daylight, the scene looked amazingly realistic. Tess went down the uneven rows of graves rearranging the head-stones slightly so they could best be seen in the pale blue glow from the lights in the parking lot several hundred feet away.

"Can you believe that?" Lane said, gesturing toward the sky. "We even have a full moon."

"I ordered it special for tonight." She tilted her head back. "Let's just hope the weather stays this nice. The forecast is for thunderstorms."

"Here come some others. I expected Tracy to be with Amy. I wonder if they've had an argument. Usually they're inseparable."

"Not anymore." Tess came closer and lowered her voice so as not to be overheard. "Have you noticed a difference in Tracy lately?"

"I don't have her in my history class until next year. What do you mean?"

"Of course I didn't know her until the beginning of school, but it seemed to me that she was friendlier and definitely more polite then than now. Lately she acts as if it's beneath her to do anything. She and Amy aren't friends any longer. At least I assume so since I never see them together."

"That happens pretty often."

"She's also changed the way she dresses."

"I've noticed that. She looks like the daughter of doom these days." Lane knelt down and tugged on the funeral grass. "Can you pull on that end? We have a wrinkle."

"Have you seen Lucy Wright lately?" Tess asked as she helped him pull the fabric straight.

"No, I don't think she's been back to the school."

"That must be hard on Tracy. You know how cruel

277

kids can be. Maybe someone has been giving her a hard time about her mother. Wouldn't that account for her change in clothing and her attitude?"

"I have no idea. You'd have to ask Ed Hudson about that."

"I have to admit I'm worried about her. Janis says that although she used to be rather introverted, she always was friendly and easy to teach."

"She should be here by now." Lane looked at the parking lot. "Looks like most of our workers have arrived."

They went around the building and into the room where the students were already trying to scare each other. Lane made a quieting motion with his hands. "Hold it down. I want all of you in your places so we can do a walk through and be sure it all works before the first of our paying customers gets here."

The boys and girls scattered. Tess took a deep breath. "I guess I'll be first."

"In case you don't make it to the other side," he said in mock gravity, "it's been fun knowing you."

"Thanks. I needed that." She squared her shoulders and entered the dark hall.

Feeling with her toes, she found the mattress and put out her hands to brace herself on the railing as she crossed it. Halfway, a blast of hot air hit her from the hair dryer. At the same time, Amy screamed.

"How was that, Mrs. Bowen? Did it scare you? I thought a scream would be good here."

"You scared me half out of my wits." Tess peered in the direction of Amy's voice. "Is Tracy here? She's supposed to be at this station with you."

278

"I haven't seen her. I tried to call her before I came, but her dad said she had already left."

"Maybe she had to go somewhere else first." Tess turned and made her way across the remaining length of the mattress and through an opening to the operating room.

Tess didn't recognize the doctor or his screaming patient, as they were drama students, not her art students. The doctor threw back his head and laughed maniacally as the strobe lights flashed from above his head. In the pulsing light, he appeared to reach into the patient's abdomen and pull out a length of intestine. Tess felt squeamish even though she knew it was only plastic tubing from one of the concealed buckets. "Very effective," she said as she backed away.

Her hands touched the black walls of masonite paneling that formed a hallway. Her apprehension was growing with each illusion, despite the fact that she knew it was all pretend, and she had to force herself to walk toward the black curtain and the light behind it. As she passed through the curtain, Mojo yanked the chain saw to life and reached toward her. Tess knew there was no chain on the blade and it couldn't hurt her, but she jumped back, nevertheless. Mojo laughed.

"You kids are too good at this," she said in a shaken voice.

"Give me an 'A' or I'll cut out your liver," Mojo bargained in a maniacal voice.

"Cut my liver out and you'll get an 'A' in biology. For an 'A' in my class, you have to cut my liver out and use it in a collage."

"Hey, that's a good one," Mojo said in his own voice. "I guess I'll let you live after all."

Carefully, Tess moved around the hairpin turn toward the next fright. Electric candles lit the head and foot of a coffin and lined the floor beside it. In that dim light, it looked like a real one and not the pressed wood transfer case that the funeral home used to transport bodies from one town to another. She knew a student was inside, but still she jumped when the lid opened and the vampire sat up, his fangs dripping the best blood the drama department could offer.

"How do I look?" Jason asked. "Is the light right for me to look scary?"

"It's perfect. I expected you, and it still frightened me."

Jason laughed and took out his fangs. "I'll be glad when it starts for real. Is it time yet?"

"The doors will open any minute. Coach Hodges, Mrs. Denkle or I will come through at intervals to be sure everything is going smoothly. If you get tired, tell one of us and we'll get the alternate vampire from the graveyard to replace you."

"I won't get tired. I get to lay here most of the time. The doctor and patient are the ones to check on. I heard Mrs. Denkle say it's hard to scream for very long at a time."

"I'll keep that in mind."

As Tess left, she almost bumped into Janis. "There you are! Lane and I were wondering if you'd had car trouble."

"No, I was reminding the living dead to stay in character and not to touch anyone. We have to stress that to everybody. None of our victims may be touched. Hear that, Dracula?"

The vampire opened his lid a crack. "Got it."

"Lane is up front," Tess said. "I'm doing a last minute walk-through."

"I saw a car parking while I was out back. We'd better get ready for the crowd."

Tess hurried away and at the next corner, ran into a body hanging from the ceiling. A scream escaped her before she recognized Chet and saw his grin. "You scared me! What are you doing up there?" She tried to get her heartbeat under control. "Does Mrs. Denkle know you're doing this?"

"No, I wanted to surprise her. Did it work?"

"Come down from there before you get hurt." She watched him chin and loosen the harness that made him appear to be hanging by the neck. "You boys were told not to do anything that we haven't discussed and approved. Give me that harness."

Chet handed it over but he was still grinning.

"Out to the graveyard. Now! I'll put this thing behind the eyeball counter up front, and you can pick it up after the haunted house is closed."

Shaking her head, Tess went back to the front. She thrust the harness at Lane. "You wouldn't believe what Chet was doing. He scared the life out of me!"

Janis looked at it. "What's this? It looks like a hanged-man harness."

"It is. I went around a corner and ran into Chet and thought for a minute he was really hanging."

"I'll go have a word with him," Janis said. "He was told not to play any tricks. Was Brady in this, too?"

"If he was, I didn't catch him. But Chet had to have had help in getting up there."

Janis left in search of her innovative students. Lane looked at Tess. "You're pale. Are you okay?"

She nodded. "It just startled me. I ran into him before I saw him."

He looked past her head. "Here come our first victims."

Tess put on her witch's wig of stringy hair and practiced her cackle as the first bunch of teenagers paid Lane for their admission.

Time passed quickly and the crowd kept coming. Judging by the shrieks and bumps from inside the halls, Tess knew the haunted house was a success. When an hour had passed, she went through the hall to see if any of the actors needed to be relieved.

Amy came to her. "Mrs. Bowen, Tracy never showed up."

"She didn't? I thought she must have come in the back way."

"No, ma'am. I'm getting worried."

"It's all right, I'm sure. Maybe she got a date at the last minute and didn't call any of us. Coach Hodges and I have been here for quite a while so she couldn't have reached us. There's no phone in the field house, you know."

"It's not like Tracy not to show up when she says she'll be some place. She's been acting weird lately."

"Are you getting tired? Do you need someone to do your job for a while?"

"No, I'm fine. I like this."

"Okay. I'm going to check on the others. If I hear anything from Tracy, I'll come tell you."

The others were also enjoying themselves, but the mad doctor's patient was already hoarse from screaming. "I'll go get your replacement," Tess promised. It had been arranged ahead of time that the living dead would fill in for the others when they needed a break.

As she hurried through the dark halls to the grave-yard, Tess again turned the corner and bumped into a hanging body. At first she was startled, but then she remembered Chet's prank. Angrily she fished in the pocket of her witch's dress for the flashlight she carried for emergencies and repairs.

"Chet!" she hissed as she fumbled to turn it on. "You're in big trouble this time!"

He didn't answer, and she heard the creak of the rope rubbing on the beam of the ceiling. Finally she found the switch and turned the flashlight on the body. It wasn't Chet.

The girl hung from a rope, her eyes glazed and half open, her tongue protruding slightly from one side of her mouth. As Tess screamed, the body swayed in the light. "Lane!" she shouted. "Janis! I need help!" She caught the girl's thin legs and felt the cold and unyielding skin beneath her skirt. This was no joke.

Tess couldn't reach high enough to untie the rope, nor could she lift the girl's weight. Frantically she ran out the back door and around the building.

Lane was selling more tickets and laughing in such a way chills ran down her spine. She grabbed him. "Lane! You've got to come with me! Now!"

"There are more people arriving. What's wrong?" He counted the money into the box as the newest victims went into the dark hall.

"We have to close the house. Something terrible has happened!"

She finally had his attention. "What's happened?"

"Somebody has been hanged back there!"

"Chet and his damned pranks." Lane reached behind the counter. "Did he sneak in here and get that harness again?"

She grabbed his arm and pulled him. "It's not Chet. It's some girl!"

He left with her at a run. They circled the field house and hurried in the back door. Tess had her flashlight on and so did Lane by the time they were inside. "Where?" he demanded. "Where is she?"

"Over this way. Oh, God, Lane, I think she's dead." Tess tried to keep her voice down in order not to scare any of the students who might overhear them. "Hurry! I hear the kids coming this way."

Tess ran to where she'd left the body but it was gone. Frantically, she looked around. "Where is she?"

Lane flashed his light about. "Are you sure she was here? It's easy to lose your way in the maze."

"Of course I'm sure," Tess snapped. "I ran into her when I came around this corner."

He shined the light up at the ceiling. The exposed grid work of the ceiling had no rope hanging from it and certainly no body.

"You must have been mistaken."

Tess glared at him, their faces eerie in the wavering lights. "How could I possibly make a mistake like that? I touched her. She felt cold and stiff." Unconsciously, she rubbed her palm on her skirt as if she could wipe away the memory. "She was right here!"

"Well, she's not here now." He looked around one more time. "Let's go find Chet."

Chet was with the other living dead in the graveyard, walking around like zombies and occasionally bumping into each other or the chain link fence. Lane

284

went to him and caught his arm. "Come over here. We want to talk to you."

"What did I do?" Chet asked with automatic defensiveness.

"Did you get the hanging harness out of the cabinet?"

"Not me, Coach. Mrs. Denkle came out here and chewed me out and told me I had to do a report on method acting. I haven't been anywhere near it." His eyes were large and honest.

Tess didn't want to believe him. "Some girl was hanging in there, not far from where you were. Was someone else planning to play a trick on us?"

"No, ma'am. Not that I know anything about. Who was she?"

"I don't know her. She did a more credible job than you did. I thought she was really dead."

"What did she look like?" Lane asked. "Maybe I'll recognize her from a description."

"Let me think." Tess rubbed her temples and forced herself to remember as dispassionately as possible. "She had short, frizzy brown hair. Her dress was long-waisted and was sort of draped around her, probably because she was so thin."

"How tall was she?" Lane asked.

"How should I know? She was hanging in the air!"

"You know who that sounds like?" Chet said, his voice quivering. "It sounds like Misty Traveno."

Lane frowned at him. "It can't be and you know it."

"I know, but Misty had all that shaggy hair, and she always wore clothes that just hung on her."

"That's impossible, and I don't want you saying things like this to the others. Your imagination is running away with you because of what we're doing here."

Chet looked doubtful, but he didn't argue.

Tess said, "We'll have to talk about this later. Whatever or whoever I saw is gone now, and we have more cars arriving."

Lane pointed his finger at Chet. "I'm keeping an eye on you, boy. Remember that."

"Yes, sir," the boy mumbled and went back to the other walking corpses.

"Maybe you're right. Maybe we shouldn't have had the haunted house this year," Lane said as they went around to the front door. "I don't know who was playing a trick on you, but this is in bad taste."

"I don't understand. Wasn't Misty Traveno one of the students who died last summer?"

"She was the one who hanged herself in the auditorium."

Tess felt slightly sick and wished she hadn't asked. Which of the students would have played such a tasteless joke? And how had they been able to carry it off so convincingly? Tess could have sworn the girl was really dead.

Tracy hurried to dress. She wanted to be out of the house before her father came home. As Kevin had instructed, she was wearing black. In the past few days, she had buried her doubts about the coven. Kevin's ideas no longer seemed farfetched; she enjoyed the rush of power she experienced around the fire with the others. She could no longer remember why she had ever thought Brooke might have been a member of the coven.

"Where are you going?" her mother asked, startling Tracy as she had thought she would get out of the house unnoticed.

Tracy turned to face her mother, trying her best to remain composed. "Out," she replied, sitting on the bed while she pulled on her black canvas shoes.

"I can see you're going out. *Where* are you going?"

"Just out, okay?" She went to the dresser and started brushing her hair, unable to refrain from using hard, jerking strokes. Her mother's questions would delay her, and she was late already.

"It's Halloween," her mother said in that same vacant tone that had become routine since Brooke's death. "When you were little, I always made Halloween costumes for both of you. You always wanted to be a fairy princess."

"Brooke was the princess. I always wanted to be something more interesting." She wished her mother would leave and stop talking about Brooke. The memories were too painful.

"Brooke was always so beautiful. She seemed to always be so proud of her princess costumes. Her hair was such a beautiful color."

Tracy slapped her hairbrush down onto the dresser. "She was happy because she got her way. Why couldn't I ever have been what *I* wanted to be? Like an astronaut or a gypsy?"

Lucy gave her daughter a blank look. "An astronaut with a fairy princess would have looked silly."

"Why did we always have to match? And why did Brooke always get her way?" She glared at her mother.

"I didn't want to talk about this, but since you brought it up, why did it always have to be Brooke who had the last say? What I wanted was just as important!"

"But you both looked so adorable in your little sparkly dresses."

"And Brooke's was always blue, so I was stuck with the pink one!"

"She liked blue. And with her hair—"

"I hate pink! And I hate fluffy dresses!" Tracy interrupted with a glare at her mother as rage welled up in her. All the anger she usually kept bottled up was bubbling to the surface. "She always got the dancing lessons, the piano lessons, the twirling lessons!"

"You never wanted to learn to play the piano; she did. You had twirling lessons. You just weren't . . ."

" 'As good as Brooke,' " Tracy finished, repeating the phrase she had heard much too often. "I never did a damned thing as good as Brooke, did I?"

Lucy looked confused as she shook her head. "But Brooke was special. She—"

Tracy couldn't bear to listen to any more. She grabbed her purse and brushed past her mother. By the time she reached her car, she was crying. Angrily, she fought back the tears. The coven was waiting for her. Once there, she would be accepted for who she was. In the coven she had a place of importance. She backed out the driveway, screeching her tires, and drove recklessly to the meeting place appointed by Kevin.

* * *

Half an hour later, Lucy Wright stood across from the school, twisting the tail of her cardigan sweater endlessly with her fingers. She didn't have long to search for Brooke; Ross would soon arrive home and notice her absence, and he had told her that he wouldn't have her coming to the school again. She suspected he might even have her committed if he knew where she was, but she had to take the risk in order to find her daughter. The unpleasantness with Tracy had made it impossible for her to stay in the house and wait.

No cars were coming, so she hurried across the street. The school loomed dark and silent above her. In the distance she could hear faint sounds coming from the field house behind the stadium. For a moment she thought it might be a football game and that Brooke would naturally be there since she was a cheerleader, but she remembered in time that it couldn't be. Not tonight.

Lucy went to the door and tugged on the handle. It was locked, of course; she had known it would be. Her thoughts went back to her days here as a student. Some of the boys she had known had broken into the school on occasion to steal tests or just to see if they could do it and not get caught, but she had never had the nerve to do anything of the sort herself. Now she wished she had learned how they had done it.

The shadows were deep at the door, and she knew she couldn't be seen. Could she get through a window? She was looking for something to break the glass with when she heard a sound at the door. She looked back to see the door swing open a few inches.

Lucy couldn't believe her good fortune. She went to

the door and peered in through the crack. "Brooke? Is that you?"

A voice answered her from deep within the building, but she couldn't make out the words. She pulled the door open wider and stepped into the building. "I can hear you, baby. Keep talking. It's dark in here."

"Here," the whispery voice sounded again, this time more clearly. "Up here."

Lucy passed the alarm system, completely unaware that the door to the control box was open and the switch that activated the alarm had been turned off. Uncertainly she groped her way to the stairs. Was that a faint light up there on the second floor?

"Mommy?"

Brooke hadn't called her that since she was a toddler. Lucy's heart beat faster. "I'm coming, baby," she called out just as she had when Brooke had awakened in the night and called for her. "Mommy is coming."

She started up the stairs. Once she had begun the climb, it wasn't so hard to do. She had only to hold onto the hand rail and concentrate on lifting her feet high enough to reach the next step.

At the top there was indeed a pale light. Lucy wasn't sure where it was coming from, but it gave an eerie green sheen to the lockers. "Brooke? Are you up here?"

"Here." The voice was so faint Lucy almost missed it.

"Where? In the art room?" This made sense. Brooke had always been good at art. There had even been talk of her going to college on an art scholarship. Naturally she would choose this place to meet her mother.

The door to the art room was closed but not locked.

Lucy opened it and stepped in. At first she thought the room was empty, and she felt a stab of disappointment. Had she been mistaken again?

"Here. Back here."

Lucy squinted trying to see through the pale green light to the spot from which Brooke's voice had come. In the back of the room tall shelves separated a portion of the room from the rest. She recalled that during open house she had noticed that supplies were kept here. "Brooke? Are you back there?"

"Mommy? Where are you?" Brooke's voice sounded much younger than Lucy had expected. It was almost as if Brooke were three again and confused in the darkness.

"I'm coming. Mommy is coming." Lucy went toward the back of the room.

When she stepped into the supply cubicle, she saw a figure standing in the corner where the shadows were nearly black. "I'm here, baby. I've come for you."

When the figure stepped forward, Lucy almost gasped. It was her Brooke all right, but her cheeks were sunken and her eyes were dark. Her red hair was hanging in tangles about her face and was such a dull color that only Lucy would have known it as Brooke's. Even her clothes looked old and were beginning to fray into rags. Lucy's heart went out to her. "Come home with me," Lucy said tenderly. "I'll take care of you."

"Cheated," Brooke said, her voice no longer sounding young and vulnerable. "You pushed me."

For a moment Lucy didn't know what Brooke meant, then she remembered the argument they had had so often. "Baby, I never meant to push you. I just

291

wanted you to have more fun than I did when I was young."

Brooke took a step forward.

"If I hadn't pushed you a little, you would never have tried out for cheerleader or any of the things you enjoyed so. I was only trying to do what's best for you."

"Pushed." The word came from Brooke, but her lips didn't move. "Gone. Forever."

Lucy felt the tears start to well. "You mean you'll never be able to do these things again? We'll find a way. I knew all along that they were wrong about you being dead. I never believed it! We'll go away, just the two of us. We'll find you a new school where they don't say such things about you."

Lucy reached out as if she would touch Brooke but stopped short. A piercing cold made her fingertips tingle. She could feel an uneasy tremble in the air as if she were standing near a powerful electric current.

"Cheated. Forever."

The whisper seemed to echo around the room. Where there other people there? Lucy glanced over her shoulder and thought she saw movement in the far corner. "Let's go, baby. Let's go home."

"Never again," Brooke lifted her head and looked at the shelves behind Lucy. "Push me never again." The words were spoken in a whispered monotone.

A voice in the corner beyond the door echoed, "Never."

Lucy started to become afraid. She looked more closely at Brooke. Was this indeed her daughter? Brooke had never let herself go like this. They had certainly had their differences, but she had tried to explain that to Brooke. "I did it all for your own good," she said as she had told her so often before she died. "I wanted you to have more than I had to settle for!"

Brooke's face paled to transparency and the shelf behind Lucy began to vibrate, then teeter.

Lucy wheeled about and stared up at it. Cans of brushes and paint and paper fell toward her as the shelf came crashing down. Lucy screamed and threw up her hands to protect herself, but she fell and was pinned.

For a moment she couldn't think. Then she felt the pain start in her legs and hips. The shelves were solid wood and heavy. When she tried to free herself, the pain cut through her, and she whimpered.

Twisting her head around, she saw Brooke standing exactly where she had been. Her expression was still cold and remote. "Brooke? Help me. Go call for help!"

Instead, Brooke looked up at the other bank of shelves. To Lucy's horror they began to move as well. She pushed against the ones holding her down but couldn't budge them. She was still struggling when the second shelf crashed down on her. Only her hand was still visible. Her fist clutched, then released as she died.

Brooke watched it all and at last something akin to a smile crossed her gray lips. A current of triumph swept around the room and down the dark halls to echo up and down the empty stairs.

Subtly the elation changed and Brooke looked toward the door. Misty was there, emerging from the shadows. An unspoken message passed between them, and they moved silently into the hall. The brief respite left Brooke. She had rid herself of the mother who had always pushed her to do more, be more, than she wanted to be. Tracy, the one who had been allowed to do as she pleased, had escaped, but her mother had not.

But already Brooke felt the dull rage building. She was still dead. She was still cheated out of her life. As if she were catching a scent in the air, she paused in the dark hall and looked about. Kevin was near. She didn't know how she knew, but she could feel a sense of him sweeping through the corridors. Kevin, the one who had cheated them most of all, was still alive, and he was near. With Misty close behind, Brooke began moving through the shadows and toward the stairs.

In the darkest corner of the school parking lot, Kevin stood looking at the field house. Cars were parked everywhere, and there was a line waiting for access to the building. For a moment he let himself fantasize getting everyone inside and blowing up the building. He had seen things like that in movies, and he considered it to be really cool.

He looked up at the full moon. It wouldn't be long now. He had come fifteen minutes early so he would be there to greet each member of his coven as they arrived. He had no doubt that the others would show up on schedule, but he was nervous about the Grand Sacrifice.

They had met earlier that evening at their usual meeting place in the woods, and he had given them his final instructions, one of which was that they were to go home and change into the black clothes they had been told to get the week before. He hadn't cared what the clothing was, so long as it was black. On Halloween no one would think anything about seeing teenagers dressed like that. Most adults didn't pay that much attention to kids anyway.

His own mother hadn't even asked him what he planned to do when he left the house. He supposed she was still mad at him for refusing to clean his room, but that was too bad. Tonight would be the most important night of his life, and he didn't want to be taken from his meditations.

He had meditated all afternoon, cross-legged on his bed, his eyes fixed on the glittering surface of the sword blade. Once more he had demanded instructions for the evenings ritual and had repeated the incantations he had designed for the sacrifice. This time he was sure he heard a voice answering in his head, and he felt confident that this time the coven's energy would be channeled into him.

A movement in the dark caught his eye. It was Mona. "The child of water comes," she whispered as she had been instructed.

"I greet you, Water," he replied.

One by one they arrived. Tracy was the last. She came to them from the shadows beside the gym. "The child of quicksilver comes. I am changing, never changing." Her voice sounded tense in the darkness, giving the standard greeting a poignancy it lacked in the meeting by the summoning fire.

Kevin bowed slightly and his lips drew up in a mirthless smile. "I greet you, Quicksilver." He lifted his arms in a position of benediction. "I welcome you, my children. Tonight you will be given a great gift. Tonight you

295

will know the name of the one we follow and your paths will never be the same again."

Mona stepped forward as if she were spokesperson of the group. "We are ready, Leader. Take us and mold us to your will."

Kevin suppressed a scowl. Mona was certainly taking a great deal onto herself. He wouldn't be sorry to see her die at all. Again he congratulated himself on having chosen this night. The full moon had been an unplanned bonus, and if he had waited much longer, Mona might have taken it into her head to split off and start a group of her own.

He looked at the school. "Let's go inside."

Tracy wasn't at all sure she wanted to do this. She had never broken into a building in her life, and she was afraid. A glance at the others told her they weren't worried about it at all. Was it because they trusted Kevin so completely, or because they were simply braver than she was?

Mona noticed her hanging back and gave Tracy a look full of derision. Tracy felt herself blushing, and she moved closer to Kevin. If Mona could do this, so could she. This, at least, was something Brooke would never have dared to do. Tonight Tracy wanted to be as different from her sister as possible. She still was hurt and was starting to feel guilty over arguing with her mother.

As if he did this every night, Kevin went to the nearest window and broke it out with his elbow. He reached in and unlocked the latch. "We enter here."

"What about the security system, man?" Rocky was staring at the broken glass. "I thought you had a key or something."

Kevin also looked at the glass and Tracy wondered if he was as confident as he was trying to appear to be. He said, "We're protected by the demons of the night. The alarm won't ring."

They waited several minutes but the night remained silent.

"See? Let there be no more faithless questions." Kevin fixed Rocky with a condemning stare. Rocky turned away and slid through the open window.

Tracy didn't want to go into the school. It wasn't just a matter of legality. She was afraid. As a child she had been terrified of the dark, and she hadn't entirely grown out of it. Only when Mona climbed in after the others did Tracy bend and crawl through the window.

They were in the wood shop. Tracy could smell the pine shavings and see the shape of saws and other machinery whose use she couldn't guess. The others were moving silently through the room. For a moment Tracy considered lagging back and escaping through the window, but now that she was inside, that no longer seemed to be an option. She kept close behind the others. When she was with them, she belonged. She wanted to feel the flow of strength and acceptance the meetings so often gave her, but it eluded her.

Kevin led them into the hall. Tracy could make out dim light from the window at the far end, but where they were, the hall was black. She bumped into Billy Joe, and he jerked away as if she had frightened him. Tracy wondered if she was the only one having second thoughts.

How had she gotten so far enmeshed in this? she wondered as she felt her way down the hall with the others. An argument with her mother and loneliness wasn't worth this. If she left now, could she go home and put her life back the way it had been?

Tracy's sense of direction was confused in the darkness and she had no idea which way to go to return to the wood shop and escape. She was afraid that she would become lost if she left the others and be locked up alone in the school all night, so she stayed close behind Billy Joe.

How long, she wondered, would it take to finish the Grand Sacrifice? As she trembled in the darkness and felt her way down the spooky hall, she promised herself this was the last time she would attend the coven. If Kevin and the others got angry with her, so be it. She tried not to bump into corners as they continued further into the school.

Chapter Thirteen

By eleven-thirty the visitors to the haunted house had reached their fill of shrieks and gory tableaus. Tess was glad. "I'm as tired as if I had carried everyone through on my shoulders," she complained good-naturedly to Lane as they waited for the last of the workers to gather their props and leave.

"I know, but admit it. You had fun."

"Surprisingly, I did. There's a certain satisfaction in playing tricks on the students for a change."

Amy Dennis came through, her arms loaded with her hair dryers and the assorted masks. "I think I have everything."

"If you don't, we'll be here tomorrow putting the field house back the way it was." Lane grinned at Amy's moan. "Tearing it down won't be as difficult as putting it up. I promise."

Amy looked at Tess. "Did Tracy call or anything?"

"No, she didn't. I'm going to have a talk with her on Monday."

"This just isn't like her. She always shows up if she

says she will, and she's enjoyed working in the haunted house ever since we got in high school."

"I guess this year it was just too much for her." Tess smiled at the girl. "Maybe if you call her you two can patch up whatever problem you're having."

"That's just it." Amy frowned and shifted her load to the other arm. "I've tried. We had an argument, and I've tried to make up with her, but she won't have anything to do with me. I guess she just decided she didn't want to run around with me anymore." Amy looked away. "I guess it was mostly my fault, but I've said I was sorry, and she still avoids me."

"I'm sorry." Tess could see the girl was really upset by Tracy's change of heart. "If there's anything I can do, let me know."

"Okay. Thanks, Mrs. Bowen." Amy shouldered the door open and left.

"Is that the last one?" Tess asked.

"I think so. Let's walk through to be sure. I wouldn't want to lock someone up in here."

They threaded their way through the makeshift halls. With the overhead lights on the maze wasn't nearly as frightening, but it was still confusing. "What a mess," Tess commented as they passed the "operating room." The fake viscera was scattered all around the table.

"It's too much to clean up tonight," Lane said. "I'll get here early tomorrow morning."

"So will I. I'll pry myself out of bed somehow."

As they made their way toward the back door, Tess hung back. "I still don't understand what I saw back here. I'm sure it was a girl and that she was hanging from the beams up there. Obviously it was a trick, but

300

it was so realistic! When I touched her, she was cold and stiff!"

"It was also in bad taste." Lane opened the back door and looked around to be sure all the fake tombstones and funeral grass had been brought inside. He closed the door and locked it.

They walked back to the front and Tess said, "I'll get my bowls tomorrow. I don't want to wash them tonight and I sure don't want to be greeted by the sight of all those veins and arteries and eyeballs in my kitchen first thing in the morning."

"That would be a gruesome sight." As he locked the field house door behind them, Lane said, "I'm glad you came to Maple Glen."

"Are you?" Tess pulled off the stringy mop of witch's hair and smiled at him. "I'm glad, too."

Lane took her hand and they walked to the car. "I never realized how lonely I was."

Tess paused. "Before you say anything else, I'm not sure I'm ready to hear it. Not yet. It's too soon."

"I know. But I wanted you to know what I feel." He smiled down at her. "We have plenty of time. All the time in the world."

They walked arm in arm to the car, and Lane opened the door for Tess. Instead of starting the car at once, he turned to face her, and drew her to him and kissed her. "I've wanted to do that all evening."

She laughed. "The way I look tonight? I'm not sure how to take that." She put the witch's wig back on and tilted her head coquettishly. "Step into my kitchen, Hansel. I'm going to make cookies." A flash of light over his shoulder drew her attention. "What was that?"

"What was what?" He turned to look behind him.

"At the school. I saw a light come on, then go off."

"No one is supposed to be there this late."

"I'm positive I saw something." She pulled the wig off and crumpled it in her lap.

Lane started the car and drove across the parking lot toward the school. "It's too bad we don't have a telephone in the field house. I should call the police."

"What should we do?"

"There's a phone in my office. We can call from it."

Tess swallowed her fear. She didn't relish crossing the dark gym, even with Lane beside her.

He parked the car in the shadows at the back of the school, where it wouldn't be seen from the windows. Moving in the darkest shadows, he guided Tess to the side door of the gym. He unlocked it and they stepped inside. It was as dark and spooky as Tess had anticipated.

"Stay right with me," he whispered. "I can find my way blindfolded."

"It's a good thing. I can't see at all." She found his hand, and they started across the gym floor.

In the center of the school, Kevin and his followers were prying open a door to the auditorium.

"Who locked this damned door?" Rocky Mancelli muttered. "It's not budging."

"Mr. Crouthers stepped up security since the Mrs. Mitchell died," Mona said in a whisper. "I heard a teacher say so."

"Well?" Matthew Greenway said to Kevin. "What

302

are we going to do if we can't get into the auditorium?"

Kevin hadn't considered that the door might be locked. "I'll ask for a sign." He lifted his hands and tilted his head back. "I call you, spirits of darkness, come to me. Make our way easy that we may serve you."

To everyone's complete amazement, the door clicked open and swung back an inch.

Kevin covered his surprise with a sardonic smile. "Now we may enter." As the others passed into the huge room, Kevin made a cursory examination of the door lock. How had it opened? Had his powers grown to these lengths? He felt as if he were already filling with the might he so desired. Performing the Grand Sacrifice in the school had been an inspiration.

"It sure is dark in here," Tracy said nervously. "I can't see where I'm going."

"Stay close to me," Rocky said. "I'm the child of the Lion. I'll protect you."

"She needs no protection other than her own," Kevin snapped. He didn't want anyone to usurp his powers at this point. All his followers must look only to him.

Kevin took some candles out of the back pack he carried and handed them around. With a cigarette lighter, he silently lit the candle he had kept for himself. Ceremoniously he passed the flame to the candle of the person nearest him. "As I gave you the beginnings of your power, so now I give you light." He moved down the line, lighting candles. "As I freed you from the mud of your existence, so now do I free you from the darkness."

He conquered the urge to look over his shoulder. He

had the uneasy feeling they weren't alone. "I feel the spirits with us. Come. Let us go to the stage."

Mona stepped out fearlessly. "I follow you, Leader. Will the stage be our place of sacrifice?"

"Why else would I be taking you there?" He could scarcely bear to talk to the girl these days. At times he had wondered if Mona had any connection at all to real life.

Single file, they walked down the aisle. Kevin had the eerie sense of this being like a warped graduation ceremony—the only one his followers would ever have. He led them up onto the stage and they formed the ring as they did at their bonfire meetings.

"Place your fires in the center," Kevin said. "They will light our final journey."

"What do you mean, 'final journey'?" Rocky asked suspiciously.

Kevin fixed him with a disdainful look. "After tonight, you'll never be the same again. After tonight, you'll be an anointed one."

"May we know the master's name yet?" Mona asked eagerly.

"Not yet." Kevin reached into his backpack and took out a jar of liquid. He had worked all afternoon on this concoction, a combination of grapefruit and tomato juice. He had hit on the idea of using tomato juice in order to make it the color and consistency of blood. After tasting it, he had added some sugar. It wouldn't do to have his followers not be able to stand the taste. After it was mixed, Kevin had added the methanol he had been distilling in the woods over the past several days. He had no idea how that might have changed the taste but he couldn't risk tasting it to find out.

He took out the paper cups he had bought for this purpose. He had found some with Halloween symbols that he thought were appropriate. Carefully he poured the mixture into the cups.

On the third floor, the shadows moved. A soft whispering began to run through the halls and down the stairs. "Again!" it said, "Again!" Another whisper answered. "Help us!" it cried to the dark rooms. "Help us!" Farther down the hall another voice responded with, "Cheated! Kill! Cheated us!"

The shadows became more solid and Troy Spaulding stepped away from the wall he'd been leaning on. At first he seemed disoriented, then he turned his head toward the stairs. Slowly he began to walk.

In the auditorium, Kevin looked around the circle as he passed out the cups. In the candlelight his black eyes were glittering like an animal's. His breath came quickly as if he had been running, and he had never felt such a rush of excitement. His followers held the cups, some of them looking at the liquid with disgust. From the reverence in her face, Mona might have been holding the Holy Grail. She was an odd one, Kevin thought.

"I call you, spirit of the night. I summon you, Mephistopheles! I command that you come to me, Belial! Heed my call, Beelzebub, Asmodeus. Lucifer! Come!"

Mona's head lifted as she recognized the names for the devil. For the first time an uncertain frown puckered her forehead.

Kevin didn't let that stop him. He could actually feel something growing inside him. There was an echoing of energy in the blackness of the auditorium. He closed his eyes and implored the entity again.

In the halls above the auditorium, other shapes formed and joined Troy. He paused and waited until Brooke Wright stepped out from the row of lockers outside the art room. Turning, his face as blank as those of the others, he lead them down the stairs toward the first floor.

The group moved in perfect silence down the stairs and past the front door in the direction of the auditorium. Moonlight from the open door touched Brooke's long red hair and Troy's shoulders before they flowed back into the darkness. The auditorium door sighed as it opened and closed behind them.

Kevin heard the door, and he wished he could glance toward the back of the auditorium. He had positioned himself with his back to it and he didn't dare break his concentration. "I call on Lucifer to sanctify this libation," he intoned. "I ask that our power become as one."

Rocky looked toward the auditorium seats as if he, too, had heard the sound of the door open and shut. He squinted but could see nothing because of the candlelight between him and the back of the room.

Billy Joe noticed what Rocky was doing and turned his head in the same direction. He was sitting closer to Kevin and didn't have to look over the candles to see into the auditorium. At first there was nothing but blackness, but as his eyes adjusted, he saw several shapes moving silently toward the stage. He couldn't be sure this wasn't a part of the ceremony Kevin had planned, but the slow progression of the eerie shapes left him uneasy.

* * *

In the gym, Lane hung up the phone. "The police are on their way."

"What should we do until they get here? Wait outside?"

"You should. I'm going to go into the hall and see if I can see them."

"You're not doing any such a thing! Or at least you're not going alone. I'm coming with you."

He hesitated but nodded. "That might be better. I don't know if anyone is outside or not, and I don't want to leave you alone."

She took his hand. "I can't believe we're doing this. Are you sure this is a good idea? What if it's not just kids?"

"Come on. We'll only peep out. If they leave before the police arrive, we may be able to identify them."

Together they crossed the echoing gym. Tess was terrified but she didn't tell him. Lane would keep her safe, and as he'd said, the vandals might already be outside the building. At the door that led into the school proper, they stopped. Lane eased it open a crack.

Tess leaned forward. "I hear something. Do you hear something?"

"Yes." He put his ear to the crack. "It sounds like chanting."

"It can't be. Why would vandals chant? It sounds like it's coming from the auditorium."

Lane pushed the door open a bit wider. "Come on."

Kevin's eyes were shut, and he didn't see Billy Joe look at Rocky and jerk his head toward the seats in the auditorium. Rocky leaned back from the circle to get a better look. He also saw the figures moving toward them and gave Billy Joe a questioning look. Tracy, too, leaned back from the candles in order to see what was happening behind Kevin.

"We come to you, Beelzebub," Kevin said in stentorian tones. "We ask that you do our bidding. Lift your cups, my coven. Lift them and drink as I do." He put the cup he held in both his hands to his lips, but he didn't drink.

Mona was in the act of obeying when she noticed Kevin's closed mouth. "Hey, Kevin's not drinking."

Everyone looked at him and Kevin jerked the cup from his lips. Trying to bluff them into obedience, he shouted. "I said to drink! Do it now!"

"No way!" Tracy said as she threw the cup away from her. "That stuff stinks! I'm not drinking it!"

"Neither am I," Rocky said. "What's in this stuff, anyway?"

Kevin couldn't believe it. He had led them right to the brink and now they were refusing to follow. For once words failed him.

Mona sat down her cup and stood. "I'm leaving. We could get into trouble being in here. I don't mind bonfires, but this could get us expelled."

Kevin glared frantically at his followers. "I'm your leader! I command that you obey me!"

"Get a life," Billy Joe said in derision. "I'm outta here." He stood and looked toward the auditorium. Instantly he froze. Unlike some of the others, he had gone to Maple Glen schools all his life and he had known all the students who committed suicide the past summer. Now he saw them all coming toward them, their faces pale and blank. He drew in a breath and yelled.

All the others turned to look at him, then followed the finger he pointed toward the nearer aisle. Their panic was immediate. When Tracy saw Brooke start up the steps, she screamed, remembering the way her sister had tried to kill her. Tracy screamed again and jumped off the stage and ran up the other aisle, the rest of the coven right behind her.

Kevin shouted at the ceiling, his rage beyond his control. He didn't look into the auditorium until he heard the last of his group scramble off the stage. Wheeling, he found himself facing Troy Spaulding.

For a moment Kevin was too stunned to move or speak.

In a whisper that grew to deafening proportions, Troy and the others began to chant the words Kevin had taught them. Brooke moved nearer, her lank red hair swinging around her head like seaweed.

Tracy almost ran over Tess and Lane in her rush to get out of the building. Tess pulled back for a second, but she was still drawn to the auditorium. At the open auditorium doors, Lane stopped and stared inside.

In the flickering candlelight, he could see students moving about. To his amazement, he recognized Brooke and Troy. Misty Traveno was there, too, as was Toni Fay Randall and all the others he had thought never to see again.

The chanting grew louder as Lane and Tess watched. She gripped his arm. "That's the girl I saw with the red hair! And the thin one on the right—she's the one I saw hanging in the field house!" She started down the aisle but Lane grabbed her arm and restrained her.

"No!" he hissed. "Come back!"

All the ghosts' attention was turned to the center of their closing circle, where Kevin Donatello stood, his face a mask of terror. He started to swing at the encroaching figures, but yanked his hand back as if he couldn't bear to touch them. They moved closer, their chant almost deafening.

As a police siren cut through the still night air, the chanting increased in tempo, Troy's face was no longer blank but burning with revenge. Brooke moved closer, her hair seeming to float around her and her lips drawn back from her teeth in anger.

Kevin shrieked and grabbed his head. His eyes were turning blood red and a rivulet of blood welled up in the inside corner of one eye and coursed down his cheek. Another trickle started from one of his ears.

Brooke moved nearer and the others let her drift into the center of the circle. The chant increased in volume, but Brooke's lips were no longer moving. She had taken command by silent acclaim as if the others knew she was the most powerful among them. Kevin had doubled over in agony, but as she approached, he straightened, whimpering and cowering. Blood was coursing down his neck and cheeks, but he didn't take his eyes off Brooke.

Slowly Brooke raised her arm, her sleeve hanging from the emaciated appendage in rags. She pointed her bony finger straight at Kevin as the chant grew to a crescendo. He seemed to suddenly realize what was about to happen because he screamed, "No!" his rage overcoming his agony.

There was a flash of brilliant light as if a bolt of lightning had erupted on the stage. For a moment afterward Tess could see nothing. Then as her eyes readjusted, she saw the stage was silent and empty.

The wail of the police sirens grew louder and seconds later the hall behind them was awash in the red and blue lights from the arriving patrol cars. Lane looked out the windows across the hall for a moment, then when he looked back he discovered that Tess was already halfway down the dark aisle. As he hurried to catch up with her, the police burst into the auditorium.

"Is somebody in here?" one of the them shouted.

"Down here," Lane called back. "We're going down to turn on the lights."

Beams of brilliant light from the powerful police flashlights flashed across the auditorium as half a dozen officers began their search of the pitch-dark auditorium. Tess knew they would find no one, although she couldn't have explained how she knew. She felt her way to the steps and around the curtain to the light control panel. She flipped several switches and flooded the stage and auditorium with light.

A shout brought her back around the curtain. The stage wasn't as empty as she had thought.

What was left of Kevin lay in the center of the stage. Blood, brains and bits of flesh were scattered all over the stage, the curtains and onto the first rows of seats. Tess could only stare.

"What the . . ." one of the policemen said.

Lane shook his head. "I don't know."

The younger policeman said, "I've never seen anything like this but once before. Remember when we came out to investigate Mrs. Mitchell's death? Her dog was in this same condition!"

Tess noticed that the officer in charge was walking toward her, but she couldn't stop staring at the marks she had noticed on the stage floor. At her feet, clearly imprinted in the pool of blood on the floor were twelve sets of bare footprints. One of the smaller pair of prints stood close to what once had been Kevin Donatello. The prints were clear but there was no sign of anyone having walked away.

The policeman frowned at Tess. "Do you people know anything about this?"

She shook her head. "We were working in the haunted house behind the stadium. As we were leaving, we saw a light come on in the school and then go off. We thought someone was breaking in. Lane opened the gym door, called you, then we came in here where we heard the sounds."

"What sort of sounds?" He had his pad out and was making notes.

"Chanting," Lane said. "We heard a kind of chanting."

The policeman looked skeptical, but he wrote it down anyway. "What else?"

"That's all. We came in the doors you just came through and saw a flash of light. Tess started down the aisle to turn on the lights and I followed her. You saw us."

"Yeah, but I don't know if you were here earlier."

"What?" Tess exclaimed.

"Seeing the way you're dressed, that's not an unlikely question," he replied.

Tess looked down at the costume she was wearing.

312

Lane was still dressed in his as well. She fought down the hysterical laughter she felt welling inside.

"That's ridiculous," Lane snapped. "There were a hundred or more witnesses that can tell you we were in the field house."

"Look here," the younger policeman said. "See those tracks in the blood?"

"Yeah, so what? There might have been more of them that we didn't catch."

"Those prints are of bare feet," the younger officer said. "These two have shoes on."

Tess stood on one leg and pulled off her shoe to show the policemen that her feet were clean.

"Okay," the older one said reluctantly. "But I want your names and addresses and identification. Don't leave town in case we want to call you down for questioning."

Tess gave him the information he wanted and tried not to look at the stage. The younger one had radioed for an ambulance, and she could already hear the siren in the distance. She didn't envy anyone the job of collecting the body.

"Let's go home," Lane said as the EMTs hurried into the building, then slowed considerably when they saw the gore on the stage.

Tess was glad to put her hand in his and leave. Once they were outside the building, she said, "What do you suppose really happened?"

"I hope we never know."

She agreed.

Epilogue

Tracy waited for Fred Crouthers to call her name. Most of her other classmates had already received their diplomas; she would be the last.

As she waited, she glanced around the auditorium. It was filled with parents and other interested parties. Last year's ceremony, the one in which Brooke would have graduated, had been small and almost silent. This year there were beams of admiration focused on the graduating seniors.

She found her father in the crowd. Beside him sat Laurie Alexander, the teacher who had taken Hannah Mitchell's place in the school. They had dated for several weeks now and Tracy was happy about the arrangement.

No one had ever been able to explain the last two deaths in the school. Kevin had been found on the stage, not a surprise to Tracy in the least. She remembered all too well looking out from the stage and seeing Brooke and others, who had died the same night, coming up these very aisles. She didn't know what they had done to him, but she and the others in her group knew he had deserved whatever it was.

Her mother's death had been ruled an accident, but no one had an explanation as to how she had been able to get into the supposedly locked school, disarm the alarm system without knowing the code, go to the art room, and have two shelves fall on her. For a long time Tracy had been haunted with the idea that her mother must have been lying in the art room while she and the others were breaking in downstairs.

Her father had gone through some extremely difficult times with her mother's death so close on the heels of Brooke's death. That was one reason Tracy had been so glad to see him start dating Miss Alexander. The past was too painful. Tracy wanted to move toward the future.

Tracy and the rest of the coven had met one last time. On the next full moon they had gathered at the bonfire site in the late afternoon. None of them had planned it, they had simply come, and all were surprised to find the others there.

Without Kevin there to keep them organized, they hadn't even bothered using the customary salute. None of them, not even Mona, had wanted to continue getting together. They all felt strangely embarrassed to be together at all. Too much had happened the night of the Grand Sacrifice.

Before they left, Mona had kicked the cold, blackened wood away from the place where Kevin had always built the fire. The others didn't stop her. None of them wanted any traces to show of what had once transpired here. As silently as they had once left the fire-lit meetings, they went to their cars and drove away, never to return.

Hearing her name being called pulled Tracy back from her reverie. Quickly she rose from her seat and strode briskly up the steps to meet Fred Crouthers in the center of the stage. He gave her a hearty handshake, a smile, and the diploma she had worked twelve years to obtain. As she crossed the stage to go down the opposite steps, she moved the tassel on her mortarboard to the other side.

By the time she reached her seat, she felt tears on her cheeks. She couldn't have said if they were tears of happiness over her achievement or of sadness that Brooke and her mother weren't there. Tracy looked over at her father, and he smiled and gave her a nod. She smiled back at him.

Minutes later Mr. Crouthers announced that the graduation ceremony was finished, and Tracy, along with all the others, threw her cap in the air and shouted with joyous release. Most of the others charged up the aisles as if they couldn't bear to be inside a school another minute.

Amy was waiting for Tracy in the aisle. "Well?" Amy asked. "Are you packed yet?"

Tracy laughed. "I'm not in that big a hurry. I'll be ready by September."

"I can't wait! I never thought they would actually let us room together! Can you believe it? What do you think the odds of that were?"

"We asked to room together." She fell into step with Amy as they headed for the area where they were to meet their families. "Why else would a college send out

316

forms like that unless they intended to pay attention to them?"

"Yes, but the University of Missouri is so big!"

Tracy listened to Amy chatter on about the college and what they might expect to see and do there. One last time she looked back at the stage. She did a double take and stared. Brooke was there, half-concealed by the black curtains that bordered the right side of the stage.

As Tracy watched, Brooke smiled and lifted her hand as if she were waving goodbye. Rather than appearing emaciated as Tracy had last seen her, Brooke looked as she had in life, her red hair gleaming and her skin only a bit too pale. As Tracy watched, Brooke vanished.

"What are you looking at?" Amy asked. "Tracy?"

"Nothing." Tracy turned away, her mind relieved at last as to Brooke's fate. "I was just remembering."

"Not me! I'm so glad to be out of here, I don't know what to do! I think I'm going to ask Dad if I can have my own car to drive to college. Do you think they'll let us have our own cars there?"

Tracy was barely listening. She, too, was more than ready to leave behind Maple Glen and its memories.

YOU'D BETTER SLEEP WITH THE LIGHTS TURNED ON!
BONE CHILLING HORROR BY

RUBY JEAN JENSEN

ANNABELLE (2011-2, $3.95/$4.95)

BABY DOLLY (3598-5, $4.99/$5.99)

CELIA (3446-6, $4.50/$5.50)

CHAIN LETTER (2162-3, $3.95/$4.95)

DEATH STONE (2785-0, $3.95/$4.95)

HOUSE OF ILLUSIONS (2324-3, $4.95/$5.95)

LOST AND FOUND (3040-1, $3.95/$4.95)

MAMA (2950-0, $3.95/$4.95)

PENDULUM (2621-8, $3.95/$4.95)

VAMPIRE CHILD (2867-9, $3.95/$4.95)

VICTORIA (3235-8, $4.50/$5.50)